BOOKS BY HELENA NEWBURY

Helena Newbury is the *New York Times* and *USA Today* bestselling author of sixteen romantic suspenses, all available where you bought this book. Find out more at helenanewbury.com.

Lying and Kissing

Punching and Kissing

Texas Kissing

Kissing My Killer

Bad For Me

Saving Liberty

Kissing the Enemy

Outlaw's Promise

Alaska Wild

Brothers

Captain Rourke

Royal Guard

Mount Mercy

The Double

Hold Me in the Dark

Deep Woods

LYING AND KISSING

HELENA NEWBURY

FOSTER & BLACK

Originally published as the three part series "*Undercover*" ("*Seduced*," "*Conflicted*," and
"*Betrayed*")
The right of Helena Newbury to be identified as the author of this work has been
asserted by her in accordance with the Copyright, Design and Patents Act 1988
This book is entirely a work of fiction. All characters, companies, organizations,
products and events in this book, other than those clearly in the public domain, are
fictitious or are used fictitiously and any resemblance to any real persons, living or
dead, events, companies, organizations or products is purely coincidental.
Cover by Mayhem Cover Creations
Main cover image licensed from (and copyright remains with) Lorado/iStockPhoto
This book contains scenes that may be triggering for survivors of rape.

ISBN: 978-1-914526-19-0

1

His voice was like slate-gray rocks grinding together, immense and powerful. A voice that *commanded.* And now and again, especially when he hit a hard *k,* the rocks clashed with an explosion of sparks that sent molten silver jetting down my spine.

When that happened, I squeezed my thighs together.

I'd been listening to his phone calls for a month.

I suspected he had a second phone. We don't listen to just anyone's calls and if he *really* only ever talked to his girlfriends, we wouldn't be interested in him. But it was the only phone tap we had on him, so I sat there each day, back ramrod straight in my typist's chair, and listened and pretended to everyone around me that it was just another boring transcription.

In reality, I listened to those long, rolling *r's* and soft, vibrating *m's* and my fingers skittered over the keyboard on autopilot. I was barely aware of what Elena or Svetlana or Natalia said—his girlfriends all blended into one mess of pouting, hurt Russian-ness as he seduced them, slept with them and rapidly spurned them.

I was only concerned with him. Luka.

I didn't get to know anything about Luka Malakov. I didn't even know what he'd done wrong to come to our attention, but clearly he was a criminal of some kind and a serious, big-time one. I told myself that meant he must be old. He was probably a white-haired, fat guy in his sixties, his nose red from too much vodka. I tried to burn that image into my mind to stop my fantasies.

It didn't work.

In my fantasies, that gorgeous voice had a body and a face to go with it, all close-cropped, dark hair and Slavic cheekbones. He had gleaming white teeth that could bite softly at neck or nipple. A wide, powerful back and big arms so that he could pick me up and—

Ahem.

I hit the foot pedal to pause the recording and took off my headphones. It was Monday and I'd been at it for an hour straight, catching up on all his calls over the weekend. If I didn't get some coffee, I was going to lose myself completely in dreams of bad guys who looked like movie stars.

The stupid thing is, I'm not even into bad guys. Every boyfriend I've ever had has been...*normal.* Respectful. When Harry took my virginity, under a tree on a warm summer evening, he asked if I was sure so many times that I eventually kissed him to shut him up. When I broke up with Greg to come to Virginia, it was polite and mature and utterly amicable—I think we even shook hands. I couldn't imagine being with a guy who seemed to treat his women as disposable items, breaking up with them after just a few days or weeks.

I couldn't imagine it but, when I listened to Luka's calls, I couldn't stop thinking about it. I couldn't stop thinking about a *bad* man who'd...*use* me.

Roughly.

I needed to get out more.

That probably goes for most of my department, to be fair. No one who works here is completely normal. You have to have a little something wrong with you, to want to spy on people all day.

I was overdue a break, so I wandered through to the cafeteria and got myself a latte. Sitting there by myself, sipping my coffee, I could have been any insignificant cog in any big corporate machine. Cheap gray suit. Long hair the color of pecans. A body that isn't slender enough to be slim, but that doesn't have the big boobs and flaring hips men go for. Even my eyes are gray, and gray's not really a color.

Trust me: if you saw me in the street, you'd look right past me.

There are no windows in our entire department, squirreled away as we are at the heart of the building. It's easy to lose track of time and place. It was easy to forget that I was in Langley in the middle of the morning, with January snow on the ground outside. In a way, I liked that. Anything that helped me forget it was winter.

But it can be dangerous, losing your sense of where you are. Sometimes, I have to transcribe one of Luka's calls live. I'm sitting at my desk in the afternoon but it's like I'm right there in Moscow at 2am, sitting just on the other side of a wall from him, as if I could push open a door and step through.

I was still sitting there, twisting a lock of hair around and around my fingers to make a spring, when Roberta sat down opposite me with an espresso. "Twenty minutes for a latte?"

Shit. Had it been that long? The coffee was lukewarm through the paper cup. I must have zoned out again. I do that, sometimes. "Sorry."

She laughed gently. "Relax, Arianna. You've earned a break. I just worry about you, sitting out here all alone." She hesitated. "Are you okay?"

Roberta is my boss. Given that we support staff are all a bunch of introverted, moody shut-ins, she also has to be part schoolteacher and part mom. Some of us would forget to go home if we weren't reminded. She's in her fifties, I think, though it's difficult to tell.

She's the person who recruited me, at college. I'd done some project on dialects in former Soviet states and she showed up, all mysterious smile and sharp suit, and asked if I wanted to make a difference. I'd thought, at first, that she worked for a charity.

I'd said I did want to make a difference. I still do.

I shrugged. "I'd just like to...*do* something. I feel like I'm stuck in a loop, here."

Roberta smiled sympathetically. "What we do here is vital. I know it doesn't always feel like it, but it is." She put her hand on mine.

"Give it another year and we can look at maybe moving you into some field work." She paused. "This is really bothering you, isn't it?"

I squirmed. She'd been so good to me; I didn't like to keep hassling her. I knew she thought she was keeping me safe, but I felt like I was dying one day at a time, buried down here. And she'd used to be a field agent herself, back in the day. Didn't she understand?

Or was it that she understood too well, and knew I wasn't cut out for it?

Roberta leaned closer. "How are the nightmares?"

Everybody knows that they screen candidates thoroughly, here. And yes, they wired me up to a lie detector when I joined and they've done it a few times since. But just because they check to make sure we're trustworthy doesn't mean we're *normal*. Over in data analysis, they couldn't function without all the Asperger's sufferers spotting patterns. And where I work, in languages, I think at least half of us are on a pill for something or other.

And then there's me. I'm broken in a much more jagged, hard-edged way, and have been for three years.

"They're still there," I said simply, and tried hard not to think about—

Falling. The crunch as we hit. Snow settling on the window. The sound of my own screams—

Under the table, I dug my fingernails into my palm. That helps bring me back, sometimes.

Roberta was frowning at me. "I can schedule you for another round of counseling...."

I shook my head. "It's fine," I said. "Everything's fine." And smiled as if it was.

~

There's the Central Intelligence Agency. Within that, there's the National Clandestine Service—when Roberta first told me that's where she worked, I snorted coffee out of my nose. But that really is what's called.

Within the National Clandestine Service, there's the Special Activities Division. And that—I'm going to come right out and say it —is where the cool stuff happens. The field ops. The excitement. That's where Nancy, my best friend and roommate, works.

Buried away at the bottom of the CIA tree diagram are the support staff—people like Roberta and me. "We're the roots," Roberta told me when she recruited me. "We hold the tree up."

Well, maybe. But being a root means being buried away underground, away from the sunlight.

Everything is compartmentalized, which is a fancy way of saying that we aren't told what's going on. I listen to Luka's calls and try to guess where he is, closing my eyes and listening for clues: the hum of a vacuum cleaner outside of a hotel room door, the traffic outside his limo.

Once, he and Natalia had phone sex. *Shalava*, he'd told her, which means, roughly, "dirty slut." *When you get here, I will push you up against the door and rip your dress and bra off. Then I will lick your breasts until you can't take it any more....*

I replayed that call fifty-seven times. The computer red-flagged it and Roberta came over to my desk, concerned. "Is there a problem?" she'd asked. "Something you can't translate?"

"Nope," I'd said, flushing beet-red. "Just wanted to be sure."

That was the closest I got to sex. I hadn't had a boyfriend since the accident. At home, in bed, I'd sometimes jill off with the help of a vibrator, thinking about movie stars and lifeguards and the guy at the coffee shop. All the people I was supposed to think about.

And when none of that worked, I thought about Luka. Dark, dark fantasies about a man who took without asking permission. Hidden under the covers, with the lights off, I'd twist the sheets into sweaty hillocks in my fists and thrash and grind and bite my lip to stop from crying out and waking Nancy. Then, afterwards, I'd want to die with shame at the things I'd been imagining. Wasn't I supposed to want sex on a white-sands beach with a guy who respected me? Not...*this*.

And then things got completely out of control.

Then I started dreaming about him.

2

I'm running through a frozen forest, running to stay warm. It's beyond cold, the air so clear that everything looks ultra-sharp. Every last little bit of heat seems to have bled out into space and what's left is a deadly wasteland.

If I stay here, I'll die.

I'm in bare feet and a long white dress, the hem of it soaked through. Freezing snow is up to my ankles. I stagger and slip but I can't stop. Because behind me is—

I can feel him watching me. Huge and dressed all in black, almost filling the path behind me. He radiates heat—I can feel it licking at the back of my neck, melting the snow I've kicked up in my wake. His warmth feels so good....

But I know that he'll be my downfall. So I run even harder.

And suddenly, he's in front of me, so close that I can't pull up in time. I slam into his chest and it's like sun-warm rock against my breasts, almost too hot to touch. I try to push myself away, but his arms have closed around me, trapping me there.

I look up into his eyes: frozen blue orbs that pin me there and make me melt inside. His eyes say, *you want this.*

And I scream *no I don't* so loudly it almost drowns out the throb in my groin.

The ground collapses and we're falling, falling. Down into the earth and into a world of darkness and hard metal, sparks and fire. I land on my back and he's immediately on top of me, his lips pressing to mine. At the first kiss, I feel the heat sluicing down through me, burning its way through the ice that's gradually filled me in the three years since the accident.

I open my mouth to take a shuddering breath and his tongue slips into my mouth, silencing me. And despite my mind fighting it, I can feel my body starting to thaw, a wave of energy waking my slumbering body and making my nipples stiffen against his chest. Between my thighs, I'm aching for him.

He grips my white dress in one massive hand and shreds it, leaving me nude. He's naked too and I have a glimpse of a thick, erect cock before he's on top of me again, pushing my legs apart. He pins my wrists. I struggle as he tells me I want it. I struggle even as I know he's right.

And then I feel him, big and unstoppable, pressing for entrance and—

I woke up with the covers twisted around me and my panties damp.

And then, the next night, it happened again.

When the dreams came, they held back the nightmares. If I was dreaming of Luka, I wasn't dreaming of snow and screaming and the sensation of falling.

But I wasn't sure which one disturbed me more.

This was my life. I rode the bus to CIA headquarters every morning, I listened to people's private conversations for eight hours, and I fantasized about a man I'd never met. I rode the bus home again and read books and went to sleep. I had no social life, let alone a love life, because, ever since that day three years ago, I didn't seem to be able to connect to anyone. My life ticked away one day at a time and none of it felt remotely real or meaningful. The only real thing, to me, was Luka's voice.

Three years ago, I'd frozen inside, to shield me from the pain. I felt numb and utterly alone. The closest thing I had to a friend or a parent was Roberta, who I knew would never let me even get close to field work.

That was my life.

And then, the next day, my life changed completely.

3

I kept my eyes on my screen when he walked in, but then I pretended to glance at the clock so that I could sneak a split-second glance at him. I looked back at my screen and then closed my eyes and studied the mental snapshot.

He was in his late fifties, with a charcoal-gray suit and a white shirt that was soft at the creases, not hard and sharp. Hazel eyes, whites a little bloodshot. He had an expensive-looking red tie on with an ornamental tie clip. I was too far away to read the lettering but it looked as if it might have been from a college. Definitely not anyone I'd seen before. I wondered if he was from a level up, or even a level above that.

I have a photographic memory. It's not as much fun as it sounds. There are some things I'd rather forget.

"Arianna Scott?" he asked, like a teacher summoning a student.

I slowly stood up. Roberta was standing next to the guy, arms folded in that particular way that means she's really mad.

The guy studied me for a moment and then nodded to himself. *What? What does that mean?*

"Follow me," he told us. No *please.* The fact he could speak that way to Roberta immediately placed him several branches up the tree diagram. Up where the cool stuff happens. I felt my heart shift up a gear.

It took two elevators and a walk to get to his office, and every step took us further from the geeky, airless cave where we toiled all day and closer to the CIA you see in the movies. When I saw the sign on the door - *Adam Kinlen, Director, Special Activities Division*, my heart started full-on racing.

There was a window that looked out over a big, open-plan office. People were busy at screens that showed world maps, fingerprints, and photos. Some of them had headsets on, talking to field agents thousands of miles away. It was the real thing.

Roberta and I sat. Adam folded his hands behind his back and stood staring out over his empire, either unaware or uncaring that Roberta was glaring at him.

"Roberta speaks very highly of you, Arianna." he told me without turning around. "Hard worker, excellent Russian skills and outstanding retention."

"Thank you, sir," I said. I could feel the heat rising in my cheeks. "I've got a photographic memory. It's easy for me."

He turned around at that. *"Really?"* He sounded genuinely interested and enthusiastic. I was starting to like him. "Close your eyes," he said.

I closed my eyes.

"What's on my desk?" he asked.

I wondered if it was a trick question, because that was easy. "There's a half-full glass of water, a sandwich that looks like pastrami on rye, your computer, your phone, a memo with a yellow post-it note stuck to it and a classified report on the French Prime Minister. The report has a coffee stain in the bottom-left corner. It starts off, *"We believe that he and his secretary—"*

"That's enough!" Adam said quickly.

I opened my eyes. Adam strode across the room, grabbed the report and shoved it into a desk drawer. Roberta was smirking.

Adam gave me a look that was halfway between irritated and

impressed. "Roberta also tells me you're eager to get out of support and into some field work."

I glanced at Roberta. She gave me a look that very clearly said *no.*

I looked through the window at the busy people doing real intelligence work. I thought of another four hours of transcription that afternoon.

I nodded.

"Good," said Adam. "I think you're wasted in support." And he gave me a smile that made my whole heart lift. I mean, not in *that* way. He was old enough to be my dad, if my dad had still been alive. But it felt as if he really believed in me. "I want you to help us on a little op. You can play the violin, right?"

I blinked. It had come so completely out of left field that it took me a few seconds to answer. "Yes," I said hesitantly. "I mean, I haven't for a while...."

"You'll have a few days to practice," he said. "You're twenty-two, correct?"

I nodded.

"I want to go on record as not liking this," said Roberta. "Arianna's not a field agent."

"She went through basic training," Adam told her.

"There's a reason they call it *basic.*"

"Ultimately, it's up to Arianna," said Adam. He grinned at me. "Would you like to try? If it goes well, we can look at gradually moving you over to field work."

It sounded too good to be true. It was exactly what I'd wanted. I glanced at Roberta and got the *no* look again. I looked at Adam and he was a hundred and ten percent *yes.*

I nodded. "I want to try," I said firmly. "What would I have to do?"

Adam's smile grew even wider. "Let's get you some coffee while we talk." Then he glanced at Roberta. "You can go."

I didn't dare look at Roberta as she walked out. I felt...*disloyal?* But that was crazy. This was good for my career. She'd want me to progress, right?

"So," said Adam. "Luka Malakov."

Oh shit.

4

My face must have betrayed something because Adam frowned. "You look like you know him."

I shook my head, then nodded. "I just remember the name from transcribing his calls," I said weakly. *You know, like that one I listened to fifty-seven times.*

Adam nodded sagely. "Do you know anything about him?"

I shook my head and braced myself. I'd been curious all this time but, suddenly, I didn't want to know. I expected it to be bad.

It was worse.

"He's an arms dealer," said Adam. "Started out in the Russian mob, just like his dad, Vasiliy. Together, they've made millions—maybe billions—selling guns. Vasiliy's getting old, so he mostly stays cooped up in a fortified mansion while Luka handles all the day-to-day running of things." Adam looked right at me. "Luka keeps everyone in line. And very, very afraid."

My stomach flipped over. I'd been fantasizing about this guy.

"We believe Luka is setting up a big deal to bring guns into the US. We need to find out who the buyer is."

I frowned. "I didn't realize arms was our thing. Isn't that more FBI or ATF?" Then I flushed. Who was I to question the head of Special Activities?

"We have our reasons," he said stiffly. "Luka will be at his place in New York on Saturday, the first time he's been over here for months."

"Can't you just arrest him? I mean, once he's on US soil?"

Adam shook his head. "We don't have nearly enough evidence. That's why we need to bug his laptop."

I swallowed. "So how do I fit in?"

Adam smiled, relaxing a little. "He's throwing a party. He's hired a string quartet and we can get you in as one of them. You play some music, slip into his office and plant the bug and then walk out. Simple."

I'd see him. Actually be in a room with the man I'd been fantasizing about. I was still reeling from the idea of Luka suddenly being...*evil.*

You moron. You knew he was a bad guy. Why did you think the CIA were tapping his phone?

"What's he...like?" I wondered. And then realized I'd said it out loud.

"Brutal," said Adam. "Unyielding. He did some jail time, a few years back, and that hardened him even more. Luka's the new prince. He's inherited the kingdom from his dad and he's not going to let anything get in his way. He's killed several times—that we know about—rivals, mostly, who've tried to encroach on his family's territory. He's not afraid to use his fists, when someone needs to be taught a lesson. People are terrified of him, right across Moscow."

And he twisted his computer screen around to show me some photos. Suddenly, I was face-to-face with Luka.

I'd thought he'd be old, but the face looking back at me couldn't have been thirty, yet. His hair was cut short—longer than I'd imagined, but still short—and it was so dark I could only just see the soft texture of it.

He had high, prominent cheekbones and a wide, sensuous mouth, one corner curling up in a smile that was all dark malevolence and sex.

He wasn't handsome. Handsome is too bland. Hollywood celebrities are *handsome.*

This guy was beautiful. Savagely, brutally beautiful, like mountain peaks that have been shaped by wind and rain.

I'd realized I was staring. It had only been a few seconds but, for someone who can memorize a face in an instant, that was a lifetime. I couldn't remember ever staring at a photo like that. I dragged my eyes away.

There were more photos below, some of them half off the screen. I got a few glimpses of his naked back, twisting black tattoos over heavy slabs of muscle. Very different from the slender, gym-toned bodies that my boyfriends had had. He looked hard...*solid* in a way they never were.

I quickly looked away.

"The party's on Saturday," said Adam. He must have read the worry on my face because he gave me a reassuring smile. "You can do this, Arianna. A few hours of violin and a few seconds of action. In and out. Easy."

Easy.

Until it all went wrong.

5

Saturday. With four hours to go, I sat in my apartment and stewed. My roommate, Nancy, was off in South America doing whatever proper field agents do—probably breaking some guy's neck with her thighs—so I couldn't watch movies with her. I'd practiced the violin until my arms ached. That left me pacing the apartment, a sick feeling in the pit of my stomach. *Maybe I'm just not cut out for this.*

But I couldn't back out now. Everyone was relying on me. The whole mission was based around me planting the bug.

It started snowing at noon, which only made me more nervous. Snow made it harder to hold back the memories and the very last thing I needed was a flashback. *What the hell was I thinking?! I can't do this!* No wonder Roberta had been pissed at Adam. She was right—I belonged safe and snug in the Language department.

I knew I'd lose it if I kept thinking, so I did the only thing I could think of: I cooked.

Nancy doesn't have time to cook. She rolls in from an assignment jet-lagged and exhausted and sometimes wincing, her arm or leg in bandages. I figure that she needs to eat properly if she's going to be able to jump out of a plane and seduce a guard and still remember to cut the blue wire not the red wire.

So I cook for her. I keep the refrigerator full so that she can just pull something out and reheat it. And sometimes, like when it's snowing outside and I really need to take my mind off things, cooking is a good distraction. I cooked a big pot of slow-cooked shredded pork with lime and garlic and some slaw to go on top, then chilled it all and stuck a note to the refrigerator door to tell Nancy it was in there.

I put on a black dress and heels and put my hair up. Choosing what to wear was easy because I only *have* one black dress, an off-the-shoulder jersey thing that only normally came out once a year for our department's Christmas party. I put on my one pair of hold-up stockings, too, because I figured string quartets were meant to look glamorous.

A horn beeped outside. Adam, in a cherry-red SUV.

Shit. I hadn't known it'd be an SUV. And in the snow, too. At least I'd be in the front, not in the back.

I'd been in cars since the accident, of course, when I absolutely had to, but only for a few minutes at a time. This was three and a half hours. *God, I'm going to be a wreck by the time I get there.*

But, if I wanted to prove myself to Adam, I didn't have a choice.

I forced my legs to walk outside.

6

I survived by looking out of the windows. If I concentrated really hard on the snowflakes whipping past the window, I could almost imagine I was safe at home and not in a car at all. Adam tried to make small talk but he could see I was distracted. He probably thought it was nerves. I wasn't clear on why he was coming along on the mission —didn't he have a whole division to run?

Maybe he just wants to make sure you don't screw it up, I thought morosely.

I focused very intently on the scenery, trying to drink it in, trying to plaster the buildings and trees and sky all over my mind to cover up the slow-motion replay of another road trip, three years before.

There are two ways to reach the highway, from my apartment. One is through town and inevitably snarled with traffic. The other is to skirt around the back roads. When Adam turned that way, I tensed up completely. The road was still covered in snow, just like—

"Can we go through town, instead?" I asked.

Adam blinked and twisted around to look at me.

"I like to see it all lit up," I said weakly.

He shrugged and then smiled indulgently. "Sure."

I wanted to hug him.

~

About four hours later, in New York, Adam pulled up outside a red-brick building—some classy performing arts college. Two men in their twenties were standing there with instrument cases over their shoulders. A cello case stood upright in the snow between them.

"Where's the third one?" I asked Adam. "Aren't there meant to be three people, plus me?"

At that moment, a head poked out from behind the cello case. The woman behind it was so small, she'd been hidden behind it completely. She couldn't have been much over 5'4".

I jumped out and smiled goodbye to Adam, as if he was a dutiful dad dropping off his daughter. I was faking the smile but, the instant I was out of the car, I felt better. I hadn't realized how much I'd been holding back the memories with sheer force of will, the entire journey.

The short woman reached out a hand. "I'm Karen," she said. "Thanks for stepping in. Our normal violinist suddenly canceled. He's *never* done that before. Stomach bug."

He didn't have a stomach bug, of course. He'd met some gorgeous woman that morning and she'd practically unfastened his pants on the spot. He'd agreed to a date that evening in a heartbeat. She'd stand him up, but by then it would be too late. He'd slink back home, despondent, and never tell his friends the truth.

This is how the CIA works. We give your lives tiny little nudges and you're not even aware we're doing it. We may have even done it to you.

I grinned at Karen. "Happy to help."

~

We got a cab to Malakov's place. Weirdly, cabs don't bother me. They don't *feel* like a car.

There was a cable TV repair truck parked a little way down the street. Even as I glanced at it, I heard Adam's voice come from the earpiece I'd burrowed deep into my ear canal. "We're right here," he said. "I can see you. And we've hacked the house's cameras, so we'll be able to see you inside. He only has cameras in the hallway and living room, but that's all we need."

Most of the time, what I do is so abstract that I forget it's wrong. It's just recordings—somehow it doesn't feel like people's private conversations. But this—watching a guy in his own house, through cameras he'd installed to keep himself safe from intruders—this made some deep, moral part of me itch.

I started to walk across the street with Karen and the others. It was overwhelming to think that all this—Adam driving me all the way here, the elaborate ruse with the quartet, the truck full of monitoring equipment—was for *me*. What if I messed up?

And then a familiar voice came through the earpiece. "You okay?"

Roberta. She must have persuaded Adam to let her tag along in the monitoring truck. It was like receiving a warm, reassuring hug. I gave a tiny nod.

"You'll be fine," she told me. "Just stick to the plan. If anything goes wrong, get out. And whatever you do, stay away from Malakov."

I gave another tiny nod and then we were at the door. It was opened by a bodyguard in a suit—a guy in his forties, massively muscled, with a ragged scar across one cheek. He checked our driving licenses. I had a brand new one, carefully aged to look ragged, with my name as *Arianna Ross*—Adam figured I'd be less likely to slip up if I only had a new surname to remember.

"In," the bodyguard said at last in heavily-accented English. He jerked his thumb over his shoulder. "Living room."

I took a deep breath and stepped inside.

7

The house was huge, extending far back from the street. An elegant staircase led up to the second floor with another suited, frowning bodyguard at the top to make sure none of the guests strayed up there. At the far end of the hallway, I could see the huge living room through an open door. And in the corner of the hallway was another door, tightly closed. The door to Luka's office.

We trooped through to the living room, sat down on the chairs they'd put out for us and got out our instruments. We'd tuned up and were just about to start when he walked in.

Some people have *presence*. I know this because I have none of it myself. I disappear into the background.

When Luka entered the room, all of us looked up. Even people who'd been facing in the opposite direction turned around. You just *knew* he was there, like a sixth sense for pure, undiluted evil.

He was wearing a black suit and white shirt, but the shirt was lazily unbuttoned at the neck and his tie hung unfastened around his neck. I could see just a hint of broad, curving pec and a glimpse of black—tattoos. The photos from his file swam up into my mind: symbols of gangs and death and brotherhood, a world completely different from mine.

He was huge—not just taller than me but broader, too, his shoulders almost seeming to brush the door frame, yet his waist was tight and perfect. He looked as if he was chiseled from stone, no softness anywhere.

It was his face, though, that really hit me. His eyes were blue but not the warm, clear blue of a summer day. They were like a winter sky when the air is so cold it hurts. And I couldn't stop looking at his mouth, at that gorgeous full lower lip pulled tight in anger, or the shadow of stubble on his cheeks.

If someone had painted a portrait of the devil, he'd have looked exactly like Luka Malakov. Evil and beautiful. Scary and tempting.

The photo hadn't even come close to doing him justice, not to his looks nor his sense of menace. It's not that he was different from a normal man, in the way night is different from day. Night is just the absence of light. Luka sucked the light right out of the room.

I saw Karen react out of the corner of my eye. Her mouth fell open. Her knuckles went white on the bow of her cello. Fight or flight, like a mouse seeing a hawk. I think she stopped breathing for a few seconds; I know I did. My heart started slamming against my ribcage, my palms sweaty. I was terrified on a deep, instinctual level I'd never felt before.

Wait. That's not true.

Once. I'd been scared like that once.

But this time, the fear was churning and boiling inside me, turning into something else. A deep, dark heat was separating out and spreading down through my stomach...down to my groin.

Fight or flight.

Flight or fuck.

There were a couple of people hanging around in the middle of the room, blocking Luka's path, but he just strode towards them and *expected* them to get the hell out of his way, and they did.

He spoke in rapid-fire Russian to the bodyguard who'd let us in—the one with the scar, who seemed to be in charge of the others. I didn't even process what he was saying, even though I'd been happily translating his calls for months. I was lost in the sound of his voice.

Like the photo, the recordings weren't the same as the live experience. Each hard, snapped-out syllable felt like my brain was being slapped with a warm leather glove. I was reeling in seconds.

This was him. This was the man I'd been secretly fantasizing about, made flesh after so many months as just a voice. And now I knew what he was: a man who sold death to the highest bidder. A man who'd kill me if I got in his way. He'd certainly kill me if he found out I was CIA.

I have to get out of here. Right. Now.

And yet I was trapped there like an insect in amber. His presence seemed to drain all the will out of me. I didn't want to run. I wanted to stay right there and look at him. And, down between my thighs, there was a lashing, snaking heat like I'd never felt before.

No. This is just a twisted crush. Desperate for excitement, I'd locked onto some fantasy guy, created in my own head from a voice. *This is the real thing, Arianna, and he's dangerous.* I needed to pull myself together and look away—

He looked at me. Just a glance at the four of us, a sweep of those icy blue eyes. But, as he passed over me, his gaze lingered.

And then locked.

8

It was as if someone had opened an oven door right in front of me. The wave of heat licked every exposed inch of flesh, from my bare shoulders to my arms to my legs. The heat throbbed and then started to pulse, burning through the fabric of my dress to the skin beneath. I couldn't seem to draw a breath, the room's air suddenly desert-dry in my throat. The warmth seemed to slide around my breasts, underneath and then over the top, stroking my nipples in an elegant caress.

Some men undress you with their eyes; Luka was full-on groping me with his. Our gazes were locked together—he seemed as unable to look away as I was. The heat was rising and scalding inside me, destroying every coherent thought. Between my thighs I could feel the arousal tighten and turn to slick moisture. *Another few seconds and I'm going to melt right into my chair.*

Then Roberta's voice, right in my ear. *"Focus!"*

I jerked and tore my gaze away. Out of the corner of my eye, I saw Luka stare at me for one more beat of my heart...and then finally look away.

Roberta knew. She'd seen me on the security cameras, staring at Luka like some lovesick puppy. She was too kind to ask me what the hell I was doing—she'd just snapped me back to reality. *I owe her one. Did Adam notice?* Maybe not. Maybe it was the sort of thing only another woman would pick up on.

Maybe I could still pull this thing off.

Luka was marching out of the room. When he passed through the doorway, the whole room seemed to take a breath. I drew in a long, shuddering gasp myself and it felt like the first one I'd taken in minutes. Under the dress, my breasts still throbbed with remembered heat.

Next to me, Karen started to say something and then shook her head and stayed quiet. Clearly, she'd been affected by him a little, too.

She started to play and, after a few seconds, the rest of us did, too.

We played our first set and it went well. I wasn't up to the standard of the others, but we were playing simple, well-known classics and I got through it with only a few mistakes. The others were friendly and sympathetic. I liked them.

All I could think about, though, was Luka.

As the party got started, he returned, tie now neatly in place. The fastened shirt didn't do anything to hide the strong lines of his chest, though. Even with his jacket on, you could see the thickness of his upper arms and the solid sweep of his back, so wide from shoulder to shoulder. I kept my eyes off of him, except when he was looking completely the other way and I thought I could risk it. A couple of times, when he looked round and I was too slow to glance away, I could feel...*something.* Something dark and thick in the air between us, shot through with bright flashes. My whole body trembled like a magnet whose opposite is nearby.

I looked, very firmly, at my sheet music until the danger had passed.

After an hour, Karen put down her bow, rubbed her wrists and said we should take our break. We all stood. The two guys wandered off, probably in search of free wine. Karen pulled out a cell phone and went out into the hallway. That left me in the living room with about ten guests.

"Now," said Adam in my earpiece.

I walked through to the hallway, trying to look as if I was just wandering and not really going anywhere in particular. On the way out of the living room, I nudged the door with my hip and then stepped through before it slowly closed, giving me privacy. The hallway was chilly—every time a guest arrived, the freezing night air rushed in. No one was hanging around out here. The bodyguard was still standing stoically at the top of the stairs but the door to the office was out of his line of sight. As long as no new guests showed up for a few minutes, it was just me and Karen.

I moved casually in front of the office door and then leaned back against it. Just an accidental push on the handle with my ass and I felt it swing silently open behind me. I took a deep breath. Karen had wrapped her arms around her against the cold and was turned away from me, trying to have a private conversation with someone—probably a boyfriend. Perfect. I figured I'd quickly step inside, slap the bug on the laptop and be back in the hallway in no more than five seconds.

I turned and took a single step into the office...and stopped.

Where was the laptop?!

I'd assumed it would be out and set up, but the desk was bare.

I reversed course into the hallway and pressed my back against the wall. Eyes squeezed shut, I stared at the after-image of the office in my mind. No laptop case on the floor. Nothing on the shelves but books. Unless it was actually hidden away in a safe or something, it wasn't there.

"No, Connor," Karen sounded embarrassed and yet turned on. "I am definitely *not* getting any more piercings. Especially not *there.*"

I knew I didn't have to say anything. I knew Adam would be watching me through the security cameras. I found the one in the hallway, looked up into it and gave a firm shake of my head.

"Shit!" said Adam. "He must have taken it upstairs with him." He let out a long sigh and I heard him rubbing the back of his neck.

"There's nothing you can do. Play the second set and then come on out and we'll pick you up."

As I walked back into the living room, I almost felt like crying. All that time and planning, all that practicing the violin, Roberta and Adam brought hundreds of miles from Virginia, all for nothing. My very first shot at a field op and it was a complete bust.

9

Karen rejoined me, a little flushed, and then the two guys. We began to play again, but I couldn't concentrate. It wasn't my fault, but that didn't matter. There was no way I'd get another field assignment after this.

Part of me was glad. This whole thing had been terrifying enough. Crawling back to the support staff sounded pretty good, in some ways.

But I remembered how Adam had smiled at me, how he'd believed in me. He'd pushed for me to be given a chance and now I was going to disappoint him.

I saw Luka a few more times, talking intently to people, shaking hands and sometimes embracing people in firm, back-slapping hugs. There was no self-consciousness to him at all, no...*doubt*. I thought of myself at a party, standing nervously in the corner and waiting for someone to talk to me. He was the polar opposite.

There were women at the party, all of them in their mid-twenties and all of them, from what I could tell, Russian. They were classily dressed and model-beautiful, mostly blonde—exactly how I'd imagined Luka's girlfriends, when I'd listened to his calls with them. All of them—every one—latched onto him at some point, grabbing his arm and looking up at him with big eyes. And he gave them a smile.

And then ignored them.

When our second set came to a close, Karen let out a little sigh of satisfaction. "Thank you," she told me. "You really came through for us."

I smiled, but inside I was dying. The whole op had been a complete washout. I sat there numbly, watching Karen putting away her cello. She paused for a moment to check her phone and then smiled adorably as she read a text from her boyfriend.

My chest ached as I watched her. Why couldn't *I* have that? Why was I so wrapped up in spying on other people's lives, instead of living my own? We'd both just done the same gig at the same party, but she was going home in the warm glow of a job well done, home to the arms of her boyfriend. I had four hours in the SUV with Adam as we drove back to Virginia, while he tried to be polite about how it had turned out and I beat myself up, over and over—

I grabbed my stuff and headed out into the hallway. With four of us all trying to get out at the same time, especially with Karen's cello case, it was chaos. Then one of the guys from the quartet came back in out of the snow, complaining that he couldn't get a cab to stop, and—

The bodyguard who was guarding the stairs hurried down and out of the door to help and—

Just for a moment, the way upstairs was open.

Roberta must have seen my expression because I heard her catch her breath in my earpiece. "*No!*"

The bodyguard was still outside, his back to us, whistling for a cab. The hallway was empty aside from Karen. "I can do it," I murmured under my breath.

"*No!*" hissed Roberta. "Abort! Get out of there!"

Adam said nothing at all for a second. Then: "You really think you can do it?"

The hope in his voice made up my mind. I grabbed Karen's

shoulder. "I just have to find a bathroom," I told her. "You get the cab. My dad'll pick me up."

Karen was trying to maneuver her cello case out of the door. "What? Oh. You're sure? Okay. I'll PayPal you your share. Thanks!" And she bustled out. In the street, I saw a cab finally pull up. Any second now, the bodyguard would turn around.

Heart thumping in my chest, I raced up the stairs.

10

W hen I reached the landing, I headed straight for the bedroom whose light was on—I figured that must be Luka's. There was no time to listen at the door. The bodyguard was probably already walking back inside. Any moment, I'd hear him mount the stairs and then—

I pushed the door open and stepped inside, holding my breath. *If he's in here, it's all over....*

But the room was empty. I quickly closed the door behind me and leaned against it. Seconds later, I heard the heavy footsteps of the bodyguard on the stairs. Had he been counting the quartet as we left and knew he'd only seen three of us go? Would he wonder where I was or just assume I'd slipped out of the house in the commotion?

The footsteps reached the top of the stairs...then came slowly towards me. *Shit!* He was thinking about checking the rooms. The floor creaked, right outside the door....

...and then faded away as he went back to his post. It was several seconds before I dared to breathe again.

For the first time, I looked around. The lights were down low, but I could see a king size bed with expensive, midnight-blue bedding. Off to one side, an open door led to a walk-in closet with suits hanging in neat rows. On the other side of the room was a closed door that I figured led to the bathroom.

And sitting right in the middle of the bed, its screen lit up, was the laptop. Luka must have been coming up here throughout the night to check his email. A workaholic.

I hurried over to the bed and dug in my purse for the bug—a wafer-thin silver sticker. I lifted up the laptop, then peeled off the sticker's backing and stuck it in place on the underside. Now, whenever the laptop was on, we'd be able to see what was on his screen.

I put the laptop back exactly as I'd found it. Now all I had to do was wait until the bodyguard took a break and I could sneak downstairs and out of the front door.

At that moment, the door to the bathroom swung open and Luka stepped out.

11

There are some moments you know you're going to remember for the rest of your life. I know this, because one in particular has burrowed so deep into my soul that it's never coming out. I remember the sickening feeling in the pit of my stomach as the car fell. It was my life, dropping out from under me. The feeling that nothing is ever going to be alright again.

This was the same and yet different. That was an ending; this was something beginning.

I'd stepped away from the bed and towards the door. That single step probably saved my life. If I'd still had my hand on the laptop, he'd have known for sure I was a spy and I would have been carried out of that room in a bloody, plastic-wrapped bundle.

I saw shock on his face and then, just for a split second, another look, one I couldn't even process, right then—I filed it away for later. Then anger, and a quick glance at the laptop.

Some instinct made me keep my eyes on him. If *I'd* looked at the laptop, my fate would have been sealed. But I just stood there, mouth open, as he closed the distance between us.

One huge hand slammed into my chest, the palm right on the valley of my upper breasts. He pushed me back against the door, the hard wood jarring me painfully. He kept coming, stopping when his face was inches from mine. The whole world narrowed down to the throbbing heat of his hand against my skin and those burning, ice-fire eyes.

"What the *fuck* are you doing in my room?" he demanded.

We stared at each other as I took panic breaths through my nose, my lips a tight line of fear. His hand, pinning me to the door, might as well have been made of warm iron. He had me so firmly that I couldn't even wriggle to the side. And despite my mounting panic, I was aware of the side of his thumb and the side of his pinky finger as they framed the tops of my breasts. Every breath made the soft flesh push and swell around them and a black, twisting energy shoot straight down to my groin. *What the fuck is wrong with me?!*

In my earpiece, I could hear panicked whispers as Adam, Roberta and the others tried to figure out what to do. Burst in and rescue me? Wait and see how it played out?

His words were replaying over and over in my head. It was the first time I'd ever heard him speak in English. His accent was heavy, softening some syllables and making others granite-hard. His *fffuck* was like a slow penetration followed by a jerk of the hips.

What the hell is wrong with me?! I wondered again. I had to answer him, had to think of some way out of this, but my mind was stuck on endless loop, replaying his words. Any second now, he was going to snap and just kill me.

So I did the only thing I could think of. I squeezed my eyes shut to try to break the loop and saw that image of him as he'd come out of the bathroom. The shock on his face, flicking momentarily to another look.

Pleasure.

Just for a fraction of a second, the ghost of a smile had touched his lips. Not the fake smile he'd given the women downstairs. A smile that actually reached those cold eyes, thawing them a little. It had been gone in an instant, but it had been there. He'd been pleased to see me.

The implications of it were still detonating like fireworks in my chest when I opened my eyes and said, "I was looking for you."

He went utterly silent. His eyes flicked over my face, fast and brutally efficient, searching for any trace of a lie.

He didn't find one because, on some level, I think I was telling the truth.

He inched his head back from me, but he didn't release me. He was getting a better look at me, I realized. He'd been entirely focused on my face, but now his eyes swept down over my chest, my hips, my legs. Something like a hot shudder went through me and I felt a flush rise in my cheeks. That feeling I'd had downstairs was back, that sense of being locked onto each other like magnets, close enough now that I twisted and turned to mimic his movements.

As he looked at me, I looked at him. He was nearly a head taller even with me in my heels, and his frame blocked out almost all of the light from behind him. With the black suit, he looked like he was made of shadow except for those blazing blue eyes. But it wasn't his size so much as the solidity of him, the *realness*. Next to him, I felt like a faded, worn-thin copy of a person.

And the weirdest part was, as I stood there pinned against the door, I could feel the energy of him flowing into me, reawakening me. After years spent frozen and slowly dying, I finally felt alive again.

He took a long, slow breath and leaned in closer to me again. He was wearing some cologne I didn't recognize, something complex and elegant and somehow old-fashioned. He moved his mouth close to my ear. Then he spoke, and each word was like a savage little kiss. "You shouldn't come looking for monsters. Men like me will eat you alive."

And then he drew back to see my reaction.

I didn't know how I was going to react either. I was operating on a whole different level, now, something deep inside me directing things. I was just along for the ride.

I took a shaky breath and whispered, "I'm not scared of you."

He stared deep into my eyes, appraising me, and said, "Yes you are."

And a deep, hot oil slick seemed to sluice through me, more complex than fear, more complex than lust.

His free hand closed on my leg, just beneath the hem of my dress. His palm cupped my flesh through the nylon, his heat throbbing into me. And he stared at me, demanding an answer.

I swallowed and stared back, and the message my eyes sent was... "Continue."

His hand rose, rasping along the dark nylon, my breathing ratcheting higher and higher with each inch. His fingers slid over my thigh...then my upper thigh. Each square millimeter he touched burned as if it was on fire, the energy crackling inward and up towards my groin. The dress was coming up along with his hand, gathering on his wrist. And then he touched the naked skin above my stocking and I realized I was panting.

He stared straight into my eyes as his fingers reached my panties. His fingertips toyed with the waistband for a second...and then continued. He moved inward, now, hoisting my dress up further with an impatient jerk of his wrist. His hand slid over my stomach and up to my chest and—

He cupped my breast, his hand weighing it in my bra. His palm throbbed warmth through the thin fabric, straight into my soft flesh. Then he squeezed—a long, lingering squeeze, and pleasure erupted in my chest and roared out to every corner of me. I tried to go up on my tiptoes, to twist, to thrash in response, but his other hand still had me pinned. I had to just stay there and take it.

I'd never been more turned on.

And then I heard a noise in my earpiece, a soft intake of breath. They're listening to this!

And my mouth said, "I have to go," even as my body demanded that I stay right where I was.

Luka had his eyes half-closed. He just remained there, studying me for another few seconds. He gave my breast one last, unexpected squeeze and I gasped as it sent a ripple of heat through me. Then he released me and my dress fell back into place.

Operating on autopilot, I grabbed my violin case and opened the door. I'd taken two steps out into the hallway before I remembered the bodyguard on the stairs. He turned at the sound of the door opening and his jaw dropped. He reached under his jacket—maybe for a radio, maybe for a gun.

But then I heard Luka emerge behind me, and whatever nod or gesture he made to his bodyguard made the man step back immediately and clear a path for me. I didn't turn around. I just hurried down the stairs, violin banging against my hip, threw the front door wide and headed straight for the cherry-red SUV. Adam was already inside and waiting and I could see the concern in his eyes. But he faked a fatherly smile and opened the door for me. I quickly climbed inside.

We roared away and the last image I had of the house, in the rear view mirror, was Luka in the doorway, thoughtfully watching me go.

There was a debriefing, back at Langley. Roberta did a lot of yelling about my "crazy stunt," although I knew most of it was out of concern. Adam backed me up. "The bug's in place," he said. "We pulled it off." He smiled at me.

We. I liked that. I felt as if I was part of his team. In with the cool kids, even if it was only temporary. You have no idea how good that feels, when you were never cool at school.

We didn't talk about what happened in the bedroom, as such. I wasn't sure how much they were able to put together, from the few words we'd said plus some rustling and panting. Thank God there were no cameras in the bedroom. Both Roberta and Adam asked if I was okay and I said yes, which was both true and not true at all.

I was still trying to process the whole thing. One minute, I remembered it as being terrifying, the next it was the hottest sexual experience of my life, actual sex included. I thought about it from one angle and I'd been an innocent, out of my depth, desperately trying to come up with an excuse for being in his room. I thought about it another way and I was desperate in a whole different way. *I'm not scared of you,* I'd claimed. But I was scared of him. I was just so turned on by him that it was overcoming my fear.

I'd complained that I was stuck in a rut- that nothing changed in the sterile, airless world I inhabited. Then, suddenly, I'd been way out in a void, dangling by a hair-thin rope over a precipice. The way I'd reacted to him was deeply disturbing, completely alien to me and yet in some weird way familiar. As if he was a dangerous drug I'd tried for the first time and found to be perfect for me. Perfect, and addictive.

The one reassuring thing was that it was over. My first op had been a success...just. And I might have pissed off Roberta, but I'd impressed Adam. Maybe he'd give me another shot.

And, whether he did or not, my future lay a long way from Luka Malakov. Aside from listening to his phone calls, I'd never hear of him again.

12

The next morning, I wasn't granted a late start just because the debriefing had finished in the early hours. I dragged myself in, eyelids only held open by coffee, and tried to avoid Roberta. I figured she'd be mad that I'd ignored her order and ran upstairs, and also that I'd gone against her wishes and volunteered for the op in the first place.

I started transcribing calls. Some banker, complaining to his friend about his wife. Then Luka, talking about another one of his women. That got my interest, but I was still half asleep as my fingers rattled over the keys, only vaguely aware of what I was typing.

Then, suddenly, I sat bolt upright in my chair.

The woman Luka was talking about was me.

"She was the one in the string quartet," Luka was saying.

Another voice. "The short one?"

"No. The pretty one."

The pretty one?!

"You think she was up to something?" asked the other voice. I recognized it, this time. Luka's head bodyguard, the guy with the scar on his face.

"I think she's an innocent," said Luka. "But I want to know how innocent. Do a check on her."

"What if she's not so innocent?"

"Then I want to fuck her."

"What if she *is* innocent?"

I could hear the smile in Luka's voice. "Then I want to fuck her even more."

The call ended. I sat there staring at the screen, feeling as if I'd just had five espressos.

He.

Wanted.

To.

Fuck.

Me.

And in a few minutes, the head bodyguard was going to call Karen. And Karen would give him my false name. And he'd discover that Arianna Ross didn't exist.

If I didn't want to blow the whole operation, I had to act *now*.

I rushed into Adam's office and told him that Arianna Ross was about to have her background checked. About two seconds after I'd finished speaking, I realized what he was going to ask next.

"Okay," he said. "Can I see the transcript?"

There followed the most toe-curlingly embarrassing minutes of my life, as Adam brought up the conversation on his screen and read what Luka had said. To his credit, he didn't comment. He just nodded a few times and then pressed a button on his desk phone. "Get me Solomon," he said.

A moment later, Solomon walked in. His tattoos, long black hair and the fact he was dressed in a black vest and jeans was strangely reassuring. For the CIA to make that many concessions to its dress code, he must be packing some serious tech credentials.

"This is Arianna *Scott,*" said Adam. "She needs her face transferred to a blank, *now,* with the name Arianna *Ross.*"

"Five minutes," said Solomon in a British accent, and walked out.

"Really?" I asked. "Five minutes?"

"He's being modest," said Adam. "More like two."

Blanks are one of the CIA's best-kept secrets.

Being a spy used to be easy. You could walk into an embassy or a trade convention in the 1970s or even the 1980s and say you were Alice Smith when you were really Betty Jones. As long as your passport looked real, no one could tell the difference. We only had to think about fooling the enemy face-to-face.

Then Facebook happened.

Now, Alice Smith doesn't just have to have a fake passport. She has to have an entire fake life, with a Facebook profile dating back years, school friends posting on her wall and ten thousand tweets conveying her every thought. And that's impossible.

Unless you're us.

Blanks are fake people. We have hundreds of them. They have birthdays and school friends and career histories. They have photos on their timelines and Twitter feeds showing them laughing in bars and falling off horses.

These are the people who unexpectedly friend you on Facebook and you never know why. They're the ones who don't message you, and never really interact except to like your funny cat pictures.

A blank's photos are posed by actors. Now, hundreds of shots of my face, taken when I first joined the CIA, were being seamlessly edited into those photos, replacing the actress's.

Maybe you've seen this happen. Maybe you've noticed a woman on your Friends list and frowned and thought, *Didn't she used to be called Jessica? And weren't her eyes green, before?* But you don't know her all that well so you shake your head and put it down to your imagination.

No more than three minutes after Solomon had left, Adam turned his computer screen to me and said, "Google yourself."

I sat down and typed my name on the keyboard. Google told me that I had a Facebook profile and a Twitter account. I had an email address with emails from friends arranging parties and nights out. I had Pinterest boards filled with book covers and recipes. *This is more real than my real life* I thought, a little sadly.

If Luka's head bodyguard checked up on me now, he'd be convinced I was real...and "innocent."

Adam sat back in his chair. "Now we need to decide what to do," he said.

I blinked. "Do?" Hadn't we just solved the problem?

Adam looked at me appraisingly. "He still wants to fuck you."

I stiffened, partially from hearing a superior drop the f-bomb, partially from the reminder. "Maybe he was just kidding around," I said, flushing.

"I don't think so."

"He's got plenty of women."

"And yet he called for a background check on you. He's interested *in you.*" Adam stared at me. "That gives us an angle."

I can be a little slow to catch on, sometimes. I didn't see where he was going. Then it hit me like a freight train in the face. "You don't mean...you want me to *see* him?!"

Adam leaned forward. "I want you to be his girlfriend. Meet him. Seduce him. Get him to confide in you."

"I can't do *that!*" I jumped to my feet. My heart felt as if it was going to smash its way out through my ribs. "I can't—" *His girlfriend. Luka's girlfriend.* Kissing him and, inevitably...*Jesus!* "He's only here for a few days."

"Yes. You'll have to go to Moscow."

I just stared at him. *He can't possibly be serious.*

But Adam just sat there, watching me calmly, seeing how I'd respond. I stood there staring at him, panting. I don't know what disturbed me more: the fear of what he was asking me to do, or the fact that there was a deep, dark part of me that actually wanted to do it.

"I'd have to sleep with him?" I said, half to myself.

Adam nodded. "I'm pretty sure that'd be on the cards, yeah."

I swayed, almost staggering. *This is not happening. I am not discussing my sex life with my boss's boss's boss.* I stared at him. How could he ask me to do this? Luka was a monster. God knows how many people he'd hurt or killed, between prison and his mafia days and now his arms business. And I'd have to smile at him and then close my eyes and open my lips for his kiss....

If I did this, if I had sex with a guy because it was my job, did that make me a prostitute?

Or—my chest tightened—if I wanted to be with him but couldn't, because of what he was, did this make it okay? Was this just the excuse I needed?

Obviously, this was insane. Obviously I had to say no. But I remembered how he'd made me feel. Not just the all-consuming lust, but that sense that I was waking up after three years asleep, that he was *real* and was making me real again. *I'd give anything for another taste of that.*

I'd been staring at Adam's desk as I thought. Now I lifted my eyes to his face. "What if he finds out? What if my cover's blown?"

"Then he'll kill you," said Adam simply.

It felt like freezing water was sluicing up my spine. But, at the same time, I felt the ghost of Luka's hand on my chest, pinning me to the wall. His other hand, exploring me. A flame sprang into life at my core, black as night yet furnace-hot. I could barely breathe.

I was terrified and yet turned on. And some indescribable third feeling, a mixture of the two.

"How long?" I asked. "How long would I be with him?"

"Until we find out how big this deal is," said Adam. "We don't have jurisdiction to arrest him ourselves. But, once we have evidence, we can pressure the Russians to act."

My legs felt as if they were going to give out, so I flopped down into the chair again. I couldn't meet Adam's eyes anymore, the twisting heat inside me out of control. God, did Adam know how I felt?! It must be written all over my face. Certainly, he must have figured out what happened in Luka's bedroom.

"Arianna," he said softly. "This is one of the hardest things an agent can be asked to do. I don't do it lightly. But Malakov is a difficult man for us to get close to. He doesn't trust anyone...except maybe you."

I nodded.

"If you say no," Adam said, "I swear to you, it won't affect your standing or whether I send you on future field ops. You have a choice."

I could feel Luka's hand on my thigh, his fingers toying with the waistband of my panties.

"Take some time," Adam said. "Think about it."

I didn't need time. There was only one possible choice.

"My answer's yes," I whispered. "I'll do it."

13

A half hour later, Adam called in Roberta. He asked me to wait in the hallway while they discussed my reassignment. While they discussed *me.*

It turned out that the soundproof walls at Langley aren't all they're cracked up to be.

"Are you out of your *goddamn mind?!*" yelled Roberta. "She's a languages geek, not a field agent!"

She'd always seemed so proud of my skills. It didn't feel that way now.

"She's smart," said Adam calmly. "She's resourceful. She handled herself well at his house."

"She could have been killed! If he'd seen her messing with his laptop—"

"He didn't. And anyway, it's her choice."

Roberta's voice rose further. "You don't know her like I know her! She's got issues!"

"Do you think I'd be suggesting this without having read her file?"

"That's not the same as knowing her! She has flashbacks! Nightmares! She can barely get in a goddamn car, Adam!"

Hot shame flared in my cheeks. I hated being a mess. I hated still feeling like a teenager.

"She's CIA," said Adam. "She's done her training. She wants to do field work. And Malakov wants to fuck her. That's good enough for me."

"You *know* that kind of field work needs a certain kind of woman," snapped Roberta. "Arianna is *not it*. Get Nancy!"

I jerked at that. *Nancy?* They'd put my best friend on this, instead of me? My stomach tensed up. Nancy was the best. That showed how hard Roberta thought this mission would be. *Maybe I should back out. Let Nancy have it.* She was the mature one, the *together* one.

But then I thought of her seducing Luka, effortlessly and professionally, and...part of me didn't want that. *Am I jealous?! That's insane!*

"Nancy's in Venezuela," said Adam. "And Malakov doesn't want *that sort of woman.* He wants Arianna."

"You can't do this, Adam! Why do you even *want* Malakov so badly? Let the Russians handle him!" Their voices were getting louder. I winced. I hated hearing them fight.

I heard Adam's chair scrape the floor as he stood. "You need to back off. That girl works here and right now we need her and she's stepped up to the plate. The only one who's not on board here is you!"

"I'm the only one who's thinking straight! Arianna is—" She must have realized she was shouting, because she lowered her voice.

A woman in a suit—someone from another division—chose that moment to walk by. She glanced at the closed door and raised voices and then at me, standing outside, and gave me a sympathetic smile.

"Arianna is *fucked up!*" Roberta hissed at that exact moment.

I did my very best to smile back at the passing woman, despite feeling as if I wanted to die.

"Sorry, Roberta," said Adam. "You're going to have to let go of your little pet. Now get out of my office."

A moment later, Roberta marched out of the office. *"Follow,"* she snapped, without even looking at me. I scurried after her, despite being close to tears at what she'd said about me.

When we got back to our department, she took me straight through to her private office and closed the door. I'd barely ever been in there. She normally liked to sit out in the open office with the rest of us.

Today, though, she closed the blinds, nodded me to a chair and then leaned against the desk, gripping the edge of it so hard that her knuckles whitened. Her dark hair fell forward, hiding her face. I imagined her counting to ten in her head. Then she took a long breath and looked up at me. "Sorry, if you heard some of that."

"It's okay," I lied. I'd been loyal to this woman for years, ever since she'd recruited me. Now I just wanted to be sick. Was that what she'd thought of me all this time? That I was *fucked up?!*

Roberta caught my expression. "I was just trying to protect you. That's all I want, Arianna—to protect you."

I swallowed, thinking of Adam and how he believed in me. "I know. But I want to do this."

Roberta sighed and sat down heavily in her chair. "It's my fault," she muttered. "I should have let you move into field work." She opened a filing cabinet and, from the very back of the drawer, pulled out a bottle of Scotch.

Roberta *drank?!* During the day?

She must have seen my look. "Only on special occasions," she said. And she poured two glasses, handing me one.

I stared at the amber liquid. My brain was still trying to catch up. "You've been a great boss," I said truthfully. *Until today.* And maybe she had just been trying to protect me. And what she'd said was true —I *was* fucked up. But I hadn't wanted her to tell Adam that and I hadn't wanted to hear her say it. Hearing that conversation had made me want to prove her wrong and impress Adam even more.

"I know you want to get out of here," Roberta said despondently. "I just—You're so good at what you do, Arianna. I need you *here*. And I don't want anything to happen to you." She looked me in the eye. "Russia's nothing like America. It's hard. Brutal. Adam should know better—he worked over there for years before he got moved up the ladder. I can't believe he's even *thinking* of sending you. I don't even understand why he wants to do this op in the first place." She shook her head. "Look—don't do this. Not Malakov."

"I can do it," I said, with a certainty I didn't feel.

"Can you? Really?" She sighed. "This sort of man can be charming, but underneath he's pure ice. He'll kill you if he finds out. He won't hesitate. Mafia guys are all about loyalty. You'll be violating that in the worst possible way. And if you *can* keep him fooled, you'll have to be with him." She sipped her Scotch. "God knows what he'll want in the bedroom. A man like that, Arianna, he's not going to be..." She sighed again. "He's not going to be like one of your boyfriends."

A chill went through me. A chill that changed to heat when it hit my groin. *God, what's wrong with me?* I flushed.

When I met Roberta's eyes again, she was staring right at me, a worried look on her face. *She can't know how I feel about him...can she?*

"Arianna, reconsider," she said. "You're about to get into shit you can't handle."

I took a deep breath...and shook my head.

14

Airports all look the same. That's what my dad used to tell me, when he returned from a business trip. But Moscow was utterly, terrifyingly alien.

There was something in the air, as soon as I stepped outside the terminal building. It felt harsh against my lips, as if they were being scoured. It wasn't just the cold, although it was snowing and a long way below freezing. It was the rawness of the air. It made the air back home seem warm and perfumed and soft as satin.

Behind me, the terminal building was like a long, green bottle on its side, all clean lines and elegant curves. Beautiful, but uncompromising. And on top of it, in huge metal letters, a sign in Cyrillic that looked straight out of the Cold War. I spent all day listening to Russian, back home, but to see the unfamiliar letters was still a shock. Your brain gets used to the alphabet, ever since you were a kid watching Sesame Street. Stumbling over letters again is like suddenly forgetting how to swim.

I hadn't been ready for customs, either. It wasn't that it had taken a long time, or that they'd asked all that many questions. It was just something in the look the officer had given me, the way he'd almost flung my passport back to me. Travelling from the US to Mexico or Canada—the only other countries I'd ever been to—I'd always felt welcome, or at least accepted. Here, I was tolerated.

Maybe it was the jet lag but, when I climbed into a cab and heard Russian pop music on the radio, I almost wanted to weep. I just longed for something familiar.

Pull yourself together! You wanted this! I asked the driver to take me to my hotel and we set off.

I couldn't wear an earpiece because, if things went well—my heart missed a beat—Luka would be getting close enough that he'd spot it. I could call Adam on the brand-new cell phone they'd given me, but even then the presumption was that the authorities might be intercepting foreigners' calls. I'd have to pretend Adam was my dad.

I'd never, in my whole life, felt so alone. There was a big part of me that wanted to tell the driver to turn around and take me back to the airport, then get the next plane home and quit the CIA. Get a normal job where I didn't have to lie to everyone I met.

But then I'd never see him again.

My reunion with Luka was meant to be accidental, so it had to be thoroughly planned.

We knew he had a thing for ice hockey—one of his few indulgences beyond women. He'd played, when he was in his teens, and in the winter he still liked to smack a puck around each weekend at Gorky Park.

Gorky Park is the Russian equivalent of Central Park. In the summer, it's full of joggers and couples pushing baby strollers. But each winter, all of the paths are deliberately iced over to create Europe's biggest ice rink. You can skate around the entire park on the paths, or there's a separate area for dancing and another for ice hockey.

Our agents in Moscow had reported that Luka usually showed up early, before his friends, and hung around near the ice hockey rink, watching the skaters. The idea was that I'd be skating and he'd see me and approach. I'd tell him how I was on vacation, starting off in Moscow before maybe taking in Rome, Paris and Venice. The team at Langley had carefully set me up with an itinerary that would give him a sense of urgency—*I'm only in Moscow for a few days*—while also leaving the door open for something to happen—*but my tickets are flexible...*

It was brilliant and ridiculous. Would he believe it was just a coincidence? My heart started thumping. Would he *want* to believe enough that he'd buy it?

And there was another problem: I can't ice skate. I mean, I might be able to stumble around with some friends, all holding hands, and the falling over would be part of the fun. But who goes to an ice rink on vacation on their own when they can't skate? I was going to look like the world's most stubborn woman. *I bet Elena and Natalia and Svetlana could skate.* During my briefing, I'd seen some long-lens photos of Luka with his last few girlfriends, finally putting faces to the voices I'd listened to for months. All of the women had been just as gorgeous and slender and blonde as I'd feared. *Why the hell is he interested in me?!*

I knew that, somewhere in the crowd, a local CIA agent would be keeping an eye on me and reporting back to Adam. But they wouldn't intervene unless things looked like they were going drastically wrong. I was basically on my own.

I went down on my ass for the fiftieth time. My hired skates were too tight, my jeans were soaked through, and my fingers were numb, even in gloves. I had no idea if Luka was watching me, or if he was even there. *What if he doesn't recognize me?* I had a woolen hat pulled tight over my ears and was cocooned in a thick coat. It was a long way from a dress and heels.

I stumbled towards a bench and clutched at it for support, panting. *What if he doesn't show up at all?*

I decided to give it one more try. I pushed off from the side, dodged a family who were all skating together and nearly collided with a young couple. Veering away from them sent me into a skittering mess, my arms circling desperately as I fought for balance, and then I went down—

Strong hands caught me under my armpits, just before I hit the ice.

I got my feet under me, blew my hair out of my face and tried to compose myself. I could feel him behind me. My chest was suddenly light with relief and a warm glow was spreading through me from where he was touching me. *Look surprised. Look surprised. Should I pretend I don't recognize him? No, that's too much. Look surprised—*

I turned and looked at him.

It wasn't Luka.

"...hi," I said. It was all I could think of.

The guy grinned. He was about my age and had sandy-colored hair that fell in tangled curls. "Hi!" he said enthusiastically. "American?" His accent wasn't nearly as strong as Luka's.

"Yes."

"It's *cold* here, yes? Want to get coffee?" He nodded to the side. A little way down the path, there were stalls set up selling tea and coffee, and you could skate right up to the counter. He was cute, in a rosy-cheeked, farm boy sort of a way.

An arm clapped around my waist and spun me around. I'd forgotten, for a second, that I was still balanced on a couple of metal blades and I nearly fell, but the arm tightened and held me.

I looked up into Luka's eyes.

"Hey," said the other guy. He sounded halfway between angry and friendly, as if he wasn't sure which would get the best result.

Luka glanced at him over my shoulder. My stomach plummeted about a thousand floors and then exploded into a deep, dark heat. The look said *she's mine.*

I heard the other guy skate away.

I remembered that I was meant to be acting surprised, but the whole thing had happened so fast that I didn't have to act. I just stood there, my back resting against Luka's muscled arm, and blinked up at him. *Up* being the operative word—I'd almost forgotten how big he was.

"You don't need to go for coffee with him," said Luka. "You are coming to lunch with me."

He asked my name, even though by now he'd have got it from the background check his bodyguard did. So we were both acting.

It occurred to me that he might suspect. Maybe my fake background hadn't been convincing enough. What if he'd approached me not because he wanted me, but because he sensed I was a spy and wanted to interrogate me? We were in a public place now but, as soon as he got me alone....

"Arianna," I said. "Arianna Ross." It's disconcerting, saying a different surname after your real first name. Like being suddenly married.

"Luka," he said. "Malakov." He was studying me very intently, his ice blue eyes searching mine. Because he liked me, or watching to see if I'd slip up?

I had time to take things in, now. Despite the cold, he wore no coat. He was in ice hockey gear, minus the padding. Several paces behind him, I could see the bodyguard from New York, the one with the scar on his cheek, watching me suspiciously.

Luka asked me what I was doing in Moscow and I spun him the vacation story. I asked what he did and he said he bought and sold things, internationally. Closer to the truth than my story. Then he reached out and touched my cheek. It was only a brush of his fingers but, immediately, I felt that connection again. The heat of him throbbed into my exposed, frozen skin and I wanted to close my eyes so that I could savor it. How could just a touch from this guy feel like the best thing in the frickin' world?

I had to remind myself to breathe.

"So...you said you wanted to take me to lunch?" I asked.

"No. I said you are coming to lunch with me."

I opened and closed my mouth a few times. "Are you always this..."—*arrogant?* — "presumptuous?"

He stared down at me, his gaze burning me up. "I remember my bedroom. Don't you?"

I felt myself flush.

He leaned close. "Still want to play with monsters?"

I didn't answer but, as he drew back and watched me, my expression must have been answer enough.

"Which hotel are you in?" he asked. "My driver will pick you up."

I told him and he said to be ready at one. And, just like that, he dropped his arm from my waist and skated away.

Did he know? Was that why he was so certain I'd agree?

Or did he detect my other secret? That, whenever I was near him, I wanted to get even closer? That I'd press myself so hard to him that we'd merge, if I could. If that was it, that was almost as scary as him knowing I was a spy. Because that dark heat inside was something I didn't even understand myself.

Back at my hotel, I sat on the bed and stared at the screen of my new cell phone. The contact name said *Dad*.

I knew it was just a cover, but it didn't stop the deep, cold ache inside me every time I saw that name.

I hit the button and Adam answered. I told him excitedly how I'd met a guy at Gorky Park and we were going for lunch. He did a pretty good job of sounding fatherly, telling me to be careful and asking which sights I'd seen.

I knew it was unusual for my handler to be someone as senior as him. His group must have hundreds of covert ops on the go—why was he taking such a personal interest in this one? Because he believed in me? Because he saw something in me that Roberta couldn't? I liked that idea.

I found a red dress and black knee boots that I figured would work for a restaurant. I'd had to go shopping, before I left. I had to look like an independent, carefree young woman who'd jet off on her own on vacation, not a geeky shut-in. I stripped out of my wet jeans and the thick sweater I'd worn for the ice skating...and then I stopped and looked at myself in the mirror.

Could Luka really want...*me?* I looked down over my body. I was just *normal.* I didn't have big boobs or long legs and I was no size zero. And he was gorgeous and—from what I'd glimpsed on his prison photos back in Langley—hard and sculpted beneath those expensive clothes.

I closed my eyes for a second and that image of his back was before my eyes. Thick slabs of muscle, strong enough to easily pick me up and carry me...or throw me down on a bed. Tattoos, and not some mass-produced, generic tribal swirls designed to make the owner look "edgy." Luka's tattoos were like a tapestry that told his life. A spider, in the center of its web: he was committed to a life of crime. A rose: he was part of the *Bratva,* the Russian mafia. Stars on his shoulders: he was a man of status, a higher class of criminal.

Criminal. What the hell was I doing, thinking about him in this way? He was the target!

I had to remain detached. This had to be an assignment, not a relationship. If I let it get personal, if I let him get under my skin, I'd be giving myself up to a man who was pure evil.

But if I did manage to keep it professional, if I slept with him and it meant nothing...wasn't that even worse?

I opened my eyes. And saw that my hand wasn't exactly between my thighs, but was tracing along the top of my panties. I jerked it guiltily away and hurried to get dressed.

The car arrived for me. A big, midnight-blue sedan, polished so bright that its flanks seemed to be made of dark water. The driver was Luka's head bodyguard. The scar across his cheek and all those muscles made him look intimidating, but he didn't seem thuggish, like some nightclub doorman. He seemed solemn, more than anything, as if he took his job very, very seriously.

I couldn't get that phone call out of my head, the one when Luka had asked him to do a background check on me. *He knows Luka wants to fuck me.* Is that how he viewed me? Did he think he was just delivering a sacrificial lamb to his boss?

Inside, the car was all flawless cream leather. I was okay until the bodyguard slammed the door. Then I felt the memories start to stir and wake. This wasn't like a cab. This was a normal car, with me in the back seat. It was daylight and it wasn't snowing, so that was something. But it still came dangerously close to triggering me.

I had to do something to keep my memory tied up so that it didn't have time to reach down into its depths and serve up my past. I stared out through the window and started to translate everything I saw into Russian. Lamppost. Dog. Tree.

It was ominously silent on the journey. There was no music and almost no road noise, the doors and windows muffling it completely. I wondered if they were armored.

I translated madly, staring at every passing building, translating *drugstore, apartment block, convenience store* as fast as I could. And then I broke off because I had a whole new problem. I noticed the bodyguard watching me in his mirror.

My stomach twisted into a knot. If Luka did have suspicions about me, he'd have told his man to look for anything suspicious. What should I do? Ignore him? Talk to him? What constituted *suspicious?!* God, this was already unbearable! *Why did I ever agree to do this?!* I was wound up tight inside, every nerve stretched to breaking point. And this was just the first date. How much worse would it get as we moved on? How was I going to keep lying to him if we had sex?!

Local CIA agents would be tracking the signal from my cell phone. There was probably an unmarked car following us, but they'd have to stay back, out of sight. Not a great comfort, if things went wrong.

I tried to relax and stretch out in my seat. There was enough room in the back that I could have put my legs almost straight out in front of me, if I'd wanted to. Was that just for show, to demonstrate Luka's wealth? Or did he want all that room so that he could ravish one of his Russian blondes on the back seat?

When we arrived, Luka came down the steps of the restaurant and opened the door like a gentleman. He'd taken a shower after ice hockey, his black hair still damp. In his expensive suit, he could have been a businessman. *Almost.* There was still an aura about him. Something that made regular people react, even if unconsciously, every time he walked past. Men took a step back. Women, I noticed, took a step forward.

He didn't give a fuck. It was the way he walked, the way he held himself. He didn't care who was watching or what they thought of him. He was taking me to lunch because he'd decided that would give him pleasure, and everyone else had better stay out of his way.

He opened the door and held out his hand for mine. Another gentlemanly act. He was polite, yet arrogant. He treated me like a lady even as he admitted to his bodyguard that he wanted to fuck me. He took women out to posh restaurants, then returned to his world of violence and death.

For a split-second, I hesitated. *Decision time.* Was I really going to get involved with this guy?

I reached out and took his hand.

16

Inside, it was all snow-white tablecloths and hushed voices. Luka already had a table and guided me over to it, his hand on the small of my back. The red dress was made of fairly thick fabric but, suddenly, it seemed to barely be there at all.

When we sat, Luka said to the waiter in Russian, "She will need a menu in English."

That was when I realized he had no idea I spoke or read Russian. That could be useful. Maybe he'd say something important about the arms deal, right in front of me, thinking I wouldn't understand. So I tilted my head curiously and raised my eyebrows.

"I said you'll need a menu in English," he repeated in English, and I nodded and smiled.

We ordered: duck, for me, exquisitely cooked and drenched in rich sauce. For him, a rack of lamb. He cut into it, the juices running pink. "Why come on vacation alone?" he asked, his accent caressing each syllable.

I'd been drilled by Adam before I left Virginia. *Keep as close to the truth as possible,* he'd said. Good advice...but what do you do when your past is something you don't share with anyone? "I thought I'd meet more people," I lied. "I thought, if I came with friends, I'd just wind up talking to them the whole time."

He nodded and chewed and then said, "Liar."

The duck turned to tasteless mush in my mouth.

He looked me right in the eye. "I can tell when you're lying to me, Arianna."

Did he know?! I was in a public place, but this was Moscow, where money and power can buy anything. He could have me down the steps and bundled into his car in seconds, even kicking and screaming.

"Tell me why you're really alone," he said.

My mind was whirling. *Why didn't I listen to Roberta? He knows! He's toying with me!* I didn't know whether to break and run and try to make it to the door or brazen it out or—

I snapped and told the truth. "I find it hard to connect with people," I blurted.

The faintest hint of a smile crossed his lips. "That's why you're alone? Not just now but...always?"

I swallowed. "Yes."

He smiled a slow smile. "That wasn't so difficult, was it?"

I relaxed a tiny amount. He did want to find out the truth about me...but not what I did for a living. About *me*. The parts of Arianna Ross that were the same as Arianna Scott. In theory, that was a relief. But the thought of that stuff coming out, of having to relive the reasons *why* I was messed up—that wasn't much less frightening.

"Are you always this...invasive with people?" I asked.

He didn't even flinch. "I don't like people lying to me."

And then I realized the edge of his foot was against mine, under the table, the hard leather of his shoe pressed against the soft calfskin of my boot. It started to slide up, a firm caress, up the inside of my shin and then up the side of my calf. I stiffened in my seat as it left the boot and rasped against the nylon of my stocking. He rested there for a moment, his toe circling the side of my knee, and I caught my breath. "Do you always do *this*, as well, with women you've just met?"

"I've met you twice, now, Arianna. And we've already been *much* closer than this."

The sound of my name on his lips did something strange to me. *He's pure ice,* Roberta had warned me. But, behind those cold blue eyes, I thought I could detect something else. Something hotter than the core of a volcano, ready to burn us both. I recognized it, because I could feel the same thing building inside me.

"Why were you so rude to that guy at the park?" I asked. "He hadn't done anything."

Luka's eyes blazed a little hotter. 'He wanted to."

"But why so rude? You just glared at him."

"I'm not a very nice person, Arianna."

"You're nice to *me.*"

"*You* have something I want."

My breath caught in my chest. "What?"

His toe slid higher up my leg. He was firm, not just brushing but pressing, kneading the soft flesh. It was a prelude to sex, showing me how he wanted to touch me with his hands. Every inch brought a new wave of pleasure, and they were merging and building, already dangerously strong. I gripped the table with one hand.

Hidden by the tablecloth, his foot angled and slid higher and higher, until it was past the tops of my stockings, right up between my thighs. Only my closed legs stopped him from sliding higher.

He looked at me from beneath half-closed eyelids.

"I—" I flushed. "No—God, we've only just met!" I looked around me. "There are *people!*" I hissed.

He waited until I'd gotten my objections out, and then he gave me the same look again. A low, smoldering gaze that felt as if it was burning my panties right off.

The heat was swirling and thickening inside me, sucking in power like a cyclone. I looked back at him helplessly, but he wasn't going to show me any mercy.

I took a deep breath...and opened my legs.

He smiled. And immediately, his foot was pushing up between my thighs, the toe of his shoe against the front of my panties. I'd never been touched by anything like that before. Fingers, a tongue...even a cock is throbbing and alive and has some give in it. But this was leather and rubber, hard and brutal, rubbing up and down against my lips. Lips that were already swollen and—*God*—wet.

This was how sex with him would be. Hard and strong and with a hint of danger, but all aimed at giving me pleasure. I stared across the table at him, my mouth slightly open, and panted as he rubbed me in slow, precise strokes exactly where I needed it. My ass was clenching and moving in my seat, both hands gripping the table, now.

"I like you, Arianna," he said. "We can have fun together. Don't you want to have fun?"

I realized that he wasn't playing around. He wasn't just going to rub me a little and then let me down again—he was actually planning to make me climax, right there in public. The heat coiled tight, twisting and thrashing like a living thing, and I squirmed helplessly in my seat. I was *close,* rushing towards it unstoppably fast. Above the table, I was just about demure. Beneath the tablecloth, my dress was rucked up around my hips and his thick, muscled leg was nestled obscenely between my thighs.

This is crazy! We've only just met!

Except we hadn't, had we? I'd been listening to his calls, fantasizing about him, dreaming about him. My body had been reacting to him for months.

I tried to speak—I'm not sure whether I was going to beg him to back off, or to keep going. But it was already too late. The heat twisted and knotted and then suddenly released and I had to squeeze my eyes shut and fight to stop myself from screaming. The orgasm tore through me, rippling outward in waves, and I bucked and shuddered in my seat, heaving air through my nose. I managed to not cry out, but I made a low moan, deep in my throat, that made a man on the next table turn and stare.

I slowly opened my eyes. I was breathing hard and Luka still had his foot jammed between my thighs. I stared at him, utterly lost.

"Tonight," he said, "You'll come out with me. And I'll get to know you much, much better."

17

I barely remember staggering out of the restaurant and into a cab. I called Adam again, telling him how much I'd enjoyed the meal and that I'd be seeing the guy again that night. Adam's voice should have been comforting but, as I sat there on the end of my bed, he sounded very far away. Langley might as well have been on another planet. Moscow—and Luka—were right there, touchable and real.

When the call was over, I fell back onto the bed and lay there staring up at the ceiling. I didn't see the smooth white plaster. I saw eyes that were so cold they pierced me to the very soul...yet with that blistering heat behind them. I reran his words in my head and every syllable licked over me, making me buzz. *I like you, Arianna," he said. "We can have fun together. Don't you want to have fun?*

Don't I?

I felt that flutter in the pit of my stomach, the one you get at the brink of the first hill on a rollercoaster. Layers of excitement and fear stacked on top of one another and twisted up tight until you don't know which is which. If it had been a normal date with a guy who made me feel like this, I would have been drunk on anticipation anyway. The knowledge of who he was—*what* he was—and what he'd do to me if he discovered my secret, made me reel. *What in the name of God am I doing?!*

This wasn't some sex game, like that boyfriend my friend Sophie had who liked to tie her up with silk scarves. This wasn't something you giggled about to your friends and that made you feel adventurous. This was a man who'd kill if one of his deals went sour. What the hell would he do if he discovered I was a spy?

And what if he *didn't* find out? What if everything went exactly as planned? Then I'd go out with him, tonight, and have a few drinks and then, at the end of the night, I'd come back to my hotel room or back to his place and we'd—

Could I really do that? Make sex into something I just...*did,* without emotion, to complete the mission? What if, when it came to it, I didn't want him?

What if I *did?*

～

The same car picked me up but, this time, Luka was in the back seat. Sprawled there, half-turned towards me, he looked too big for the car, even huge as it was. As I slid in beside him, the top-to-toe appraisal he gave me made me catch my breath.

I'd gone back and forth several times on what to wear. In the end, I settled on a little black dress that I hoped would pass for classy. I knew my clothes weren't nearly expensive enough to match up to whatever Luka would wear, but then I was meant to be just a tourist —not one of the super-rich.

The dress seemed to meet with Luka's approval. I could feel his eyes on my legs, stroking upward along my thighs. I self-consciously tugged the hem down a little. His gaze was unnerving and a turn on but it had another effect, too. For the first time in years, I was able to almost forget that I was in a car. I found I only needed to do my translation trick a little to keep me calm.

The car slid through the streets of Moscow and, again, there was almost no sound. We were cocooned in our own little world inside and it hit me for the first time that the windows were tinted. We could see out, but nobody knew we were in there. We might as well have been invisible—ghosts, flitting through the streets.

Luka looked, if it was possible, even hotter than before. He'd changed into a black shirt and expensive-looking black jeans. The lack of color only emphasized the blue of his eyes. His collar was open just enough to reveal that enticing triangle of hard, tan chest I'd seen at the party. Those broad shoulders and thick biceps looked even better under the more casually-cut shirt and I could see his powerful thighs as they stretched the denim tight. I couldn't help thinking about what all that muscle would mean in bed. Brutal and hard and able to take me for hours.

I flushed. I didn't normally think of men in that way. It was like a pheromone or an aura he put out, sweeping my senses every time I was close to him. I was starting to find that my mind went to shreds every time I was around Luka Malakov, reducing me to animal instincts and base needs.

As we sped through the city, he didn't say anything. He just looked at me, his eyes shining in the dim light from the streetlights. Being looked at like that isn't something I'm used to. And it wasn't like the restaurant or the park or even at his house in New York. There was something about being in that private little cocoon with him, like being trapped in a cage with a hungry tiger. I should have been terrified. I *was* terrified, on some level. But I could feel that same connection I'd felt before, crackling in the air between us.

If I was trapped in a cage with a tiger, that made me the deer. The prey. And part of me just wanted to shake my hair away from my neck and offer it up to him to be savaged.

"Where is it we're going?" I said, more to break the silence than anything.

He gave me a sly smile. "There isn't a direct translation for its name. The closest I can get is, *"the underside of heaven."*

We pulled up right outside two huge, smoked-glass doors. Before the car had even stopped, the doormen were putting their hands to their earpieces, telling someone we'd arrived. They unclipped the velvet rope and showed us straight past the waiting line of people and inside.

The nightclub was vast—one massive room with a ceiling at least three floors above us. The dance floor itself was another level down, a sea of bodies lit up by blue and green lights. At one edge of the room, a shining bar made of what looked like glass stretched most of the length of the club. There must have been twenty bartenders behind it, but they were still working flat out.

As we descended the stairs, I realized my little black dress was horribly out of place. There wasn't a single woman there without something that shone or sparkled. Even their shoes had crystals or sequins or both. And it wasn't that their clothes were flashy but cheap —they were flashy and expensive. Designer bags, big rings and pendants—everyone was displaying their wealth. The men were slightly more subdued, but there was still plenty of jewelry on display. I saw a few women glance at me and then away, disinterested —I was too drab to be competition. And then they'd see Luka, behind me, and their perfectly-painted lips would open in shock.

"Do you come here a lot?" I asked over my shoulder. All of the women around me were supermodel-gorgeous, all long legs and high cheekbones. I wondered whether he'd met Elena or Svetlana or Natalia here.

He shrugged. "Sometimes. Is good place to let off steam." I could tell he was relaxing because his English slipped slightly. Then he smiled. "But it's more fun with someone new." And, as I turned to look at him, his fingers brushed my cheek. They left a scorching, tingling trail behind, like the feeling you get when you touch ice fresh from the freezer and it burns instead of freezes.

He took me downstairs and headed through the crowd to the bar. I could feel the energy rise up around us as we plunged in. Back home, I didn't exactly spend much time in clubs, but I'd been to some at college. Some of it was familiar: the swell and ebb as the crowd reacted to the music, the wide-eyed grins and panting faces as they worked out the stress of the week. As Luka had said, a good place to relax.

But the clubs I'd been to hadn't had dancing like...*this*. On the fringes of the crowd, away from the hardcore thrashers, couples were going far further than just necking and groping. A couple of guys had their shirts mostly off and some of the Russian beauties were grinding against hands slid up their skirts and thrust into their tops. It really was like the underside of heaven—people who looked like angels, bathing in sin. A wave of fear mixed with heat rippled down my body. Was this why he'd brought me here?

His bodyguard joined us and followed behind, eyes everywhere. No one in the crowd questioned his suit and tie or thought his stony expression was weird amongst all the excitement. *In a place like this,* I thought, *they're probably used to bodyguards.*

We neared the bar, where the crowd was three deep. I prepared to settle in to wait, but Luka just stepped forward. As he moved in behind people and they turned to see who it was, I saw their faces go deathly pale. They slid aside, a few of them waving him forward, most of them too scared to speak. Within seconds, there was an empty stretch of bar six feet wide.

Luka acted as if he hadn't even noticed, as if that's just what crowds did by themselves. It hit me that it probably felt that way to him, by now. I tried to smile politely at the people who'd parted for us, but they just gaped at me. One or two of them wouldn't even dare meet my eyes.

It started to sink in just how feared this man was. The one who—I caught my breath—suddenly had his hand on my ass.

I braced my hands on the bar and jerked back in surprise. It was wet, and freezing cold. Literally. The whole thing was a giant, sculpted block of ice, glossy smooth and slippery. Intricate tunnels had been bored through it and, at a few words from Luka, the bartender lifted a bottle of vodka and poured a generous shot into a hole in the bar's surface. The clear liquor raced through the twisting tunnels, heading downward.

"You better catch it," said Luka with a grin. "Or it'll spill."

I looked down. The tunnel ended at the front of the bar in a little ice spout. Probably, you were supposed to hold a glass there to catch your drink. But Luka hadn't given me a glass.

"Hurry," said Luka. His eyes were sparkling.

The spout was at roughly groin level. The symbolism wasn't lost on me. I could see him watching me, gauging my reaction. It was a test, to see if I'd play by his rules.

Drinking a shot like that, with everyone watching, was *not* the sort of thing I did. But, as I stared into his eyes, I felt the excitement spiraling up inside me. Arianna Scott, languages geek, wouldn't do it. But Arianna Ross, carefree vacation girl...maybe she would.

Maybe being undercover could be liberating.

Keeping my knees together as demurely as I could, I crouched. By tipping my head back and pressing my chest close to my legs, I just managed to get low enough to put my mouth on the ice spout. Slippery hardness nudged my lips.

Arianna, what the hell are you doing?

Ice-cold vodka exploded into my mouth, colder than I'd ever tasted it. Smoother, too, with none of the harshness of the vodka I'd tasted in the US. And there was a lot of it—the equivalent of two or even three shots back home.

Throughout the whole thing, I kept looking up at Luka. His eyes never left mine for a second, not even to lick over my body as I crouched in that submissive pose.

I swallowed.

What really shook me was that not a single person around us laughed or leered at me. The moment was all about me and Luka - everyone else was too scared to do more than watch.

As I got to my feet, I caught the look the men were giving Luka. *Longing.* I'd never known that men could look like that. They wanted his lifestyle, his money. But most of all, they wanted that attitude he had, that aura of pure, undiluted evil. They wanted to be intimidating like him. But I knew they couldn't be. It wasn't something you can buy or learn. It wasn't something Luka had acquired because of what he did. It was something he was born with—maybe it had even driven him into crime.

And that same aura was doing something to me. Something about the way he looked at me, like a king looking at a favored maid. Wondering if he should take her off to his bedchambers or just ravish her right there.

His eyes sparkled and then he smiled. If it had been a test, I'd passed.

"We'll take the bottle," said Luka in Russian and the bartender nodded and thrust it at him. No money changed hands, so I took it that he had a tab. Given how expensive the whole place seemed and what bottles went for in clubs, I didn't even want to guess at how much money he'd just spent—and we'd only been here a few minutes.

On the way through the crowd this time, he saw me looking at the other women. Every movement made some part of them flash as it caught the light: rings topped with diamonds, bracelets encrusted with crystals.

"Bling," said Luka, his accent giving the word a whole new, disapproving tone. "Less of it now, than a few years ago. But here, people still like to show off."

It wasn't just the fancy clothes, though. The short skirts and strappy tops were showing off long lengths of gym-toned thigh and perfect, slender arms. They were all graceful as swans. "I feel a little...drab," I muttered.

Luka suddenly gripped my arm and spun me to face him, pulling me closer at the same time. I think I let out a little gasp of surprise— he did it so abruptly, with no thought for paltry American concerns like *personal space.* When I met his eyes, I saw the anger there at what I'd said. "There's nothing wrong with the way you look," he said in a voice that wouldn't be argued with.

I blinked up at him, amazed. But, at the same time, I felt my heart unfold from the tight little knot it had become. We stared at each other. For an instant, I saw that arrogant, iron-hard exterior fracture and I glimpsed the man underneath.

It was gone in a heartbeat. But what shocked me to the core was that, no matter how many times I played it back in my mind in the days to come, he always looked the same.

For a second, he'd looked like I felt: helpless.

He turned away from me as if embarrassed and I looked away, too, trying to get control of myself. *Pull yourself together! You can't go gooey just because he says one nice thing! Remember what he is!* I tried to imagine what Nancy would do. Probably karate kick him out of a window. *He probably says that line to all the women he meets—all of those Russian blondes.*

And, even as I thought it, I saw one of them right in front of me. A little taller than me, with a tiny waist and pert, thrusting breasts under her sparkling blue top. She had arrow-straight, gleaming blonde hair down to her shoulders.

And she was glaring at me with total, unreserved hatred. Maybe it was because Luka wasn't looking in her direction, or maybe she was simply too angry to be afraid, but she looked as if she wanted to jump on me and tear my throat out.

To my relief, Luka pulled me in the other direction, towards the edge of the club. He showed me to a table surrounded by low, black leather armchairs. Every seat was taken.

When we were still ten feet away, the people sitting there nudged each other, stood up and scattered. One of them even wiped the tabletop with his sleeve.

I shook my head in disbelief as we sat down. Luka sat back in his seat. "What?" he asked.

"Everyone's afraid of you."

He glanced around and then shrugged, as if that was their fault.

I remembered that I wasn't meant to know what he did. "Why?"

He gave a wry little grin. "Some people are scared of how I do business."

He lifted the bottle of vodka. He hadn't brought any glasses, I realized. I watched as he took a long pull. "How *do* you do business?" I asked.

He locked eyes with me and slowly lowered the bottle. "Without limits." He passed me the bottle. "Have you ever tried living without limits, Arianna?"

18

I took the bottle with shaking hands. I'd already had the equivalent of a couple of shots. But I put the glass neck to my mouth and tipped it back until the liquor ran like silver fire over my tongue and down my throat. I lowered it and took a long breath, the club's warm air suddenly freezing next to the burn of the alcohol. "Limits are good," I rasped. "Limits keep things safe."

He smirked at that and patted his leg. It took me a second to realize that he wanted me to sit there. I stood up and walked over to him, my legs trembling.

I went to sit sideways on his leg, like a princess riding side-saddle on a unicorn. He admonished me with a little shake of his head and an amused crush of those sensuous lips.

I swallowed, stood slightly, and sat again. This time, I sat back on his leg so that I was astride it. I managed to keep my knees together, though.

I kept my eyes forward because I thought that, somehow, if I did that, I might not lose control. I felt his hand on my back—so warm!—and then sweeping up through my hair, letting the strands spill and play over his fingers as his thumb ascended my spine. I arched my back in response, trembling.

Suddenly, he lifted his knee, taking his foot off the ground and raising me into the air as if I weighed nothing. I slid backward, my thighs opening, my heels skittering for purchase on the floor. My ass pressed against his groin. His mouth was at my ear, his accent wrapping each syllable in ice before it slipped into my brain. "What are you *really* doing in Moscow, Arianna?"

My whole body went tense. My feet were still off the ground—I had no traction, no way of struggling up from his lap. I tried to lurch forward but that only made my ass grind more firmly against the hardness I could feel at his groin. Cold fear erupted inside me, freezing my brain, numbing my response. I opened my lips but nothing came out. *I'm blown. I'm blown!*

But then his mouth was at my ear again. "You come on vacation by yourself, but I don't think it's to meet people. You are too..." he fumbled for the phrase in English. "*In own head.*"

Introvert. *A language geek,* I thought. *I'm just a language geek.* I nodded, still rigid with fear.

His hands were on my thighs, steadying me as I balanced precariously on his leg. He still hadn't lowered his knee. I glanced up for a second and spied the blonde again. She looked even angrier than before, and her gaze was locked on my open legs, and on Luka's leg between them.

His hands started to slide upward, tugging the dress with them. I gulped. We were in the shadows, but still in open view of everyone. I watched as the hem rose up my stockinged thighs. "I think," Luka said, "You came here to find something you couldn't find at home. Something you needed."

I shook my head. My cover wasn't blown but I didn't like the way this was going.

His lips were even closer, now, stroking the super-sensitive edges of my ear as he spoke. "I think you lie awake in America thinking of bad men."

I felt myself flush with embarrassment, remembering the way I'd played his phone calls over and over. I *had* fantasized about him, but I hadn't come out here to chase after him....

Had I?

One hand settled on my shoulder and then slid down my collar bone to my throat. I swallowed slowly. The feel of it resting there, massive and powerful, was frightening. Intoxicating. *Dammit, how does he do this to me?!*

The hand slowly rose, stroking up my throat to the underside of my chin and tipping my head back. My hair cushioned my head against his shoulder. Now I was nestled in his lap, my eyes looking up at him. My legs were either side of his, the hard bulge of his cock between the cheeks of my ass. Why wasn't I running? Why was I just sitting there, staring up at him? I could feel the heat starting to build inside me, spiraling up in urgent waves.

He was looking at me with hooded eyes and his voice had gone deeper than I'd ever known it, almost a growl. The music was loud, but he could have whispered to me from twenty feet away and that voice would have carried. "I think you came looking for me," he said.

I stiffened. The heat was rolling through me, leaving me throbbing and drunk with desire. My arms reached up and grabbed for him, seeking anything solid to cling onto and finding his shoulders. His fingers lightly touched my wrist and then traced all the way along my arm until it reached my upturned face. He brushed my cheek. "And I think that maybe...I've been looking for someone like you."

I swallowed. "What am I?" But I already knew, because I'd already heard him say it.

He smiled a lazy, cat-like smile. "An innocent,"

I thought of all those sophisticated, beautiful Russian women. "Why do you want an innocent?" I croaked.

His lips twisted, the smile growing cruel. "To corrupt her."

A deep, liquid heat pooled at my core and then rippled out to fill me, leaving me breathless. My own reaction scared me. But there was something else. When he'd said it, there'd been another flicker in those burning, frozen eyes. A glimpse of something behind the mask, a need that went beyond just lust. I felt my heart lift and open a little, tentatively unfurling for the first time in many years.

And then I saw him lean down, his eyes closing, and—

Oh God, he was going to—

I had time for a single, overwhelmed breath before his lips came down on mine. My hands came up off his shoulders in shock and I grabbed for his head—I'm not sure what I had in mind. Push him away? Pull him in harder?

His fingers knitted with mine, holding my arms out from my body.

The kiss was as urgent as that need I'd seen inside him, a release of something that must have been building up all day. His lips brushed mine and I just had time to take a shuddering breath. I could feel his need to own me, to possess me utterly. His tongue toyed with the chink between my lips. He didn't want to force his way in; he wanted me to open up to him.

I opened.

His kiss was like a drug entering my body, one made entirely of blackness and heat and sin. I felt my insides turn to liquid, my legs at last relaxing and slumping either side of his, no longer caring who saw. My hands squeezed his and he squeezed back. His tongue thrust deep, exploring me, filling me, and I saw stars. I drew in air through my nose but it didn't do anything to cool me or clear my head. I was sinking into him, becoming one with him, my ass grinding unconsciously against his cock through his jeans.

I felt as if some part of me that had never been connected before had just been hooked up to a live wire.

He broke the kiss, then kissed me again, open-mouthed and panting. His leg lifted more, tipping me, and I slid back until my whole back was pressed against his chest. I could feel my skirt sliding higher, pulled by his raised knee. I could feel air on the tops of my hold-ups, on my bare thighs. *How much is on display?!* But I was past caring.

The kiss went on and on, dark heat soaking down from my lips to my core...and I drank it down hungrily. Because on the way through me, the heat was awakening something, coaxing it from a three year slumber. Not my lust. Not even my closed-off heart.

Something deeper and more vital than that. It felt as if he was waking up *me.*

He finally lifted his lips and it was like something had been ripped from me. I actually tried to pull him back towards me. He was staring down at me with an expression that I guessed matched my own.

Total. Loss. Of control.

But then he shook his head minutely and glanced towards the dance floor.

I sort of shook myself and returned to reality. I was still nestled in his lap, much tighter against him than I had been before. I flushed as I realized I was basically sitting on his groin, legs spread languidly either side of him, my dress up around my hips.

I let out a strangled groan and shoved the hem down as fast as I could, jerking it awkwardly out from between our bodies. I heard him give a low chuckle and the sound of it made me shudder in a way that was worryingly pleasant.

Get it together! This is not a guy you can lose control with! But I already had. Would again, as soon as he touched me. The vodka had made me merely tipsy, but I was drunk on Luka Malakov, utterly wasted. *Right now, I'll do anything he wants me to.*

"Let's dance," he said in my ear, pushing me up to standing. I didn't really have a choice, even if I'd been lucid enough to protest, because he almost lifted me to my feet. As we walked towards the dance floor, I wondered why he'd interrupted the kiss to go do something as tame as dance. Did he want to slow things down? That didn't seem like his way at all.

Then we were in among the press of bodies. He stopped us in the shallows of the crowd, where bodies ground and twisted against each other. Where dancing was just an excuse.

Oh.

He swung around in front of me and suddenly I was up against him, as close as we had been in New York. Then, I hadn't been able to move back; now, I didn't want to. He was so damn *big,* up close, his chest like a solid wall. I laid my hands on his shoulders and pushed back to give me time to think but, as soon as I lost the warmth of him blazing through his shirt, I couldn't think at all. I pressed myself close again. I needed that contact with him like I needed to breathe.

I looked up at him, lost..., and immediately lost myself even more when I saw the hunger in his eyes. There was an edge of anger to it...as if he resented wanting me so much. As if he'd make me pay, for making him want me. *But I'm not doing anything!*

We began to dance.

19

I didn't dance, ever. The few times I'd actually been to clubs, back in college, I'd been too self-conscious. I'd done everything possible to stay off the dance floor while trying to look as if I was having a good time. Now, though, as his arm captured my waist and snugged me tight against him, I was beyond caring what other people thought.

I forgot about my body, my nerves, even the people around me. The only thing that existed in the world were his eyes, gazing down into mine. I could feel the deep bass throb of the music pounding through my bones, lifting me like a wave, and I started to unconsciously move to it. He followed my movements, our bodies joined from thigh to neck, until I wasn't sure if I was moving him or he was moving me.

I closed my eyes and just let go, flexing and swaying and twisting with him, my breasts crushed against his chest, my groin pushed hard against his. I could feel him throbbing there, the two of us separated by a few inconsequential layers of fabric. And I could feel my own response, the twisting heat inside me turning to slick moisture.

The beat shifted, the DJ mixing in another track, and Luka

twisted me around so that my back was to him. His hands ran up my sides and drew my arms up and around his neck so that I was stretched out like an offering, almost hanging down the length of his body, my front exposed.

Immediately, his palms were on my hips, stroking upward, and it felt as if they were pulling the heat inside up with them. I still had my eyes closed, shutting out everything else as his palms moved up over my sides...up to the sides of my breasts. He rubbed there for long seconds, his thumbs just nudging the soft flesh, keeping me on the razor sharp line between where I'd allow it and where I'd stop him. He could sense me, somehow. He knew exactly how far I'd let him go.

And he was going to keep tempting me further and further. Leading me astray. Corrupting me. He wasn't hiding it. He'd damn well promised it. And I was letting him.

For the mission. Just for the mission. I have to.
Bullshit.

His hands suddenly swept down my body, his fingers catching the hem of my dress. He began to slide it up my thighs, and this time we weren't in the shadows. This time we were right out on the edge of the dance floor, with people all around us.

I didn't open my eyes. I tried to tell myself that I was embarrassed, that I didn't want to think about all those people watching us. But a deep, hot squirm inside me reminded me that wasn't true. The feel of their eyes on us, the feel of the cool air against my—*God, my bare thighs, how high has he got my skirt?!*—was turning me on. Grinding back against him, letting his hands run all over me in the middle of a nightclub, I was more turned on than I could ever remember being, even during sex. *Is this what letting go feels like?*

His fingers were on my thighs. My *inner* thighs. Thumbs stroking at the very edge of my panties, then moving inward—

I had to open my eyes. That would nudge me over the line from arousal to embarrassment, and I'd stop him.

His thumbs drew a line upward, less than a fingers-width from the line that separated the lips of my sex. I groaned.

I didn't want to open my eyes. I didn't want it to end.

His thumbs lifted. Returned. Another line, this time practically touching my lips. I could feel his breath hot in my ear. He was as turned on as I was.

The next, one, I knew would be right on my lips, and then I'd be completely lost. I was liable to let him bring me off, right there on the dance floor.

My eyes fluttered open.

Either we'd drifted, as we danced, or the couples around us had gotten friskier. Immediately in front of me, a woman with long red hair was clinging to her partner, her legs wrapped around his waist as they kissed, his hands up under her skirt. To my left, a dark-haired woman was pressed between two men, one in front and one behind. The one behind her was kissing her neck. The one in front had unbuttoned her blouse all the way to her waist and was palming her breasts.

I pulled free of Luka's hands. He let me go immediately. When I twisted around to look at him, there was no anger—if anything, he looked amused.

"I need to—" I realized I was panting. I pushed my dress down to cover me, my groin still throbbing with the memory of his hands. "I'll...be back in a minute," I told him. And turned and stumbled from the dance floor.

I didn't even know where I was heading, at first. I just aimed for where the music seemed quietest and the lights seemed most steady. My whole body was trembling, my legs like rubber. I felt like I'd mainlined something. Every sense was intensified, every nerve ending twitching. I wanted his touch; I wanted his lips; I wanted *him*.

I found the bathrooms and almost fell through the door into the ladies room. In there, the lights were white and bright and I could think—just. A few other women were in there, redoing their make-up. I grabbed onto the edge of a sink, trying to get my breathing under control.

Staring at myself in the mirror, I replayed the evening in my head. I'd been completely unprepared for how I'd react to him, once things got started. I'd known that I liked him. I'd fantasized about his voice and then about his body. But I was realizing—too late—that something else was going on here, something far deeper than just an infatuation. It made no sense. I knew he was the worst sort of man. I knew the sort of things he'd done. I shouldn't *be able* to like him. And yet I felt something between us, something soul-deep and undeniable.

He wanted me because he thought I was an innocent. I *was* an innocent, in some ways, probably far more innocent than he suspected. And, at the same time, I was lying to him, preparing to betray him. I'd seen that flicker in his eyes- that need for me that no man had ever shown. And I'd felt myself waking up, big chunks of ice that I hadn't even realized were there cracking and splintering inside me as I was roused. Now that I was alone, I could feel myself shutting down again, closing up.

I couldn't process it, standing there in a bathroom. I needed time alone to figure it out. But it was almost as if I'd briefly come back to life, after being frozen for—

For three years?

I stared at myself and shook my head. I didn't like the implications of that. I couldn't handle the idea that he might be that important in my life.

I noticed something out of the corner of my eye. The woman next to me, thrusting her make-up bag into her purse so fast that a lipstick went skittering across the floor. She almost ran out of the room. And I realized that the other women had left, too. I seemed to be alone.

And then, in the mirror, I saw the blonde from the dance floor step into view behind me. I had time to blink in surprise, just once, and then she grabbed the back of my head and rammed my head into the mirror.

20

M y forehead struck first. There was a cracking sensation that I
prayed was the mirror and, an instant later, white-hot pain
flooded my brain.

She still had hold of my hair. She used it to yank me backward
and I stumbled in my heels.

"Blyadischa!" she yelled. *Whore.* Something cracked against my
cheek and I fell sideways, landing on my knees. My face burned and I
thought I tasted blood. She'd slapped me, with the full weight of her
oversized rings.

Tears sprang to my eyes. My head throbbed so hard I couldn't
think. *Why does she hate me?!*

"American *shalava!*" She was calling me a slut. She'd been glaring
at me all night, ever since she'd first seen me with—

Oh no.

She kicked me, then, aiming for my breasts but fortunately
hitting me in the shoulder. I sprawled backward, almost going full-
length on the tiles. My brain was trying to catch up with what was
happening. *I'm being attacked. Things like this don't happen to me.* I'd
never been in a fight in my life. Part of me wanted to curl into a ball
and pray that, if I just took it, she'd run out of steam and stop.

But she wasn't even close. Hitting me just seemed to make her madder. *"Yob tebye suka!"* she screeched, almost hysterical. She grabbed me by the hair again and I had to scramble onto my knees or she would have ripped it out by the roots. She half-dragged me forward, into a stall.

Don't panic. A voice from my past, one that was meant to cut in at times like this. I just had to listen to it.

She rammed my head into the toilet bowl and there was a sudden roar, deafeningly loud. Freezing water filled my ears and nose. I clamped my mouth shut.

The woman screamed something, muffled through the water. I tried to lift my head but her hand was shoving my head down, holding me under. My hair was being pulled around by the currents, wrapping around my face like seaweed. My lungs screamed for oxygen.

Panic won't help you. The voice had an accent. A Texas drawl. Rick Espiano, my unarmed combat instructor, back when I'd done my basic training. I hadn't been good at it, not like Nancy.

But I *do* have a good memory.

Don't panic, I heard Rick say, as fear clawed at my mind. *Just think. What do you have? What can you use?*

I drove my foot back, *hard,* and felt it connect with something. There was a muffled scream and my head was released.

I pushed myself up, vision half-blocked by my tangled, soaked hair. I heaved in a huge lungful of air, tossing my head to try to clear my eyes.

The woman was staggering back from me, gripping her bare thigh with both hands. There was a satisfyingly large red mark there.

She came at me again, nails ready to slash like claws across my face. But my memory had kicked in, now. I ducked under her arm, my shoulder against her thigh, and used her own momentum to throw her over my back. She screamed and I heard her land hard. When I turned around, she was sprawled on the floor, groaning.

Luka's head bodyguard put his head around the door, saw what was happening, and ran in. Luka was right behind him.

My legs wouldn't hold me anymore. I sank to the floor, my back against a sink. My hair, face and shoulders were soaked with water—thankfully, the place was classy enough that the toilets were clean. But I could feel tears running down my cheeks, no doubt taking my make-up with them in long, ugly streaks. My hair was over my eyes and, when I tried to sweep it back out of my face, it stuck to my hands in wet ropes. I sobbed.

Luka marched over to the woman on the floor. She was still half-dazed from the throw but, when she saw who it was, she tried to scramble backward away from him. He looked between me and her and the look on his face was one of raw protective fury. He reached down and grabbed the woman by the front of her sparkling top, lifting her easily into the air until her head almost brushed the ceiling. "This woman hurt you?" he asked. Emotion made his accent thick and heavy.

I nodded. And then my stomach lurched because his expression went from *angry* to *murderous*. He was going to kill her, for touching me. His bodyguard was by his side in an instant, ready to help.

"Wait!" I croaked. "Don't—don't hurt her!"

Luka glanced at me, but didn't release his grip.

"I don't need you to," I said.

He looked back to the woman. He was going to do it. *This is the only way he knows.*

"I don't *want* you to!" I blurted.

Nothing happened for a second. Then he turned his head slowly towards me, as if I'd said something absurd. He held my gaze for a moment and, just for the briefest second, I saw that flicker again, the hint of something underneath. Something—some*one*—who needed me.

He suddenly tossed the woman away like a bag of garbage. She yelped with pain as she hit the floor and quickly crawled away from him, terrified but alive.

Luka strode over to me and crouched, then scooped me up into his arms. I wanted to run away and hide, humiliated by the way I looked and still shaking from the sudden violence. I twisted my head away from him.

But he put his hand on my cheek and coaxed me to look at him, as gentle as he had been brutal a moment before. He was frowning at me. "You don't ever have to hide yourself from me," he admonished, his voice heavy with emotion again. He jerked his head at the bodyguard and the man nodded and ran off ahead of him. To ready the car, I realized.

"Where are we going?" I rasped, my throat raw from crying.

"To my apartment," he told me. "You can shower, and wash that bitch's touch off you."

His apartment. And after I'd cleaned myself up...*sex?!* I was still reeling from the suddenness and brutality of the attack. I was having a hard time getting my mind back onto the date...and the mission. I just nodded. Then, as he carried me to the door, I glanced back at the groaning woman on the floor. "How did your bodyguard know?" I whispered. "How did he know there was something wrong?"

"Yuri sees everything," said Luka with a sort of grim pride.

Yuri. The man with the scar now had a name.

Outside the bathroom, a crowd had gathered to see what the commotion was all about. When they saw Luka stride out with me in his arms, they parted like the Red Sea. Through the open door behind us, the blonde woman was visible, still lying on the floor. I saw a couple of women look from her to me to Luka, their expressions incredulous. Then one of them muttered something to the other. "*Tupa Karova!*" Stupid cow! About the blonde, not me.

The next comment made me freeze inside...yet, worryingly, my heart gave a flutter. "*What was she thinking? Couldn't she see the American girl's his?*"

⁓

I looked at the flawless, pale leather as I climbed into the car and thought about how many ways I was about to ruin it. But Luka didn't seem to care about the toilet water in my hair or the mascara running down my face. He just set me carefully down on the back seat and climbed in beside me. I was starting to breathe again, but I was still lost. I could taste blood in my mouth and my head was ringing. I was mentally and emotionally exhausted. For a moment, as his strong arms released me and he brushed a strand of wet hair off my forehead, I just allowed myself to...be. I let myself sink into the soft leather and enjoyed the stillness, forgetting where I was.

With me, that's an incredibly dangerous thing to do.

As we started to move, Luka leaned across me and did up my seat belt. The metallic click resonated through my entire body.

That was all it took.

It all came together: the car; the feeling of a man doing up my seat belt, just as my dad had done for me that day; the snow whipping past the windows.

I was too wiped out to use my translating trick to distract me and my emotional defenses had been shattered. I could feel my sense of time and place sliding as I was ripped away into the past.

21

Part of me wants to say that I was normal. The sort of girl who went to crazy parties and had a million friends, as if I was perfect before it all went wrong. But the truth is that, even back then, I probably hit the books a little too hard and played it a little too safe.

So no, I wasn't normal, back then. I was a little geeky. But I was happy.

In a lot of ways, I was at a tipping point. I'd just left my teens behind and turned twenty. I was halfway through my languages course at Berkeley. I'd broken up with my high school sweetheart a few months earlier, my last teen-style relationship, where the sex was still furtive and awkward. But I hadn't yet had what felt like a real adult relationship, where sex would be expected...and, I hoped, awesome. I was just about to move out of dorms and into a shared house with my friends. As I prepared to go back to college that January, I felt as if a whole new section of my life was about to begin.

And then everything changed.

Three Years Earlier

"We're not lost," said dad from the driver's seat.

"Lost," said mom, next to him.

"Lost," I said from the backseat, smirking.

"We're *not* lost."

It had been a spur-of-the-moment thing. A drive out in the snow that was one percent about seeing some beautiful scenery, nine percent about spending time together as a family because I was heading back to Berkeley in a few days and ninety percent about dad getting to drive the new SUV away from the highway. It still had that new-car smell and my seat belt lock had been so tight, dad had had to wrestle it in for me.

Now we were deep into the back roads of Wisconsin, surrounded by thick forest, and even the GPS just showed a spider web of faint lines that could be anything from logging roads to footpaths. We'd already had to backtrack twice and the sky outside had turned from dark blue to black. We could see the snow whipping past in the headlights but little else.

Inside the SUV, though, it was warm and snug and we were taking turns to Bluetooth music to the stereo and it would be my turn next so I was going to put something decent on instead of dad's endless seventies rock.

My mom craned her head to look up at the sky through her window. "The moon's over *there*. That means we should be going *that way*." She pointed behind us.

"You're navigating using the stars, now?" My dad was smiling. Being lost was just another adventure, to him.

"Can't be any worse than relying on the Force, or whatever the hell you're using," she told him.

He leaned across to her. "You should show me some more respect. Or I might just—" He whispered in her ear in a way that made her blush and swat at him, and he chuckled.

I groaned and lifted my book in front of my eyes. *Gross*. Going back to Berkeley couldn't come soon enough.

I felt the car slow, just a little. "Does it...?" said my mom.

I lowered my book. They were both straining to see the road ahead through the windshield.

"I *think* it does," said my dad. "I think we—"

And then he said *fuck* so loudly it actually hurt my ears, and I jerked forward against my belt as he slammed on the brakes. But the feel of the road beneath us changed from a vibration to a smooth swish as the tires stopped gripping and started gliding. And then, quite suddenly, there was no road feel at all.

We started to fall.

My mom snapped her head around to look at me, her eyes wide and panicked. I saw her terrified realization that she was going to die, and that I might, too.

There wasn't time to scream. There wasn't time to do anything. The car started to tilt forward as it fell, the heavy engine making the SUV fall nose-first. Everything was black, outside, so I couldn't see the ground coming.

The impact was so fast and so sudden that it felt like an explosion, like the front of the car had just been blown apart. One second, we were falling and the car was perfectly normal. The next, the whole front of the car had moved. The front cabin, where my parents were, was squashed down to half its usual size. My mom and dad were resting on fat white airbags that looked like oversized marshmallows and I was hanging in mid-air, supported by my seat belt.

Then the car groaned and tipped and I threw my arms up instinctively to protect my head. There was a huge bang as we fell onto our side, the ground whacking into the door just inches from me.

And then everything went still. And very, very dark.

I only found out later that we'd driven onto an old, rarely used logging road and, disoriented by the snow, we'd been steadily climbing up into the hills. My mom and dad had seen the gap in the trees ahead of them and thought that the road simply dipped down slightly. They hadn't realized they were driving right off the edge of a sheer drop.

We'd fallen almost eighty feet and now the SUV was lying on its side. The headlights had gone out and there were no streetlamps, out here. Everything was utterly black.

"Mom?" I asked.

No reply.

I hit the button on my seat belt, but the buckle didn't release. "Dad?"

No reply.

I reached out into the darkness with both arms, trying to find the back of my dad's seat. Straining forward, I found his headrest and then the softness of his hair. I rubbed it. Tears were forming in my eyes, now. "Dad?"

His head was heavy and didn't move. He was either unconscious or....

"*Mom?!*" My voice was cracking, now. I reached out towards her, but she was diagonally across the car from me and I couldn't reach her. After a moment, though, I heard the most welcome sound in the world: breathing "Mom! Mom, wake up! We crashed! Dad's hurt! Wake up!"

But she didn't stir. Unconscious. *Maybe dad's just unconscious, too. Maybe he's just breathing too quietly for me to hear him.* I started to wrestle with my seat belt, but the buckle was firmly jammed in its socket. I seemed to be unhurt, but I couldn't move. Eventually, I gave a howl of frustration.

And then something dripped onto my leg. Something warm and wet, from up above me and in front, where my mom was sitting. I rubbed it between my fingers. Thick and sticky.

Blood.

"Mom?" Tears were rolling down my cheeks, now, and threatening to choke my voice off completely. "Mom, you have to wake up now!" I banged around in my seat, trying to make a noise, but it made no difference.

I waited for all the things you see on TV: wailing sirens and firefighters cutting us free and wrapping blankets around us, and doctors hurrying to help my parents. But nothing happened. No one came. It hit me that there'd been no one behind us on the road. No one had seen us go off the edge.

Going out for a drive had been a spur of the moment thing. No one knew we were out there.

And it was still snowing. Now that my eyes were adjusting to the darkness, I could just make out the shape of the flakes, softly settling on the side window that was now directly above me. The snow would cover up our tire tracks.

Suddenly, the car lit up with sound and light. My phone. *My phone!* It had shot off my lap during the crash and was now somewhere in the front of the car. I couldn't see it, but I could hear the insistent, slightly tinny dance music I'd set as the ring tone and see the glow of its screen. My friend Dana. All I had to do was hit *Answer* and I could tell her to call for help.

I strained against my seat belt, but it wouldn't release. I tried to pull it away from me so that I could wriggle out from under it, but something had happened to the reel the belt comes out of. It let me have half an inch of belt and then locked tight, refusing to pay out any more. However much I twisted and struggled, there wasn't nearly enough room for me to slip out.

Dana gave up, and the music stopped. A few seconds later, the screen powered down and the car was plunged back into blackness. After the glow, it seemed even darker than before.

There was a tiny groan from my mom and I heard her move slightly. I screamed her name as hard as I could, but she didn't wake. Another drop of blood hit my leg and then another, falling faster, now.

For the next few hours, I tried everything I could think of. I used my feet to try to reach for my phone, but it was too far away. I tried to gnaw through the seat belt with my teeth, but I barely made a dent on the fabric. I knew that no one would be able to see the car in the darkness and I prayed for morning.

But the side window, above me, grew darker and darker, shutting out even the faint light of the stars. The sound of the wind grew muffled and then stopped altogether. There was utter silence, as thick and terrifying as I'd ever known it, and utter darkness. The snow was burying us. By morning, there'd just be a drift.

The temperature started to drop. Without the heater on, the car shed all its heat into the snow. By midnight, I was losing feeling in my hands and feet. Then I started to shake and couldn't stop. The air in the car started to grow stale and I wondered how tightly we were sealed in.

I screamed my mom and dad's names more times than I can remember. But neither of them woke and all I could do was fixate on my mom's ragged breathing, willing her to keep going.

A faint light filled the car, sunlight filtered through a layer of snow. Each time I thought I heard a distant car, I yelled until I was hoarse. But I knew it was useless. I was in a sealed car, under snow, and the other drivers would have their windows shut against the cold.

And then, just as the light outside grew brightest and I figured it was noon, my mom stopped breathing. And the cold in the car crept into me, burrowing down into my heart and my soul and froze me solid.

I was in there for two days. Towards the end of the second day, I passed out. I woke up in the hospital.

The doctors told me that I'd been dehydrated and suffering from hypothermia. They told me that my parents were dead.

A guy walking his dog had found us. He'd leaned against the buried car, thinking it was a rock, and some of the snow had fallen away. The newspapers called it a miracle. It didn't feel like one. It felt as if the ice that had frozen me inside isolated me from everyone else.

I was twenty, so I was old enough to bury my parents and go back to college. I concentrated on my studies and gradually edged away from my friends. It was easier to be on my own. I couldn't really connect with them. The ice dulled everything.

I existed like that for over a year. And then, just as I was about to enter my senior year, single and almost friendless, Roberta showed up. She was elegant and professional and yet warm and kind, and the same age as my mother would have been. She asked if I wanted to help my country and I said yes. She bought me hot chocolate and said that she knew a place where she thought I'd be happy, and all I had to do to get there was to make sure I aced all my classes.

So I did. I wanted to make her happy. And a year later, I went to work for the CIA.

I did my basic training and then I started translating phone calls. If anyone noticed that I was a little cold or that I didn't seem to have a social life, they didn't say anything. As I said before, a lot of us in the CIA aren't exactly normal.

I worked. I slept and ate. But the ice inside me never melted. I was twenty-two, but I still felt twenty, unwilling and unable to think about things like relationships and marriage and my career. I did what I was told and I tried to keep Roberta and then Adam happy. I'm not sure why their opinion mattered so much to me, but it did.

And now I was in Moscow, and the ice should have been an advantage. This was the one situation where I couldn't afford to let myself feel. And yet, for the first time, I'd felt things crack and thaw inside me.

22

"Arianna."

My name, but not the sound I recognized. This was all harsh *R*s and long *A*s that sounded like poetry. My name, but made beautiful.

A hand slid around the back of my neck, warm and strong, the thumb rubbing at my hairline. I could feel the heat pumping into me, and that was when I realized how cold I was.

"You're freezing," said Luka. He told Yuri in Russian to turn up the heater. Then I heard the concern in his voice. "It's not just cold, is it?" he asked. His hand was still rubbing at the back of my neck and now his other hand started to stroke up and down my bare arm. Not a sexual touch—a healing touch. One I wouldn't have thought him capable of.

I turned my head to him. Somewhere, alarm bells were clanging hysterically, reminding me that I was meant to be being the perfect dream girlfriend, that I was meant to be sexy and happy and laugh at his jokes. But the alarms were muffled by the ice. I didn't feel sexy—I was dripping wet and bedraggled. I opened my mouth to tell him that everything was fine, but nothing came out. He studied me, those blue eyes searching deep inside me, straight past any barriers I could throw up. I saw his frown as he realized something was really wrong.

It didn't make any sense. Guys, if they looked at me at all, just thought I was distant and cold. How could this man—this monster—be the one to see past that?

He reached across me and I felt my seat belt disengage. I shuddered. Just the sound of it hissing back into its reel, that glorious sound that I'd imagined so many times when I was trapped, was enough to fill my eyes with tears.

And then he was shoving one big arm under my legs and another around my back and I was being scooped up again. He lifted me—powerfully, determined but with great care. He didn't want to hurt me but he was damn well going to cuddle me, *now*.

I landed in his lap, but it wasn't like at the club. This wasn't about sex. He wrapped his arms around me, leaning forward at the same time and nestling his head into my cheek, and it was as if he was wrapping his whole body around me. His warmth, his life, throbbed into me and I felt the ice inside me break. What had been cold and solid but at least smooth became jagged and vicious. A strangled sob escaped me.

Luka whispered something in my ear. "*Shh, myshka.*" *Shh, little mouse.*

That sent me over the edge. I forgot that it didn't make any sense, that this couldn't possibly be Luka Malakov being tender and concerned. I forgot who I was and who I was meant to be. I just remembered being cold, *so cold,* in that car, and no one coming, and, suddenly, I couldn't stop crying.

The pain rolled down my cheeks in big, hot waves, dripping onto my dress and onto Luka's muscled arms. My wet hair was soaking his collar and now my tears were soaking his sleeves and I was a disgusting mess but he didn't seem to care. He just wrapped me tight in his arms, so tight I could feel his heartbeat thumping against my back, and he held me.

I don't know how long it took us to drive to his apartment. But I know that, eventually, the tears slowed and the memories crawled back to their homes in my chest and the ice re-froze. Thinner than before, though, and with cracks like a spider web.

I sniffed and blinked and took some deep breaths and said, in a small voice, "I'm alright, now."

He made a disapproving noise, as if to say that *no*, I most definitely wasn't and he knew it, but that he'd accept it for the time being. He squeezed me and then held me against him until the car pulled up.

His building was a skyscraper whose concrete base looked solid enough to withstand an apocalypse. A doorman dashed to open the doors for him before we were even out of the car and he led me straight inside, his arm around my waist. Both the doorman and the woman behind the reception desk did an incredible job of ignoring my soaked hair and the make-up running down my face.

There was an elevator at the far end of the reception hall. Luka didn't have to press a button and wait. He just turned a key in a lock and the doors slid open, the elevator already waiting for us. Inside, there was only one button.

I swayed a little in my heels as the floor pressed upward under our feet. A hundred floors sped past. We were going to the penthouse.

There was a short, bare corridor, with a camera pointing right at the elevator door. His front door was a huge slab of polished wood, as strong as it was beautiful. Luka turned another key and heavy bolts clunked back.

We emerged into a huge, two level living room. There was a sort of pit sunk into the floor with cream leather couches on three sides and I caught a glimpse of a kitchen area off to the right. But I barely looked because in front of me was...Moscow.

The walls were floor-to-ceiling windows, with no drapes or blinds. But we had privacy, of a sort, because we were the highest building for miles. The city lay spread out around us like a map, traffic just glowing worms of light far below.

Luka put a hand on my arm and led me gently to a door. Behind it was a wet room finished in dark gray slate. The edges of the room were in darkness, giving the illusion that it went on forever. In the center, recessed spotlights picked out a gleaming metal shower head and the circle of floor beneath it.

"Take your time," said Luka. "Clean that bitch off you. Dump your clothes outside the door and I'll have them cleaned."

I swallowed and looked around for a bathrobe. "Do you have anything else to wear?"

A smile touched his lips. His accent stroked each word, elongating the *E*s, turning them into vibrations that traveled up and down my spine.

"You won't need anything to wear."

23

I closed the door, shutting out Luka and his world of violence and money and isolating myself in the silence of the wet room. I locked the door. Then I leaned my back against it.

You won't need anything to wear, he'd said.

This was it. He wanted to have sex. Luka Malakov wanted to have sex *with me.*

The fact that it had been in the cards all along didn't make it any less of a bombshell. He was everything I stood opposed to. He was the literal enemy, the sort of man I'd sworn to protect the US from. And I was going to give myself to him?

Give yourself to him? A mocking little voice spoke up inside me. *As if it's the supreme sacrifice?*

I felt the heat roll down my body, making my breasts tingle and my belly throb, finishing in a hot ache between my thighs.

If I slept with him because it was my job, because I had to...did that make it okay? Or did that just make me a whore?

All this on top of the fact that even simply having sex—normal sex, with a normal guy—would have been a major event in its own right. It was six months since I'd dated, and that had only lasted a couple of dates. It was just over a year since I'd had sex.

And this wouldn't just be sex. I remembered Roberta's warning: *God knows what he'll want in the bedroom.*

What *would* it be like? To be with a man as big and powerful as him? To lie under him, while he...

I squeezed my thighs together.

This is nuts. I should call the whole thing off. I should tell Adam I needed to bail and fly home to the US and even quit the CIA if I had to. *I can't have sex with a guy like him!*

...however much I want to.

I reddened guiltily.

Except that, because it's my job, I don't have to feel guilty.

Guilt-free sex with a truly evil man I knew I shouldn't get involved with but couldn't resist. Perfect. Except for the part where, if he suspected for an instant that I was CIA, he'd break my neck.

I closed my eyes and leaned back against the door. *What would Nancy do?* Probably somersault backwards through the air, firing a gun in each hand. *Not all that helpful.*

A shower. I'd take a shower and hope that cleared my head. Except that meant taking off my clothes, and there was nowhere to put them in the wet room where they wouldn't get soaked. I could dump them outside the door like Luka had said to, but if he really did take them to be cleaned, I'd be trapped there...naked. Taking a shower *was* making a decision.

I took a deep breath and stopped thinking. Instead, I felt. I remembered the feel of his hands all over me, at the party in New York and his foot between my thighs at lunch. But that wasn't what decided me. It was when I remembered the warmth of his chest against my back in the car and the tenderness of his gaze, those few times he'd let his defenses slip. There was more to him than the raw evil I'd been told about. And yet, worryingly, I was aware that the evil —and the *fuck you* attitude, the not caring what anyone thought— turned me on as much as the tenderness. I wanted his cold strength as well as his hidden, blazing center.

I unzipped my dress, still damp from the toilet water, and peeled it off. I stripped off my bra, panties and heels and then stood there, naked, biting my lip, the bundle of clothes in my arms.

All at once, I unlocked the door and pulled it open, half expecting Luka to be standing right there. But there was no one in sight. I laid the bundle down outside the door together with my purse and closed and relocked the door, then stepped quickly towards the shower before I could change my mind.

The slate tiles were warm underfoot—the place must have underfloor heating. There didn't seem to be any controls for the shower but, as I stepped under it, the spray came on, strong and just the right side of scalding. The shower head was as big as a car's wheel with about a million holes for the water. Standing under it was like being immersed rather than showered and the sensation left me gasping. But I could feel the jets pounding the heat into my body like hammers, forcing back the Moscow chill. And that took me back to a different sort of cold.

What exactly had happened in Luka's car? I hadn't had a full-on flashback like that in a long time and the intensity of it scared me. And yet, at the same time, it had felt as if something important had changed inside me. I was still frozen inside but I'd definitely felt things crack and move before they'd hardened again.

On the few occasions when the memories had hit me at full strength like that, I'd just had to endure it, the pain turning back in on itself again and again, like a beam of light in a hall of mirrors. But with Luka there, I'd actually been able to vent some of it. A little of the pain had escaped and it had felt...incredible.

Had he *healed me,* in some way? That made no sense. He killed people and sold things that killed people. What did he know about healing?

He'd called me *Little Mouse.* That wasn't how I'd expected him to react, faced with a woman ugly-crying in his car. I would have expected him to kick me out and pick up a couple of Russian escorts, instead.

When the water had sluiced the dried tears from my face and the toilet water from my skin, I rummaged around on the shelves by the shower, looking for shampoo. Translating the Russian wasn't a problem. Reading the labels in the moodily-lit bathroom was. *Who does he think he is: Batman?*

The bottles all looked like men's products—black, silver, and blue bottles. They had a quality feel but they didn't look trendy. That didn't surprise me. I couldn't imagine Luka reading up on which hair products would make his hair softer and more manageable. I was surprised he didn't wash it in coal tar and engine grease.

Right at the back of the shelf, I found a half-empty bottle with a definite feminine feel. Something Elena or one of the others had left there. I washed my hair like I've never washed it before, until all traces of the fight in the club bathroom were gone. I gently felt my face. My cheek still throbbed a little where the woman had slapped it, but there didn't seem to be a bruise. My forehead was tender but hadn't swollen up and my lip had stopped bleeding. I'd been lucky.

I found a bottle of what I hoped was shower gel. As soon as I opened it, I recognized the scent from being around Luka—it was the one he used, citrusy and with a hint of cold, stormy skies. I soaped myself down until I felt completely clean, suds trickling down over my breasts and stomach. I don't know how much time passed but, by the time I finished, the attack felt as if it had happened to someone else.

I shut off the water and then took a look at myself in the mirror. Without make-up remover, I'd had to just scrub at my ruined make-up as best I could. It was pretty much all gone, which looked a hell of a lot better than a clown face. But now I was completely bare.

What I needed was my purse, so I could at least apply a little lipstick. It had been a long time since I dated, but I hadn't completely lost touch with my feminine instincts. I looked around for a towel...and then realized there weren't any.

I poked my head out of the door. My clothes, as Luka had promised, had gone. So had my purse. I was now stranded, naked, and dripping wet. I swallowed. "Um. Hello?"

Nothing. But, if I strained my ears, I could hear something coming from the open-plan living area. A crackling sound. The penthouse seemed to be mainly in darkness, with only the occasional spotlight and the moonlight coming in through the windows to light my way.

I took a deep breath...and stepped out, naked, to find him.

The penthouse had cream carpets, the pile so deep that my feet almost disappeared. I squelched across them, wincing. First I'd probably ruined his car's upholstery, now his penthouse. But he had stranded me without a towel...possibly deliberately. A deep, hot throb went through me.

As I rounded the corner, I saw him. He was standing by an enormous fireplace in which a fire was blazing, the logs stacked as high as my hip. The scale of it would have dwarfed any other man, but not Luka. He was still in his black shirt and black jeans and yet, despite the fine clothes, he looked...*rugged.* The fire was lighting up his high cheekbones and solid jaw in reds and oranges and I couldn't remember ever seeing anything more beautiful. He was like a statue to male power, cast in granite.

And then he turned and saw me and I saw his eyes gleam in the darkness. I felt his gaze rake down my naked, dripping body and I swear half the water just evaporated right there, my whole body going warm under his eyes. I felt my core dissolve into liquid heat.

He beckoned with his finger.

I stepped towards him and, as I passed a framed photo on the wall, I saw my reflection in the glass. My pale skin was gleaming wetly, still beaded with moisture. My hair was a twisted, wet rope down my back. My nipples had already hardened from the sudden transition from hot shower to cold air. But I was just...me. *Why does he want me?! This should be Svetlana or Natalia or...hell, Nancy, stalking around in their high heels with their perfect make-up. Why me?*

I started walking towards him and, with every step, I could feel that charge in the air between us, tingling and sparkling against every inch of exposed skin. I wasn't sure how much he could see but I knew I was still mostly veiled in shadow. Every step brought me closer to the firelight and put more of me on display. I started to breathe faster.

When I was still ten feet away, I could feel the heat of the fire. I looked down and saw that the warm light was hitting my calves, now, allowing him to see them. Another step, and it was over my knees. Another, and it was all the way up my thighs. The room was so quiet that I could hear my own ragged breathing.

His eyes ran down and then up my body and he gave *that* smile, the one that seemed to mean he approved, and the heat started to build faster and faster, as if a switch had been thrown. How could just a smile, just the knowledge that he wanted me, do that to me? God, I was completely at his mercy.

This time, he didn't beckon me. He said, "Come here," and I could hear the thick layer of lust under his words.

My legs seemed to move of their own accord. I closed the remaining distance between us, the last shadows retreating up my thighs, stomach, and breasts until they disappeared completely and my whole body was wrapped in flickering orange light. It made the soft curls of brown hair between my thighs gleam. As I neared him, I stepped right in front of the fireplace and the heat was like a furnace.

I stopped. There were no more than a few feet between us, now, but he didn't reach for me or tell me to come closer. I felt the fire beginning to dry the water from my body, the heat of it almost too much to bear on the side of me that was closest. And Luka was just as close—*how is he not hot?* But he just stood there as if made of rock and I didn't doubt that he could stand there all night if he wanted to.

His own comfort didn't seem to bother him at all. He was only interested in one thing, at that moment, and that was me. His gaze traced every line of my body: my cheekbone, the curve of my lip, the shape of my neck. It went lower and I felt it like a touch on my breasts, the nipples puckering even more as his eyes swept over them. Down over my stomach, down between my thighs—

I swallowed. The heat inside me coiled and tightened.

His gaze moved down my legs, all the way to my toes, and I shifted my weight from foot to foot. It felt as if he was consuming me, savoring each piece.

His eyes rose to mine and locked there and he made the tiniest circling motion with one finger. I realized he wanted me to turn and dry myself. And, at the same time, show off my entire body to him.

I lifted my arms out to the sides and began to turn. The blazing hot skin on one side of me went blessedly cool as it rotated away from the fire. Then my back and ass were facing the fireplace, the violent heat of it vaporizing every drop of moisture. I kept turning, because I knew that if I stopped, I might not have the courage to start again.

I turned until my ass was towards Luka and my other side was towards the fire. I felt his eyes sweeping over my back and down the curve of my spine, following it down between the cheeks of my ass, and I tensed.

Then I was rotating again, my front towards the fire, and the heat was so intense that I had to close my eyes. I felt the fire blasting my eyelids, my cheeks, my breasts. The heat soaked into me and I swear I felt my breasts swell as they warmed. My nipples had been hard because of the chill; now, they stayed hard thanks to the heat inside me. I felt my sex absorbing the heat, too, swelling, *aching,* the heat inside and out melting me, my arousal turning to slick moisture.

I faced him again and opened my eyes. He was staring right at me and he was breathing hard, that massive chest moving in ragged heaves, as if he was having to hold himself back.

I could feel my heart pounding in my chest. *Say something, Arianna, say something or it's going to happen, it's going to happen right now, say something SAY SOMETHING—*"I—"

Too late.

All in one movement, he stepped forward, put his hand under my chin, and tilted my face up. His lips were on me instantly, crushing against mine, the kiss open-mouthed and hungry, and it was less than a second before my own lips flowered open and let him in. His chest pushed up against my naked breasts, the soft cloth of his shirt rasping against my nipples, and I groaned into his mouth.

Then one of his huge hands landed hard on my ass, pulling me powerfully up, and I yelped as my feet left the ground. I grabbed for his neck instinctively and my legs went either side of his. My naked sex bumped against his jeans and I went weak, squirming and then clinging to him, my legs wrapping around him to hold me up. His tongue was exploring my mouth while the hand under my ass squeezed and fondled each cheek in turn, every press of his fingers making me gasp. His other hand played up and down my spine, each sweep of it drawing the fire inside higher and higher—

Suddenly he spun around and pushed me away from him, almost throwing me down. I staggered and almost fell. He turned his back on me, staring at the fire. He was between me and it, now, silhouetted against the flames. "Luka?" I asked, worried. "What—"

"You shouldn't be with me," he said. "You're a good person."

I'd like to say that I pretended to be naive. That I played the part of the American tourist who didn't know what he did for a living. "You are too, I'm sure," I said.

But the truth is, I said it because I wanted it so badly to be true. I wanted it all to be a huge mistake, and for him to turn out to be the good guy after all.

He shook his head, his back still turned. "No," he said. "No, I'm not."

I had my way out. I could just ask for my clothes and leave and never see him again. Tell Adam I'd done my best and go home to a hero's welcome for having tried.

But I didn't want to go. I wanted to be with him so badly it hurt. I stepped forward and put my hand on his arm.

His hand came down on my hand, trapping it there. He slowly turned to face me and I almost gasped when I saw the pain in his eyes, the debate that was raging there. "Don't start what you can't finish," he told me.

I swallowed. And nodded.

His eyes were stroking over me, hotter even than the fire had been. "I don't know what you're used to," he said. "But you won't be used to me."

Something deep inside me, something I hadn't even known existed until the party in New York, twisted and throbbed, releasing a dark, dark heat. *He's not going to be like one of your boyfriends,* Roberta had warned me.

I didn't want him to be. I felt a rush of shame as I admitted it, but...part of me wanted to welcome that darkness into me.

I nodded. And instantly, I saw the change in his eyes as he slipped over the edge and out of control. I felt as if I'd just cut the rope tethering a balloon to the ground and now it was surging skyward, dragging me with it. He grabbed my hand in a death-grip—

OhGodwhathaveIdone?

—and pulled me towards the bedroom.

24

I had to run to keep up. If I'd stumbled, I honestly believe he would have dragged me along the carpet.

We burst through a door into his bedroom. A huge room, with a bed that looked bigger than king size, covered in a dark red satiny comforter that gleamed in the low lighting. Luka heaved on my hand and I squealed as my feet left the floor and I flew headfirst through the air —

I landed on my back on the bed, the air knocked out of me. I lay there gasping, looking up at him, trying to come to terms with the reality that *he just threw me onto his bed*.

He was undressing. He didn't rush, despite the headlong dash through the apartment. It was as if he wanted to savor this part. His fingers worked the buttons of his shirt, his bare chest gradually appearing. I lay there panting, staring up at him. He was a huge man anyway but, looking up at him like that, he looked like a giant.

The smooth expanse of his pecs slowly came into view and, with it, the first of his tattoos. The spider at the center of its web, picked out in black against the smooth tan flesh. His chest was so wide, so solidly hewn that I wanted to run my hands over it in wonder. Then, as the shirt loosened around his shoulders, I saw the tattooed stars there, the ranking that lifted him above the others. What had he done, to earn those? How many men had he beaten or shot to rise up the chain of command? I should have been terrified—*was* terrified—but I imagined leaning around him from behind and softly kissing every point of each star, telling him that I knew what he was...and that I wanted him so much I didn't care.

His broad chest gave way to a tight midsection, the muscles hard ridges beneath the skin. As he slid the shirt down his arms, my eyes locked on the Bratva tattoo of a rose on his bicep. It wasn't just him who would kill me, if he found out what I was. The entire weight of the organization could be turned, with one phone call, into an apparatus for tracking me down and putting me in a shallow grave. I was on their turf, where the games were played by their rules.

The thought made me close my eyes for a second in fear but, when I opened them again and took in the whole of his naked torso, I knew I wasn't going to run. The sight of him was short-circuiting my brain, going straight past every bit of common sense I possessed. I was acting on instinct and need. His body was sheer power, shaped not through vanity but through brutality. The ink was the final evidence, if I needed any: this man was as bad as they came. And he was staring right between my thighs.

I closed my legs, out of instinct.

He smiled, as if that was amusing.

What have I done?!

He kicked off his shoes and unfastened his expensive leather belt. When he pulled it through the loops, it whistled and snapped. There was something about the way he did it that made me go weak inside. *God, does he use that on his women? Does he tie them up and—*

He lazily pushed his jeans down, taking his jockey shorts with them. I got my first look at his cock. Big. Thick. And already—God, already hard and primed in his fist as he climbed onto the bed—

I moved away from him, my ass scooching up the bed. I don't know why—primal instinct at the sheer size of him, I think. It wasn't that I didn't want it.

And it didn't make any difference. His hand seized my ankle and dragged me back down the bed. I let out a kind of strangled groan.

He looked meaningfully down at my pressed-together thighs.

I swallowed, the air rattling in my nostrils I was breathing so hard. And I opened my legs for him. I felt cool air hit my delicate flesh and I could feel myself throbbing, wet with need for him. *God!* I'd never felt like this, ever.

He moved up the bed, kneeling between my legs and hulking over me, planting his hands either side of me. His thickly-muscled forearms might as well have been made of solid steel, imprisoning me.

You wanted this, a little voice inside me reminded me.

His knees moved up between my legs. God, his lower half was just as heavily muscled. That solid mass you get on a heavyweight boxer, dwarfing me. *What was I thinking?!*

I felt the first touch of his cock against my inner thigh and the hot, throbbing weight of it made me gasp. Then he was leaning down over me as if to kiss me, his lips only an inch from mine....

But he didn't kiss me. This wasn't going to be that sort of sex. His mouth moved down my neck, a soft exhalation sending little currents of air dancing across my skin. He moved down to my chest and—

My upper body came up off the bed as his mouth enveloped my breast in its hot, sucking depths, his lips spread wide to take as much of me as he could. Then his hand was on my shoulder, ramming me hard back down to the bed. I gasped and stared up at him; the look in his eyes was clear.

I wasn't to move. He was in control.

His tongue started to lash over my quivering nipple, his lips massaging the soft flesh around it, and I ground my thighs together, trapping him between them. His hand remained planted on my shoulder, pinning me down, even though I had no intention of moving. His other hand started working on my other breast, squeezing and rubbing, his thumb sliding back and forth across the nipple. My ass came off the bed a little, my thighs grinding harder.

Looking down, I saw that his hand was so big, it covered my breast completely. A deep, hot throb went through me at the image.

He switched his mouth to my other breast and slid a hand down over my stomach to my groin. The flat of his palm pressed against my pubis and suddenly that, too, was rammed down onto the bed, my grinding thighs held motionless. I was pinned by both his hands, now, shoulder and groin. *Held down.* I felt something rise and spiral inside me, black smoke shot through with sparks of pure fire, hot enough to blazing right through the ice. Fear...but the kind of fear that propels you out of the way of an oncoming truck. Fear that makes you feel alive.

I pushed against his hands. Not because I wanted to escape; because I wanted to feel them holding me down. I might as well have been straining against solid rock.

His fingers started to explore the soft folds between my thighs and I automatically tried to roll my hips...but I couldn't. I couldn't move away, either, or cover myself. His knees kept my legs open and his hand kept me pinned to the bed. I was his, and all I could do was give myself up to it.

Being unable to move and respond meant that all I could do was feel. Every sensation was magnified. I could feel how thick and strong his fingers were as they played up and down over my lips, tracing the shape of them. I could feel that massive palm rocking and rubbing against me as he held me down, sending quaking pleasure through me. I could feel my wetness building with each passing second, the pleasure rolling out in hot, tight waves.

His fingers rubbed and rubbed—and then, quite suddenly, two of his fingers slid into me. I felt myself spasm around them, my breath coming in quick, shocked pants. God, I could feel every knuckle. They slid in and then scissored open, spreading me, and I trembled. Then his palm was lifting off my groin and his whole body was shifting lower. One big hand pressed down on my breast, pinning me to the bed as his head—

...went between my thighs.

"*LUKA!*"

I hadn't even been aware I was going to say it. It just escaped from me as his mouth settled over my sex, his tongue lapping at my clit. I was overcome, not just by how incredible it felt but by the fact he'd done it. I'd thought he was going to take what he wanted, not give back. I hadn't realized that he wanted much more from me than simply to fuck me. I stared down and I knew the sight of him, of his strong, muscled back as he knelt between my thighs, would be burned into my mind forever.

His lips sealed around my clit, his tongue teasing it from its hiding place with quick, expert strokes. The pleasure arced outward, lighting up every part of me. It throbbed upward through my stomach and chest, stealing my breath. It flash-fried my brain, driving out any thoughts outside of this incredible, beautiful man and what he was doing to me.

His fingers began to pump at me. The thickness of his fingers and his heavy, rounded knuckles made me quiver and gasp with each stroke. The waves of pleasure became trapped in a hot ball that began to slowly expand. I was thrashing under him, now, but that strong hand on my breast and the push of his head against my groin locked me to the bed as securely as iron chains.

His head drew back from me a little—far enough that he could glance up at my face, but close enough that, when he spoke, I could feel each word as a hot wind against my sticky, engorged flesh. "You are beautiful," he told me, and underneath his strong accent I could hear his rising lust. "Come for me, now, Arianna."

His tongue lashed out again, circling just where I needed it most, and the ball of pleasure inside me was stretched and glowed blindingly bright—

One of his fingers slid from me, quickly replaced with another as he continued to piston them in and out. Then the slickened finger slid underneath me, between the cheeks of my ass—

My eyes went wide, my hips helplessly trying to rise as the orgasm overtook me. My eyes screwed tight, my head grinding into the bed as I bent like a bow, spit-wet breasts straining for the ceiling. "*Nggghhhhhhh!*"

His tongue lifted from my throbbing heat, but his voice started up again and it kept the orgasm going better than any amount of physical attention. He was talking to himself in Russian, unaware that I could understand. "*I am going to take you, Arianna. I am going to end your innocence in every conceivable way. I am going to make you beg me to stop and then beg me for more.*"

I exploded. The climax roared through me, shredding me into tiny fragments of stardust that sprayed out into the void. I gave myself up to the idea of being his, that this monster of a man was going to do whatever the hell he liked to me. And that I was going to love it.

I thrashed and shook and it felt like minutes passed. When I came back to myself and opened my eyes, I was bathed in sweat and my chest was heaving.

"*Wow,*" I said in a tiny voice. It was all I could manage.

He smiled down at me, a cruel grin that was all mastery and knowing confidence. The same smile, I guessed, that he wore when he'd done this to Elena and Natalia and his other Russian blondes. A smile that said he'd won, that he'd held me down and played my body like a maestro, shown me pleasure I'd never known before. All of which was true. And yet—

There was something else there, just a flicker of it in his eyes. A deep, burning need that went beyond just sex. It went beyond just extracting pleasure from my body for both of us. It was about something deeper and more permanent. It was darkly possessive and powerful enough that it came close to making him lose control. Not tonight, maybe. But, if it grew, then someday.

That flicker gave me hope. And raised a dangerous flutter deep in my frozen heart.

The look in his eyes was gone in an instant, though, and I was back to being his plaything. I gasped as I felt his fingers pull from me and then his body was moving up to cover mine. He bore me down on the bed as his hips pushed my thighs apart. He grabbed my knees and spread them wide and then wider, so wide that my inner thighs ached. I heard the rubber sound of a condom and then, with one long push, he was filling me.

My arms came up to clutch at him, hugging him to me. It didn't hurt, but the deep stretch of it made me catch my breath and he wasn't even all the way in. My fingers dug hard into the muscles of his back as he slid back and plunged in again—*God!* That feeling of his hardness opening me up, making me his....

Deep. *Deeper.* His girth stretching me tight. *God!*

His face drew level with mine and he laid kisses on my forehead as he filled me completely.

He waited there for a second, allowing me to adjust to his size. I could feel myself tight around him, and the press of my groin against his. God, the feeling of him being rooted in me, my body so fragile and pale under him. Part of me wished there was a mirror on the ceiling so that I could see all of him. I knew that if I could glimpse the tan cheeks of his ass pushed hard up between my thighs, I'd come just from that alone.

He began to move and it became buttery-smooth and perfect, every millimeter of the thrust a delight, ribbons of pleasure zig-zagging upward. I reached up to touch his face, my fingers stroking over his cheeks. He allowed it for a second and then his hand was capturing mine, bearing it down to the bed above my head and grabbing the other one, too. His hands were big enough that he was able to pin both of my wrists with just one, giving him a hand free. He used it to trace a finger down my cheek, then over my gasping lips and down to my breast. Taking his weight on his elbows, he started to stroke at my slickened nipple as he thrust, twirling his thumb and forefinger around and around the base of the hardened flesh.

I drew in great, heaving gasps through my nose. It was all...too...much: the spirals of fire coming from his fingers on my nipple; the silken perfection of his long, hard thrusts; the feel of that strong hand, holding my wrists down.

I began to thrash again, bouncing the back of my head into the bed again and again as I tried to vent some of the pressure that was building inside me. His thrusts were faster, now, the strong muscles of his legs and ass propelling him effortlessly into me, his groin slapping against mine.

He'd angled himself lower and his chest was rubbing over my breasts with each thrust, my nipples hard as rocks. The ball of pleasure expanded for the second time, until it filled my whole chest. The power of him was incredible—his thrusts were so hard, so fast, that the huge bed was banging against the wall, yet they seemed effortless. Again and again, the silken push of him filled me and stretched me. He was just going to keep going and going for as long as he liked and there was nothing I could do—

Nothing I could do.

The pleasure expanded again, my climax rushing towards me. I bucked and wriggled under him and every press of my body against his, every reminder of how firmly I was pinned, made me hotter and hotter. *God, I'm going to come again.* I had no hope of escape. I just had to lie there and take the pleasure he was giving me. He had me exactly where he wanted me, trapped under his muscled body, helpless—

Helpless.

My back arched and I screamed in ecstasy as the pleasure exploded. I felt myself spasm around him, my whole body shuddering. I heard him grunt, a low, animal noise, and then the hot pulse of him inside me.

My wrists pushed and pushed against his restraining hand and my fingers just managed to find his and knit together with them. We stayed there for a moment as we both rode out our peaks, and then he relaxed atop me. I noticed he was careful to support himself on his arms, preventing his hard body from crushing me. *A gentleman,* I thought dreamily. *However much he used me.*

Used me. Now that it was over, reality started to come back. With it, the first stirrings of outrage and fear. God, he'd picked me up and *thrown* me on the bed. Pinned me down while he'd...

...given me the best orgasms of my life. I flushed. When I looked up at Luka with confused, guilty eyes, I saw that flicker again, just for a second. A hint that maybe he'd lost control, too, or come close to it.

He got off me and walked to the other side of the room. The sudden lack of his body was like a physical loss, the cool air of the apartment making me quiver as it wafted over my shining nipples and the wet folds of my sex. God, I'd been...*ridden.* My legs lolled wantonly apart, too tired to close. My breasts were throbbing where he'd ravished me with his mouth and fingers. Inside, I felt a deep and very pleasant ache where he'd stretched me.

What had I done?

What had I let him do to me?

I knew, instinctively, that this was the way sex was, for him. This was the way it had been with his other girlfriends. But with me...what was it I'd glimpsed, that had made it different?

He was leaning on a countertop before a mirror. I saw him looking at himself and wished I could see his reflection from where I was. I wanted to know what was in his eyes. Guilt? Anger—at me, at himself?

He finally turned around and walked back to the bed, still completely naked. "Are you okay?" he asked.

He sounded...wait, was that...was he *scared?* Scared that he might have hurt me?

"Yeah," I said. "Yes. I'm fine." I gingerly closed my legs and sat up, hugging my knees. I ached a little, but there was no pain.

He nodded quickly, as if relieved. And, now that the fear was gone, he looked almost confused. I was getting to know that feeling pretty well myself, when I was around him. That *what the hell am I doing* feeling, the disconcerting sensation of being not quite in control. I couldn't understand the hold he had on me. *My* confusion made sense.

But why would *he* be feeling that way?

"Will you stay the night?" he asked suddenly. And then he sort of coughed and said, "You'll have to stay the night. I sent your clothes to be washed."

At three in the morning? But maybe anything was possible, if you were rich enough. The real question was, what had come over him? He was suddenly behaving like a nervous teenager, all his hard man exterior gone.

"Yes," I said. "Yes, I'll stay."

He nodded gruffly as if that was what he wanted to hear. He pulled back the comforter to reveal soft cotton sheets and I slid between them. A second later, I felt him spoon me, the hard press of his muscles against my back comforting. He wrapped an arm around me and I felt a warm swell of emotion. It was the first time I hadn't slept alone in a year.

But this isn't real. You know how he treats his girlfriends. It's just sex.

And even if that wasn't true, it can't be real. This is just a mission.

He's using me. I'm using him.

I knew that. I kept repeating it to myself.

And yet the warm press of him against my back felt so very, very good.

25

I woke up alone in the bed. It felt wrong, as if I'd already gotten used to the feel of him against me. And that was ridiculous, after just one night.

I could feel that the covers were warm behind me, though, so Luka couldn't have been up long. Without moving, I opened my eyes. The blinds behind me must have been open because the room was bright with sunlight. I was about to sit up to look for Luka when I saw something. On the dresser, right in front of my eyes, was a steaming black coffee mug. And reflected in its shining surface I could see—

I snapped my eyes closed again and then studied the image in my mind. In the reflection, I'd seen myself, lying on my side in the bed. And behind me, sitting in an armchair across the room, was Luka. He was sipping an identical mug of coffee and he looked fantastic in black jeans and a white shirt that he hadn't bothered to fasten up yet. That glorious strong chest thrust out between the shirt's open sides and my eyes tracked down, over the hard ridges of his abs and along the deep centerline, then back up over his pecs.

But it wasn't his body that had caught my attention. It was what he was doing.

He was staring at me. He was sitting there watching me sleeping.

Why would he do that? In his phone calls, he'd always seemed like a guy who could barely spare the time to talk to his girlfriends, even when they looked like supermodels. Clearly, I'd slept in—the sun seemed to be high in the sky. Had there been a clock anywhere in view? I searched through the remembered image. Shit! 9:47. What the hell was he doing, still watching me slumber in his bed?

I kept my eyes closed and let out what I hoped was a good fake yawn, flopping over on my back and stretching my arms above my head. Possibly, I overdid it a little because the covers rode down and my boobs popped into view. I'd forgotten I was naked.

I opened my eyes. Luka was up out of his chair and gazing nonchalantly out of the window as if he'd never been looking at me at all. "Good morning," I said, quickly covering myself.

He turned. His face was back to its icy mask. "I made you coffee," he said. Then, "It's good that you're up. You should go. I have a meeting."

I nodded, confused, then pretended to see the time on the clock and made a big show of looking surprised that I'd slept so late. I glugged some coffee and ran off to the shower.

Standing under the spray again, I tried to figure things out. He was coming across as indifferent—cold, even. He was giving the impression that it had just been a one-night stand and that now he wanted me out. I would have bought the act completely if I hadn't seen him watching me so intently as I slept. And why had he asked me to stay the night, only to kick me out in the morning?

The callousness made sense—I knew what sort of man he was. But what he was hiding underneath...that didn't make sense at all.

Outside the bathroom door, I found my clothes, freshly laundered and neatly folded. He really *had* got someone to clean them at three in the morning. I dressed and went to find him.

He was standing behind the kitchen counter, reading the newspaper that was spread out across it. That meant that approaching him was awkward. The closer I got, the more the counter seemed like a barrier between us. "Um. I'll be going, then, I guess." Was he going to kiss me? Talk about the night before?

I knew I should be thinking of the whole thing as a spy. Analyzing, probing for weaknesses. That's what Nancy or one of the other professionals would have done. I just wondered, heart aching, if he was even going to look up.

Then he did and I saw that pain in his eyes again, the blue ice burning for a second. "I called you a taxi," he said. "It's downstairs. It'll take you back to your hotel. I already paid for it."

"Thank you." *Now what? Kiss him? Ask him what's next?* Maybe I'd been wrong, before. Maybe he really *was* just kicking me out and that's all there was to it. I was to be just another one-night stand in a long line of them. I hesitated for another second and then stepped towards the door.

I had my hand on the doorknob when he said, "Arianna."

I turned back.

He stared at me for another beat, his eyes searching my face. In that second, despite his size, he looked...helpless. Then he was storming out from behind the counter, his open shirt flapping with the movement. He covered the distance between us in a few short strides and the sight of him, all muscle and tattoos and those intense blue eyes, made me tense as he drew near. Luka could *loom* like no man I'd ever met.

I raised my eyes to look up at him just as he brushed my hair back from my face. That conflict in his eyes again. Confusion, as if he didn't understand his own feelings. I opened my mouth to ask what the hell was going on and—

And he was kissing me, his hand coming up to hold my cheek and then caress it, his tongue pushing my lips apart. His thumb rubbed in slow circles on my cheekbone and I could feel that massive chest moving against me as he panted like some barely-restrained beast. The contact was like an electrical surge ripping through my body. I felt as if I could lift my feet off the floor and I'd float there in mid air. He lifted his mouth and kissed my lower lip, biting it lightly between his teeth, and I went heady.

When we finally parted, we stood there with lips almost touching, as if neither of us wanted to back off. We were so close that I couldn't see his eyes. "I want you again," I heard him say.

I caught my breath at the thick lust that had entered his voice. I remembered what he'd said when his head was between my thighs, those words in Russian I wasn't meant to understand. That he was going to end my innocence, in every conceivable way. I remembered how it had been: brutal and hard, pinned to the bed...and feeling alive, for just a few minutes.

I was meant to be getting involved with him. I was meant to be becoming his girlfriend. But this thing that I'd inadvertently unlocked between us, this darkness in him I was drawn to and the innocence he was drawn to in me...that was something altogether more dangerous. I couldn't.

He gripped my arm, hard. "*I have to have you,*" he said.

I felt my legs weaken under me. I swallowed and then, in a voice that didn't sound like my own, I whispered, "Yes."

He moved back far enough that I could see his face. "I have to go on a trip for a few days," he said. "You'll come." Not *do you want to come? You'll come.*

"A trip?" I asked uncertainly.

"It's on a yacht," he told me. He grinned, getting a little of his confident charm back. "We will be away for a few days. I will have to go to a meeting, but the rest of the time...." He kissed me again, slowly but with no less heat than before.

I had no idea what to do. Go away with him?! *Where?* That wasn't even vaguely within the scope of the mission. But I was meant to be getting close to him...and the idea of more time with him sent thick, dark tendrils of heat straight down to my groin. "Okay," I said.

For just a second, he smiled like a child at Christmas.

I stepped back from him and opened the door, thinking fast. I had to somehow find out where we were going, so I could tell Adam. "I'll have to get something to wear," I said. "Where are we going? Will it be hot? Cold?"

He smirked. "Cold," he said. *Damn!* I needed a location—at least a damn country! But I couldn't push it too hard or it might look suspicious.

He picked up a pad of Post-It notes from the counter, wrote on the top one and gave it to me. "Tell the taxi to take you there. Tell them I sent you."

I looked at the note. The name of a store and an address. Luka's handwriting was all bold strokes and sharp angles, powerful but precise. "Okay," I said doubtfully.

I backed out of the door. As I reached the threshold, he suddenly reached out and grabbed the collar of my dress, preventing me from moving further. Then he dragged me back inside and kissed me again, hot and long and slow, his lips owning me totally.

"I will collect you from your hotel at three," he said.

And he gently closed the door.

26

The cab was waiting for me, just as he'd said. And the driver took the Post-It note and drove me there without complaint, even though he'd only been paid to take me to my hotel. Did Luka have some sort of bottomless credit line with these guys, or were they just too scared of him to complain?

The thick Plexiglas partition between the driver and me helped cement it in my mind as *cab* and not *car* and that crucial pathway in my broken brain didn't light up. No flashbacks. But the fact that it could happen so easily, as it had in the car with Luka, was terrifying.

I hunkered down in the back, arms folded across my chest, and tried to process. Was it just about sex, with Luka? That certainly made sense, given that we'd barely spoken from the moment we got to his apartment to the time he—I flushed. And that morning, he'd seemed ready to hurry me out. And yet he'd sat there watching me, when he thought I was asleep. And even during the sex, I'd seen that flicker in his eyes, gotten that feeling that, however much he treated me like something to simply be fucked, there was a lot more going on inside.

And what about this trip on the yacht? I kept Adam informed of where I was. In theory, if I got into trouble, he could get me out. But that didn't apply if I was off in the middle of the ocean. I didn't even know which country we were going to.

I tried to focus on the mission, but I couldn't help wondering what it meant, that Luka wanted to take me away with him. Did I qualify as a girlfriend, now? My last relationship had been in college and had followed the same pattern as the ones in my teens: flirting and kissing and dating and then, eventually, something more physical. This was completely different. Was I a *lover,* now? That sounded like something out of a 70s French movie. Was this how grown-up relationships were—you fucked the guy and then you hoped that you started to mean something to him?

I went around and around thinking about it, getting more and more worked up. Just when I was about to wind down the cab's window and scream to vent some stress, my phone rang. I presumed it was Adam and grabbed it. "Hello?"

"Arianna. Thank God. What in the name of fucking fuck do you think you're doing?"

Nancy.

And suddenly, everything was okay. At last, I had someone I could talk to. Someone who'd understand what it was like to be undercover.

Of course, we'd have to talk in code. Our calls were probably being intercepted by the Russian authorities and there'd be hell to pay if they thought the CIA was running an op in their country. We had to sound like a couple of typical twenty-somethings. "I thought you were on that business trip," I said.

"I got back last night and found you gone. Your...*dad* told me about your vacation in Moscow." She sounded casual and cheery, while letting just enough of a hint of fear bubble through that I understood her real message.

"Yeah, well...I figured it was time I saw the world. You know I've been wanting to do that for a long time." I'd moaned plenty of times to Nancy about wanting to try field work.

"Sure, sure. But *Moscow?* I didn't think the travel *company* you use even did that sort of trip."

I frowned. *The Company* was slang for the CIA. She was hinting that the op didn't make sense. Roberta had said something similar. Why was the CIA—and Adam—so interested in Luka? And why had he sent me, not someone experienced, like Nancy?

I pushed the disquiet down inside me. This was my one chance. I wasn't going to start second-guessing my new boss. Maybe she was just jealous, although that wasn't like her at all.

"Don't you think you might have rushed into things a little?" Nancy asked. "Your dad says you've already fallen for some guy out there. I don't want to see you get your heart broken, Arianna. And this guy sounds like a real heartbreaker."

"I'll be fine," I said with a confidence I didn't feel. She wasn't talking romance. She was talking about my body being found floating in a Moscow river.

"You don't know what these Russian men can be like," she said. "A lot of them have big families. Lots of *brothers.*" She was talking about the brotherhood, the Russian mafia. "It makes it difficult for them to form attachments with women. In fact, they don't get on with women at all. Do you remember I told you about my old boyfriend, Dmitri? *He* was Russian."

I felt sick. I remembered Dmitri. She'd told me, one night after too much wine, about how one of her first missions had required her to steal documents from his office. He'd caught her, beaten her and tried to rape her. "I remember," I said in a small voice. "But Luka isn't like that."

"I really think you should come home," said Nancy. "I know your dad thinks it's good for you to be out there, seeing the world, but I'm really worried you're going to get your heart broken. Just come home, Arianna."

"I'm fine," I said again. The car was slowing. "I have to go. Take care." And I ended the call before she could argue.

I wanted nothing more than to speak to her. Hearing her voice after so long with nothing familiar around me was like coming home. But if I kept talking to her, she was going to persuade me to bail. God, she didn't even know about the trip on the yacht, yet. If she knew I was planning to do that, she'd freak out completely. And the scary thing was that she was absolutely right—I was way out of my depth.

The cab pulled up outside a boutique that was all soft lighting and artfully displayed mannequins, a world away from the places I normally shopped at back home. My stomach tensed. In theory, I had the new Arianna Ross credit card Adam had given me, but my instincts took over. *Shit! I couldn't afford this!*

As soon as I took a step inside, a woman in an immaculate black designer dress stepped from behind the counter. Her blonde pixie cut was so precise I suspected it was styled with a laser. Something about my clothes clearly marked me as a tourist, and not a rich one. "Can I help you?" she asked in English.

There's a certain way that store assistants can say *Can I help you* so that it sounds like *Please get out of my store.*

"Um," I said. "I think I need some clothes. Quite a lot of clothes. I'm not sure exactly what." We stared at one another. *Well done, Arianna. Very decisive.* I looked around. "I'm not sure I can afford this place..."

The store assistant gave me a smile so incredibly patronizing, it felt as if she'd kicked me in the chest. "There are some cheaper stores a few streets down," she said sweetly. And she picked up the coffee she'd been drinking and leaned against the counter, smirking. Even her coffee mug was designer, with some achingly cool clothes company's logo on the side.

A hot flush rose in my cheeks. She made me feel as if I was something she'd scraped off her shoe. I turned to slink out and then remembered something. "Luka Malakov sent me," I mumbled.

There was a crash as the designer coffee mug hit the floor.

I thought I'd offended her. I thought maybe his name was so despised that she'd thrown the mug down in anger. I headed for the door.

She *ran* in front of me, slipping and almost falling on the marble floor, and blocked my path. And now I saw how the color was draining from her face. She babbled at me in Russian for a few seconds, begging forgiveness, before she remembered I was just a dumb American tourist. "I'm sorry!" she said in English. "I didn't know! Alina! *Alina!*"

I'd seen people go pale, but I'd never seen anyone go *white* before. She looked as if she was about to throw up.

A slightly older woman with dark hair came running in from the back. At first, she frowned at the commotion, especially when she saw the coffee all over the floor. Then the blonde woman hissed in Russian, "*She's from Luka Malakov!*"

Alina stopped dead in her tracks and then swallowed as if she was trying to choke down a football. Her hand played nervously with the necklace at her throat. "You work for Mr. Malakov?" she asked in Russian.

"She's American!" the younger one said in a terse whisper, still in Russian. Holy shit, there were tears in her eyes. "I think she's his...." She looked up at her boss with huge, scared eyes. "*I was rude to her!*"

Alina stared at her and then at me. I actually saw her knees weaken. She spoke in English for the first time. "You are Mr. Malakov's..." She swallowed again. "You are *with* Mr. Malakov?"

I nodded, growing more freaked out by the minute.

Alina glanced at her assistant and then at the spilled coffee and smashed mug. She spoke in English, so I knew she wanted me to understand. "Clean this up," she snapped at the store assistant. "Then collect your things. You're fired." She looked back at me, eyes wide with concern, clearly hoping this would appease me.

I was too shocked to react. The scariest thing was that the store assistant didn't even argue. She just nodded, head down, and ran to fetch cleaning things.

"Please allow me to help you," said Alina. She stressed the *allow me,* as if nothing could be a greater honor.

"I—" I was completely freaked out, now. All I wanted to do was run. "I'm not sure I can afford this place."

Alina reacted as if I'd said I was thinking of drinking bleach. "There's no *charge!*" she said, aghast. "We would never charge you!"

For the next hour, Alina showed me dresses and jeans, jackets and shoes. She picked out long woolen coats for above deck and figure-hugging dresses for below deck. I soon had more clothes than in my closet back home. And then we started on the shoes—towering heels I could barely walk in, but that did wonderful things to my legs and ass.

"And will you be needing...underneath?" asked Alina, her English failing her. She yanked her dress away from her chest and pointed to her bra.

"Um..." I flushed. I hadn't even thought about lingerie. In my suitcase back at the hotel, I had the same plain briefs and bras I always wore. Would those do? "I don't know."

Alina flushed too. "For Mr. Malakov," she whispered, "I think you need—" She gestured at her breasts and groin in a *va-va-voom* sort of a way. "Upstairs," she said.

She led me up to the next floor and shooed away the sales clerk there. She started to bring out artful constructions of lace and satin, mainly in black, purple or red. I didn't doubt that one of Luka's blondes would have looked fantastic in them. Was this what Nancy did on assignment: pick out underwear to seduce her target? Or did she have a secret closet full of it in Virginia that she packed into her suitcase along with her guns? *I am so out of my depth.*

I tried to imagine myself in one of the lingerie sets and couldn't. Then I remembered what Luka had said. "Do you have anything more...innocent?" I asked, red-faced. "White?"

She blinked at me. "Like bride on night of wedding?"

"Exactly like that. Innocent but good quality and"—*am I really having this conversation?*— "sexy."

She nodded quickly, but gave me a look that was almost pitying. Aghast, maybe, at the idea of an innocent in Luka's hands. She brought out white bras and panties, hold-ups and suspender belts and even a corset. They were all strokably soft and gorgeously made. I told her I'd take them, along with some of the tamer black sets.

When I finally returned downstairs, the coffee was cleaned up and the clothes and shoes had already been packed into my cab. The driver was still waiting patiently for me, even though it had been over an hour. Luka's money was going to take some getting used to.

"Please," said Alina, squeezing my hand. "Give Mr. Malakov our regards." Her eyes were wide with fear when she said his name.

I felt bad about the store assistant. She'd been rude, but she didn't deserve to lose her job. "Please...you don't need to fire that woman. Could you...get her back?"

From Alina's astonished face, compassion wasn't high on the list of traits when it came to Luka's previous women. Maybe, when you were that powerful, people started to look like bugs to be stepped on. And now everyone thought *I* was one of those women.

"Of course," said Alina. "Whatever you wish."

The scary thing was, I sensed that I could have asked her to fire the woman, or get her back, or cut off one of her fingers and she would have done it, without question. And it was Luka who had instilled this fear in them.

The man who wanted to corrupt me.

27

B ack at the hotel, I dumped the shopping bags and then called Adam, telling my "dad" excitedly about how the guy I'd met wanted to take me on his yacht. He was silent for a moment. Then he told me he had a surprise for me. "I'm here," he said.

"Where?"

"*Here.* Let's meet. Gorky Park."

What?!

I got a cab there and waited on a bench, watching couples laugh and cling to each other on the ice as I sipped a coffee. When a man sat down on the bench next to me, I had to study him for a few seconds before I really believed it. "You're *here?!*"

"I flew in last night," said Adam. He pulled his winter coat tighter around himself. "God*damn,* I forgot how cold it gets here."

My head was spinning. Someone as senior as Adam didn't normally leave Langley, except to go to Washington. They certainly didn't jet off to Moscow to meet up with field agents. Not for the first time, I had that twinge of unease. This was my first mission, so I had nothing to compare it with...but still, nothing about it seemed normal. What if Roberta and Nancy had been right? "Why—Why are you here?"

"We followed Luka's car to the nightclub, then back to his penthouse. You stayed the night. I assume you...hit it off?"

Deep, hot embarrassment rose up in me. Only the icy wind stopped me turning beet-red. "Yes."

"That's when I thought I should come out here. Things may move very quickly, now, and I want to be on site, where I can help. You've done well, Arianna."

Despite my unease, the praise triggered a deep, warm glow inside me. It was almost scary, how much I'd needed to hear it. "What are we going to do about the yacht?" I asked. "I don't even know where we're going."

"Go with him," said Adam without hesitation. "We think this trip is tied in with the arms deal. Stick to him like glue and see if you can find out who the buyer is."

"But I'll be...alone with him. Out at sea." There'd be no way anyone could tail us, out there, without being seen. I'd be totally without backup.

Adam put a fatherly hand on my back and leaned close. "You can do this, Arianna. I wouldn't have sent you here if I didn't believe you could."

Again, his words sent a wave of pride flooding through me and that helped to counter my fear. I tried to look at it rationally. If I wanted to bail, this was the time. Adam would be able to get me on the next plane out of the country. Luka would be pissed, but would think his new girlfriend had gotten cold feet and run home. I could go back to listening to his phone calls from a safe, cozy office.

And I'd never see him again.

He'll kill you if he finds out. Roberta's words. I didn't doubt they were true. I thought I'd seen glimpses of warmth in him—vulnerability, even. But that didn't change who he was. And whatever lust, whatever affection he held for Arianna Ross, American tourist, it didn't extend to Arianna Scott, CIA spy.

But Adam believed in me, in a way that Roberta didn't seem to. He'd seen something in me that she hadn't seen in years. I wanted to prove something—to him, to Roberta, to myself.

Mainly, though, what was going through my head was the feel of Luka's hands in my hair. The things he'd whispered in my ear as we stood by the door of his penthouse. *He had to have me.* No man had ever wanted me with that intensity and it sat like a burning coal at my very center, glowing through the layers of ice. Maybe even melting it.

He's going to end my innocence. In every conceivable way. Was it worse that he wanted to do it, or that part of me wanted him to?

"I'll do it," I said quietly. "I'll go with him."

28

I'd seen luxury yachts in movies. That didn't prepare me for *this*.

The thing was the size of a house, all smooth white lines and smoked glass. The sort of yacht a movie star charters when they want to party away from prying eyes. I'd put on some of the new clothes from the store: a short gray jersey dress with a scoop neck teamed with thick black stockings so that my legs didn't get frostbitten; a pair of shining, four-inch pumps with scarlet soles that were very hard to walk in and a long black woolen coat that managed to be fashionable *and* warm. But, even in the expensive outfit, I felt out of place. This was millionaire—maybe billionaire—territory.

It had taken us all afternoon to get there. First a drive to the airport, then a first-class flight to St. Petersburg, where the yacht was moored. Luka had already disappeared inside, talking to the captain about getting underway.

I climbed carefully up the gangway and then stopped, eying the polished teak decking. I clung to the rail and balanced there unsteadily, trying to take my heels off without falling over.

"What are you doing?" asked Yuri from behind me. The bodyguard was looking his usual gruff self—scar, somber suit and the bulge under his jacket that I was sure was a handgun. The only thing that spoiled the effect was the six shopping bags he was carrying.

"Taking off my shoes. Aren't you meant to do that? So you don't scratch the deck?" I was sure I'd heard that somewhere.

Yuri pushed me forward onto the yacht. "Who gives a fuck about the deck?" he muttered.

It was a wake-up call. The next one was the crew. I was expecting smiling guys with tans and polo shirts. Instead, the deck was patrolled by men with crew cuts and muscles, all dressed in black combat fatigues. And of course the sundeck was covered in an inch of snow.

This was not a holiday. This was a luxury yacht pressed into service as transport and carrying something that had to be very well protected. I wasn't there for some romantic getaway. I was—I tensed —I was Luka's entertainment, a distraction from something very serious indeed.

Inside the yacht, it was more like what I'd expected. The freezing weather couldn't spoil the luxury of the stateroom Yuri showed me to—bigger than most hotel rooms and with a huge, circular bed and—

And with a mirror on the ceiling. In fact, the decor of the whole yacht was pretty *bling.*

"It belonged to a German," said Luka, walking in. "A businessman who liked to party." He slid his arms around my waist from behind.

"Really?" I asked. "What was his business?" I had to remember to play dumb.

"Chemicals," said Luka.

I had a pretty good idea what sort of chemicals. "And what happened to him?"

Luka exchanged a look with Yuri. "He tried to expand into Russia. And found that he'd overreached."

He hadn't even chartered this thing. He'd taken it as a trophy after —I shuddered as I thought of what must have happened to the German drug dealer.

Luka wrapped his arms around me a little tighter. "You're cold," he said, his face so close to my neck that I could feel each word. "Let me warm you up."

"I'll get the rest of the bags," muttered Yuri, and left, leaving the door open.

Luka's hand stroked down over my stomach, the heat of his palm soaking through the fabric of my coat. He started working at the buttons, popping them one by one. At the same time, he started to lay kisses on the nape of my neck, his stubble rasping gently against me.

At the first touch of his lips, I felt the room spin. I tried to cling onto the memory of what I'd just felt, the cold fear and the lurch of my stomach as he'd basically told me that he'd killed a guy. But however much I focused on the wrongness of it, I could feel myself getting hotter with each kiss. And it wasn't that his evil was overridden or that I ignored it. The scary thing was that it sort of twisted together with the pleasure, enhancing it. There was a sort of power coming off of him, an aura. Everywhere we went, people got the hell out of his way and I understood why. It wasn't just his money or his power or his armed bodyguards. He could be unarmed and alone in an alley and people would still run from him. It was just something he had, maybe something he was born with. And something about it made me—

He finished with my coat's buttons and whipped it back off my shoulders. It tangled on my arms, trapping them. He didn't seem to be in any hurry to release them.

Instead, his hands worked their way around my front, sliding around my waist and then up to my breasts. My back was arched a little because of the way the coat was tangled behind me so my breasts jutted out, practically thrusting into his hands. When his warm palms enveloped them, I felt the heat begin to build and spin inside me. He wasn't gentle. His big hands squeezed while his thumbs rubbed, finding my nipples through the layers of fabric. I squirmed and shifted under his hands, closing my eyes for a second. My wrists pulled at the coat, but the fabric was folded back on itself around them, too tightly bunched too pull the sleeves off over my hands. "Luka..." I said warningly.

His response was to bring one hand up and under my chin, tilting my head back so that he could kiss my upside-down face. His lips came down on mine, savage and hard, our teeth clacking together in our urgency, his tongue thrusting into my mouth. I drew in a shuddering breath through my nose and jerked my wrists again. This time, it wasn't an attempt to get free. I just wanted to feel the cloth trapping me.

What the hell is wrong with me?!

He kept his hand under my chin, forcing my face up to meet his, while his other hand roughly massaged my breast. I writhed, sparkling hot pulses of pleasure twisting down from my engorged nipple to my groin. Then his hand was sliding down my body.

And I remembered the open door.

My eyes flew open. Even as I watched, one of the black-uniformed thugs strode past the doorway. He didn't look inside, but Yuri would be back any second. "*Mmmffp!*" I said through the kiss.

Luka ignored me. The kiss was deepening with every passing second, his mouth open and hungry and mine was opening, too. Despite my protests, I was losing myself in him again. I knew we had to stop, but it felt so *good.*

His hand cupped my groin through the dress and I groaned. Then he started hauling the dress up my body. I suddenly felt the cool air of the cabin on my stockinged thighs, then on the bare skin *above* my stockings and that woke me up. I managed to pull my face away from him. "Luka!" I gasped. "Yuri will be back!"

I could hear how his breathing had changed, his huge chest expanding and contracting against my back like that of a bull about to charge. "Fuck Yuri," he growled. His fingers ran lightly over the front of my panties, feeling me through the soft black fabric, and my knees buckled at the sensation. I could feel myself throbbing with need behind the material, my arousal already changing to wetness.

And then he hooked two fingers into the waistband of my panties and ripped them off.

"*Luka!*" I hissed. I thrashed with my trapped arms but...I don't think I was trying to get free, exactly. I was embarrassed, scared of being exposed, but the pleasure he was giving me easily topped that. I could feel the darkness of it, the *wrongness* of it overwhelming me and dragging me down towards something dark and deliciously hot.

Luka's fingers slid down over the lips of my sex and I moaned. Then they were spearing into me, spreading me with their thickness, and I bent forward, my legs going rubbery. Luka took my weight easily. His fingers slid up inside me, thick and knobbly and *God* I was wet—

A rustle of paper, in front of us. My hair had fallen forward over my face when I bent forward, so I had to toss it back to see.

Yuri was in the doorway, crouching slightly to set down the paper store bags he carried. He was carefully keeping his eyes on them. I felt myself flushing.

And then, as he stood, Yuri looked up and stared straight into my eyes and I felt a deep, hot jolt go through me. I could feel his eyes on my squirming body, on Luka's fingers buried in me, and I saw a flicker in those normally emotionless eyes. Lust, and maybe sorrow.

Then he turned and was gone, and I was desperately breaking the kiss. "Luka!" I said, panting. "St—*ahh!*"

He'd started to stroke his fingers in and out of me, hard and fast, while simultaneously circling my clit with his thumb. A shudder went through me, the pleasure spinning faster and faster. "You want me to stop?" he asked, a smile in his voice.

I flushed even deeper as the heat spiraled out of control. *Yes. No.* I didn't know what I wanted. We were in public, with people walking past the door and Yuri had just seen us and this was wrong but *God* it felt so good. I was wetter than I'd ever been, his fingers sliding easily in me and I could feel the hardness of his cock against my ass. But this was *wrong.* I couldn't just let him use me like this, all restrained and...*trapped.*

"*Nrrrggghhhh!*" I groaned. Stars exploded in front of my eyes. My whole body went mannequin-stiff against him, my hips grinding against his thrusting fingers, and his mouth recaptured mine. I panted my orgasm between his lips, my breath coming in shuddering gasps.

He supported me as I trembled and shook and finally relaxed. Then, as he released me, I staggered forward and my dress fell back into place. I shrugged my coat back onto my shoulders and tossed my hair out of my eyes, and I was decent again.

Apart from the ripped panties on the floor.

"What was...*that?!*" I panted.

"Didn't you enjoy it?" he asked innocently.

It would be ridiculous to say *no*. I glared at him, but he had that hint of a smile on his lips that completely disarmed me. I settled for, "You can't just do things like that! People could see! Yuri saw!"

"So? He's seen me plenty of times. Sometimes, in the back of the car."

So I'd been right about why he wanted all that legroom.

He reached out and grabbed my hand, pulling me up against him. Dammit, he was gorgeous and so assured in his power. He knew he could do whatever he wanted. "And usually," he told me, "the girls are naked."

I thought about how I must have looked: dress hiked up, panties gone, his fingers inside me. How was I going to look Yuri in the eye again? I shook my head. Now that the sexual heat had died away, I was starting to get mad. At him, for doing it and at myself, for letting him. I was meant to be on a mission. I was meant to be the one in control. The anger rose and bubbled. I could have said *stop* but—I flushed—I'd been enjoying it too much. I didn't know how to say any of that, so I lashed out in another direction. "Is that what I am, then, just another one of your girls to—to fuck whenever you like? Another Natalia?"

He froze. "How do you know about Natalia?"

Because I listened to your phone calls. Every drop of blood in my veins turned to freezing sludge. *Shit!*

29

I thought about saying *aren't all Russian women called Natalia or Natasha?* But I was pretty sure that wouldn't fly.

"You said her name in your sleep." It was the first thing that popped into my head.

He frowned. "I don't talk in my sleep."

I thought I was going to be sick.

Then he frowned more deeply, looking uncertain. "Do I?"

Nancy had once told me that the best way to make a lie believable was to believe it yourself, to convince yourself that you were telling the truth. I imagined Luka spooning me, so close that I could feel his breath on my ear. I could easily imagine that sexy Russian accent, muttering a name. "You did last night," I said confidently. "You kept muttering about her."

Luka's jaw set. I could tell he believed me, but tentatively. He seemed disturbed that I'd supposedly discovered a weakness. "What did I say?" he asked.

My mind flashed back to all those phone calls. When he'd dumped her, she'd angrily reminded him, in her precise, clipped tones, about all the wonderful things she'd done for him. The things she'd let him do to her.

"You were telling her"—I felt myself redden, which hopefully made it seem authentic –"you were telling her you were going to take her up the ass again," I said.

And for the first time ever, Luka dropped his eyes from mine. Was that a tiny hint of a blush in his cheeks? If it was, it was gone in a second. "Okay," he said.

Whew.

Then he frowned. "How did you understand what I was saying?"

Shit! I hadn't thought of that. I wasn't supposed to understand Russian, let alone muttered Russian sleep-talking. I decided to go for broke. "You said it in English," I said nonchalantly, digging my nails into my palms.

He frowned again. Then he seemed to remember something and nodded to himself, as if he now understood. "Ah. I see."

"What?"

He shook his head. The matter was closed. But, now that the danger was passed, I was intrigued. "No, tell me—what?"

"Is sex thing, is not for you." His English always got mangled when he was flustered, or excited.

"Because I'm an innocent?" I asked, raising an eyebrow.

"Yes."

"But it's okay for you to corrupt me when you want to?" I asked.

Now there was a gleam in his eye. "Yes."

I kept staring at him and, eventually, he relented. "I must have been dreaming about a sex game I used to play with Natalia," he said. "I used to speak to her in English, when we played it."

"Why?"

"I'd be interrogating her."

"*Interrogating*—"

He smirked. "She used to pretend to be an American spy."

My stomach did a full somersault and then plummeted into my feet. "Oh."

He patted my shoulder. He'd cheered up, now, amused at how shocked I looked. "We will be sailing, soon. I'll go and see about some dinner." He nodded at the torn panties on the floor. "You find some new ones. Or just leave them off." He kissed the top of my head and strode out the door, his shoulders almost brushing the door frame.

I sat down heavily on the edge of the bed. Now that he'd gone, the adrenaline washed through me, leaving me a trembling mess. I'd come *that close* to blowing my cover. I'd got angry and Natalia's name had slipped out. All it had taken was for me to lose control.

And around Luka, losing control was inevitable.

30

It soon became clear that Luka had dispensed with all of the crew who'd normally look after the yacht and its guests on a voyage. I figured there must be a captain, somewhere, to steer the thing, but there were no cleaners, maids or deckhands. Just us, Yuri and all the guys dressed in black. From their muscle and haircuts, I presumed they were ex-army, maybe even ex-*Spetsnaz:* Russian Special Forces. They didn't smile at me or glare at me. They treated me like luggage Luka had brought aboard.

There were huge refrigerators in the galley stocked with plenty of food, pre-prepared for easy reheating. We loaded up and, back in the stateroom, we sat at the table and feasted. There was pork with marinated apples, gravy and mushrooms and some very good red wine.

As we ate, I felt the throb of the engines. We were underway. Heading off into the night across a freezing, dark ocean, heading who-knew where. My stomach tightened at the thought. And, at the same time, I was getting into some sort of twisted relationship with Luka. I didn't know where *that* was heading, either, and that was even more dangerous.

"No," said Luka suddenly. "You're not another Natalia."

"What?" I'd zoned out for a second.

"You're not another Natalia."

I caught my breath. "What am I, then?"

He looked at me for a long time, then gave a wry little laugh and shook his head, muttering something I couldn't quite hear.

"What?"

"Nothing."

I played it back in my mind, over and over. I couldn't be sure, but it had sounded like he'd muttered *spaseniye*.

I was his salvation.

After dinner, Luka said he had to make a phone call. And then there was an awkward silence.

We were too far away from shore, by now, to use a cell phone. And the ship-to-shore phone system aboard the yacht used handsets, built into the walls, so it wasn't like Luka could go outside to make his call. He needed me to leave. But I wasn't supposed to have any idea what he did for a living, so I had to play dumb.

"Business?" I asked.

He nodded. "I need to arrange things with my father. He's meeting us."

I smiled innocently but my mind was racing. His father, Vasiliy. The one who'd built the family empire before passing over control to his son. For him to emerge from the shadows, something big must be happening. Was the arms deal going down on this trip? I needed to warn Adam...and I had no way to contact him.

I couldn't say any of this to Luka. I had to play the oblivious girlfriend. "Will *I* meet him?" I asked brightly.

"Yes," he said. But he sighed as he said it, as if that was a whole other problem. I felt an uneasy chill pass through me, a dense fog that threatened to numb all the parts that Luka was bringing back to life. What did *that* mean? That his father wouldn't like me? That he wouldn't...*approve?*

Stop thinking of it like a relationship. I was undercover. I was just pretending.

"I'll go explore," I said. "Or maybe go to the galley and find some dessert." I felt a flash of guilt, at that. I'd just stuffed myself with pork and gravy, but there'd been some pavlova in the refrigerator that looked divine....

He smiled at that. "Yes, get dessert," he said. "Eat plenty. You'll need your energy for later."

I caught my breath again, eyeing the huge bed, and backed out of the door.

"Stay on this level," he called after me. "Or go up top. Not down."

I nodded quickly and smiled, then closed the door to give him privacy for his call. I leaned against the wall in the companionway for a moment, thinking. I pushed all thoughts of me and Luka out of my head and focused on the mission. If the deal was going down on this trip, I needed to get my head in the game and do my job. While he was busy making his call, I had the perfect opportunity to scout around and find out what was on board. And he'd just told me exactly where to look.

31

The yacht was divided quite clearly into two worlds. There were the decks where the guests were supposed to go, all polished wood and soft lighting. Then there were the lower decks, where only the crew would go.

Down there, everything was bare steel and rooms were either lit up by harsh fluorescent lights or were shadowy pits with tangles of ropes and cables to trip over. Walking quietly on metal staircases in high heels was impossible, so I slipped them off and walked in stockinged feet, wincing at the touch of the freezing metal. Luckily, most of the guards seemed to be up top. That made sense, now that we were out at sea. Anyone trying to steal our cargo or harm Luka would have to board first. They didn't realize that they'd invited the enemy right into their midst.

Something twisted inside me, at that. A pang of guilt. *Stupid.* I wasn't the enemy; Luka was the enemy.

In the third room I checked, I found what I was looking for. A huge pile of crates, reaching higher than my head.

I leaned closer. Russian lettering. Batch numbers, which I memorized, and the symbols for the Russian Army.

Weapons, originally meant for the military. The deal, whoever it was with, was going down on this very trip...and I had no way to warn Adam, or call for help. We were way out of cell phone range.

I heard footsteps coming from the next room. The rooms were arranged in a chain, one leading to the next, so there was no place to run but onward, into the next room. Another storeroom, this one empty. No place to hide. I could still hear the footsteps behind me, moving through the room I'd just left. *Shit!*

I hurried into the next room...and stopped dead.

The walls were lined with lockers. A TV on the wall was blaring and there was an ashtray on the table, smoke still rising from a butt. It must be the break room, where the guards hung out between patrols. And now the ones right on my tail were coming back here.

And it was a dead end.

32

Time seemed to stretch out. My eyes searched the room for a door I'd missed, a hatch...anything that would let me escape. But there was nothing. The guards would be there in seconds, and they'd catch me. And they'd know that, to get there, I must have gone straight through the room with the weapon crates. There'd be no chance of *"Oh, I was looking for a bathroom!"* They'd take me straight to Luka, and he'd think back to how he'd found me in his room in New York, and he'd realize what I really was.

My eyes fell on the lockers. *That's ridiculous.* If I hid there, I'd be trapped until they left.

The footsteps were right behind me. I pulled open the nearest locker and flung myself inside, pulling the door shut behind me.

Two guards strolled in. Now that we were out at sea, they didn't have to hide the fact they were armed. Both of them had stubby submachine guns slung around their necks.

They slumped down into cheap plastic chairs that creaked under their muscled bulk. They had the same crew cuts and powerful bodies as the others I'd seen, definitely ex-soldiers. One was blond and one dark, but otherwise they could have been brothers. Bored, they glanced up at the soccer game on the TV and lit cigarettes.

In the locker, I tried to breathe silently. There were vents cut into the front of the door, so I could see, but it was so narrow that my elbows were pinned to my sides. And I was going to be stuck there until they left. If they didn't discover me and either shoot me or take me to Luka, first.

"You see his new one?" the blond one asked in Russian.

The dark-haired one laughed and nodded. "You know she's American?"

Oh great. They were talking about me! I wanted to put my hands over my ears, but the locker was so small that there wasn't room to lift my arms.

The other one laughed and shook his head, sucking on his cigarette and then blowing out the smoke. "Why'd he bring her aboard?"

"I don't mind. Nice to have something to look at."

My cheeks reddened.

The blond one shook his head. "I don't want something to look at. Not when I can't fuck her." He shifted in his seat, nodding down at his groin. "Fucking frustrating."

The dark one grinned. "I don't mind. I hope she's a screamer. He took Elena—remember Elena?—to a hotel in Paris one time and I was in the room next to theirs. I listened to them all night."

I was beet-red, now. I made a mental note to stay very, very quiet during sex.

The blond one shook his head. "I don't want to be walking around with my dick hard all day. Why couldn't he leave her in Moscow? It's only a couple of days."

I felt a chill run up my spine. Why *had* Luka brought me along? It made no sense.

"He's keeping her sweet, idiot. Don't you know anything about women? He's letting her think he's in love with her. She's probably off doing her nails, now, expecting a ring and a house and children."

I felt hot tears prickling at my eyes. *Don't!* Not in here. I wasn't sure I could cry silently. *Save it for later.*

The dark-haired guard stubbed out his cigarette. "I give it a week.

Once he's fucked her ten different ways, he'll get rid of her like the rest." He stood up. "Come on."

And they strolled out. I stayed there in the locker with the tears trickling down my face and no way to wipe them. I just had to stare through the blur as I heard their footsteps die away.

And what was I crying about, anyway? This was a mission. I was *meant* to be just another one of Luka's girlfriends. I knew damn well that he used them and tossed them away. I'd listened to their tears when he'd dumped them. Why was I surprised?

Had I actually believed that I was different?

I snuck out of the locker and retraced my steps. I made it back to the stairs without running into any more guards and then hurried upstairs and back to the stateroom. By the time I got there, my tears were just about dry. *Focus!* I'd gotten the information I needed and that was all that mattered.

Right?

When I opened the door, Luka was just putting the phone down. I closed the door behind me and sniffed, willing my face to cool down.

When Luka turned, he looked troubled. Bad news in the phone call? Then he saw me and, for a second, it was as if all his worries had been lifted. A smile half-formed on his lips and the idea that I could have that effect on him made me swell inside in a way I hadn't experienced in a long time.

But he's just using you. He just wants to fuck you and then he'll dump you.

Maybe they're wrong about him.

He looked closer and saw my expression. His smile was gone in an instant. "Are you okay?" he asked, stepping forward. "What's wrong?"

Nothing. Nothing's wrong, I thought sadly. My *job* was to be another short-term fling. But, back in Langley, I hadn't thought it would be this difficult.

I stared up into his eyes. I swore I could see something there— some tenderness, beneath the ice-hard exterior, beneath the lust. But that was crazy. If he wanted a proper relationship with anyone, he'd want it with one of his Russian blondes, with their perfect hair and their legs up to their armpits. Not me.

"I'm fine," I lied.

Immediately, he gave me that look. The one that said, *don't lie to me.*

"I just got cold," I said. "I went out on deck, and I hadn't taken a coat, and I didn't want to come back in here and disturb you."

He shook his head and sighed, then gave a tiny, affectionate chuckle that made me melt. Pulling me to his chest, he wrapped his arms around me. Immediately, his closeness made me feel better. It was like resting my head against a warm rock face, infinitely solid and strong.

"You need to think about yourself more," he told me. "You always put everyone else first." He put his hands on my cheeks for a second and pushed me back so that he could look at me. "If you keep doing that, you'll freeze."

How could a man as evil as him be so gentle, so thoughtful? I nodded.

He frowned. "You seem shorter," he told me. He looked down. "Where are your shoes?"

Shit! Out in the corridor, near the stairs, where I'd taken them off.

"It was icy, outside," I said. "Have you *tried* walking on ice in four inch heels?"

His lip curled in one of those little smiles he sometimes gave, when I amused him. He didn't seem to do it with anyone else. Then, as he looked me up and down, his expression changed. I could see his eyes glazing with lust and the sight of it sent a deep throb right through my body.

How can I do this? How can I have sex with him knowing it's only ever going to be about sex? I'd never do that back home, ever. I didn't do flings.

It's your job, I thought sternly. And felt the guilt wash through me, because I knew that was just an excuse. I wanted him. God, I wanted him so bad it was like an ache inside me.

I gulped and looked up at him. And something about that look—maybe the need he could see in me—sent him over the edge.

He gave a growl, put his hands on my waist and pushed me backward, slowly at first but faster and faster, until I had to stagger back quickly or fall. My back hit the wall and I gasped, the air knocked out of me.

And then my feet left the floor. He'd gripped my waist and was lifting me straight up, like some ballet dancer lifting his partner. He didn't stop until my head was almost touching the ceiling. I stared down at him, going weak at the sight of him. He was standing there not even breaking a sweat, handling my weight as if I was a doll.

I realized that his face was level with my groin. He used his thumbs to inch the hem of my dress up and then his teeth to lift it the rest of the way. I squirmed just from the feeling of his eyes on my panties, staring at them, *through* them, to the soft flesh beneath. My breath began to come in shuddering pants. *I am completely out of control with this man.*

"You are mine, Arianna," he said. "You were mine as soon as I saw you at that party. Do you understand?"

"Yes," I said weakly. The arousal and the more powerful, soul-deep need within me were joining together, making me forget everything else. I was *his.*

He leaned forward and licked me through my panties. "*Oh God!*" I cried out, my legs kicking in mid air. His tongue was exactly the right mix of firm and soft and the barrier of silky material meant that the contact was teasing.

He shifted his hands one at a time, palming the cheeks of my ass. He pushed my legs up and I bent them at the knees, sitting in mid-air with my back against the wall and my weight supported by his hands. Then he moved forward, burying his head between my thighs. He took long, slow licks at me, each one drawing the silky fabric across my lips and then releasing it. I groaned and reached for something—anything—to clutch at, and found his hair. I buried my fingers in his soft, dark locks.

He started to really work at me, then. He spread my legs open wide enough to make me gasp, then started to lick fast and steady, his nose rubbing over my clit on each stroke. My breath was coming in quick little pants, now. The fact I was hanging in mid air, pinned to the wall, made it even better. There was something about the feeling of being...*handled* so easily, the way he could just hold me there effortlessly.

The heat inside me began to circle and twist, whipping faster and faster around my frozen core. I felt *alive,* as if someone had pressed "play" on my life after three years on pause. My ass started to grind against the wall, my eyes fluttering closed. I could feel my panties getting wet, then soaking, as his tongue lashed over me again and again, the material clinging to my lips, taking on their shape.

He pushed deeper, teasing just inside me, and I groaned louder and jerked my hips forward to meet him. The panties were keeping me right on the edge, the heat inside me spinning at cyclone speed but not quite fast enough to release. I wanted them gone. I wanted to be naked against him and for him to be inside me. Another few seconds of his mouth and it felt as if the fabric would melt under our combined heat anyway.

Suddenly, he pulled me from the wall and carried me across the room, my head almost brushing the ceiling. He swung me down and I dropped onto the bed on my back, bouncing a little, my legs in the air.

He didn't even let them come down. He caught my thighs and pushed them up and back, opening me, and dug in his pocket for a condom. He shoved his pants down to mid-thigh and pushed my soaked panties to the side, not even bothering to take them off. Then he was inside me, filling me in one long, hard thrust, and I arched my back and shuddered at the perfect, silken stretch of him, my hands finding his muscled shoulders.

We rolled back on the bed, him on top and my legs bent up between us, my feet high in the air. He pushed my shoulders down into the bed and started to fuck me with fast, brutal strokes and I felt the orgasm coming at me almost faster than I could handle. We were both almost fully dressed, almost decent apart from our naked groins and our desperate, open mouths as we kissed and broke and kissed again. My tongue was in his mouth as hard and urgently as he was inside me. I'd given myself up to him utterly. The fact I wanted it—wanted it at least as much as him—made me feel more helpless than any amount of him throwing me around.

The bed rocked and squeaked, despite its size. His physical power was breathtaking—I could feel the muscles of his shoulders bunching as he pounded me. The hard slap of his groin against me made me heady. I was even more open to him, like this, and I could feel him even deeper than before.

I ran my hands down over his back, tracing his muscles, marveling at the size of him. I half-opened my eyes and saw movement above him and had to do a double-take. I realized I was looking at our reflection. I'd forgotten about the mirror on the ceiling. Before, it had seemed tacky, like something you'd find in a Vegas hotel room. But now, looking at his muscled form, his hard, tanned ass rising and falling as he fucked the woman on the bed, I felt myself getting hotter and hotter. The sight of it—the reality of what I was doing—fought with everything I knew about myself. *I can't be doing this,* I thought. *This is not me. I'm not like this.*

And then I looked up into those icy eyes and saw the raw lust in them, and I didn't care anymore. I flexed my pelvis, pushing it up to meet him and cried out his name as the heat consumed me completely. I felt myself clutching at him, shuddering around him....

And then I heard him call out *my* name as he came, too.

Afterwards, as we lay side-by-side on the bed, he gazed at me, pushing the sweat-damp hair back off my forehead strand by strand. I could see the worry in his eyes. "What?" I asked.

"Tomorrow morning, you'll meet my father." He paused. "And there'll be...business. My meeting."

"So?"

He stared at me. "You'll come with me. It's safer than leaving you here alone."

I had to pretend I had no clue about the deal. "Safer?"

He sighed and rubbed his eyes. Then he got up off the bed, pulled up his pants and poured vodka into a glass, handing me one, too. I took it, propping myself up on one elbow. I was ready for him to spin me some story about how he was a legitimate businessman, but sometimes he had to do business with shady types. I was ready for him to say that everything he did was legal, but had to be done on the quiet to avoid paying taxes.

I was ready for the lies because it was obvious from his calls with Elena and Natalia and Svetlana that none of them had had any clue what he really did.

I was ready for anything except what he said next.

"Arianna," he said. "I sell guns."

33

It should have been hard. I had to pretend to be stunned, when I'd known what he did all along. But the weird thing was, it *was* a shock. Firstly, because he'd told me. The one thing I'd never considered was that this man who lived his life behind a veil of lies and secrecy would open up to me.

Secondly, I didn't want to believe it. I had his file memorized. I'd seen his tattoos. I knew what he was on an intellectual level...but on a deeper level, on the level that lived in my chest, I hadn't believed it. I'd had some stupid, childish dream that maybe it was all a mistake. Maybe he'd been set up. It didn't make any sense, but I'd stuck to it anyway. It was a jolt, now, to realize I'd been thinking that...and to have it so suddenly ripped away.

So when I stared at him and said *"What?!"* it sounded absolutely real. I sat up fully, my vodka sloshing in the glass and nearly spilling on the bed. My soaked panties pulled tight against my lips, still swollen with arousal, a reminder of what we'd just done. Moments ago, I'd had sex with Luka: my boyfriend, my lover. My biggest problem had been my guilt over doing it when I knew it was just a short-term fling for him. Now he was back to being *Malakov, the arms dealer* and I felt like a fool for ever forgetting it.

He slowly unbuttoned his shirt and showed me his tattoos. "Do you know what these mean?" he asked. To my surprise, his voice was thick with emotion. "Do you know what *this* means?" He pointed to the rose.

I swallowed. I had to pretend to be innocent...but not stupid. "It means...you belong to something?"

"It means I belong to a brotherhood. The strongest brotherhood there is. My father, too." He sat down gently on the edge of the bed. "We make order where, otherwise, there'd be chaos."

I nodded slowly.

"What I do...*part* of what I do...is guns."

I didn't know how to react. This was not something I'd ever discussed, when I'd talked with Adam. I wasn't ever meant to know that he was an arms dealer. Should I lie and say I understood? Would he buy that?

In the end, I went with what I really thought. "You sell...death," I said, my voice cold. "To who? To armies? To street gangs?"

"To anyone with money," he said.

I shook my head in disgust.

"I arm people. I don't make them fight."

"You make it so they *can* fight. If they were punching each other, they'd do a lot less damage. Bystanders wouldn't get shot."

He sighed. "If I didn't do it—"

"Oh, *someone else would?!*" I shook my head.

He went quiet. I could sense the anger building inside him, now, could see it in the set of his shoulders, the white of his knuckles as he clenched his fists. Sooner, not later, he was going to lose it. And the thought of a man as big as him, as violent as him, getting out of control was terrifying.

I tried to calm things down by going quiet myself, but that only seemed to add to his frustration. "Say something," he said, his voice almost a growl.

"Why are you telling me?" I said. "What do you expect me to say?"

"You had to know. You'll be at the meeting tomorrow."

"But why—"

"I already told you: it's safer than leaving you here alone."

I shook my head. "But why bring me on the trip at all? Why not just leave me in Moscow, oblivious?"

He lowered his head, brooding. He reminded me of an animal, when he did that—a huge bear, solemn and deadly. When he raised his head again, he stared straight into my eyes. "Because I can't be without you."

I believed it. Not just because I could see the need in his eyes, but because I was feeling that tug, too. But I knew it wasn't the whole story. "You could have waited one night. Why did you *really* bring me?"

I saw it, then, that vulnerability I'd glimpsed before. A need, deep within him, that went beyond simple lust and maybe even beyond love. Something soul-deep. I stared back at him, willing him to open up just a little more.

But he jumped to his feet and yelled his frustration instead, hurling his glass across the room. It shattered into a million shining fragments against the wall and I recoiled at the sound. He stood there for a moment, panting. The muscles in his back and shoulders were so hard with tension, they stood out even through his shirt. Part of me expected him to grab me and hurl *me* against the wall.

But, somehow, I knew he'd never do that.

He suddenly stalked across the room and hurled the door open so hard it banged against the wall. Then he was gone down the companionway and I was left sitting there in shock.

I knew I couldn't just leave him like that. Somewhere out there, Luka was hurting. Angry, sure. Dangerous, definitely. But I'd caught a glimpse of the parts of him he hid from the world. There was some sort of battle going on inside him, and it was driving him crazy.

I wasn't the same woman who'd left Langley to go to that party in New York. Meeting him had changed me forever, given me a glimpse of a happiness I used to have. And however fucked up it was that a man who sold death had brought me back to life, I owed him for that.

I'd done this to him. I'd brought this vulnerability to the surface.

He'd given me the hope that maybe I wasn't beyond repair; I had to see if, somehow, I could fix him, too.

I found a pair of sneakers in my luggage that looked ridiculous with the stockings and dress, but it was quicker than running back to the stairs to retrieve my heels. I picked my way carefully past the glass on the floor and looked up and down the empty companionway. It was late at night, now, and the yacht was silent apart from the throb of the engines. Where would he go, if he wanted to be alone?

I headed upstairs and out onto the deck.

Immediately, I knew I'd made a mistake. The cold was like a physical thing, as if someone was jamming knives into my exposed arms and face. I gasped and saw my breath as a rising cloud. I was going to freeze out there in just a few minutes. But I could at least have a look for him before heading back inside.

The yacht was moving fast across ocean that looked as still as black glass. The moon was out and there was no land in sight. I felt my insides shrink down to nothing at the thought of how alone I was out here. No backup. No police. No one who could help me.

I saw him standing at the rail, right at the prow of the yacht. What if I was wrong about him? What if he was still mad and he just tossed me over the side in his rage?

I remembered how I'd felt, after the accident. How I'd shut down and closed everyone out. I'd functioned, but not lived. Luka seemed to be the opposite: he lived like a king, went to clubs, had a string of girlfriends...and yet, when I looked in his eyes, he didn't look happy. He looked trapped.

I took a deep breath...and moved towards him.

34

W hen I was still ten feet away, and with him still staring out to sea, he suddenly snapped, "What are you doing out here?"

I caught my breath and stopped where I was. "I just came to talk."

He shook his head, still not turning around. "Go to bed."

I took a tentative step towards him. "Luka—"

"Got to *bed!*" he roared.

I stood stock still in the middle of the freezing deck. He was pushing me away, closing me out. Just as he'd shut out Elena and Natalia and Svetlana, I realized.

I'd thought the same as his guards: that he was a callous womanizer, using them and dumping them. What he'd actually done was break up with them before they could get too close.

This is perfect, a little voice inside me thought. *I know about the crates, now. I have the batch numbers. I'll find out more at the meeting, tomorrow. He'll dump me when we get back to Moscow, I report to Adam and I can go home. Everything will go back to normal.*

All I had to do was turn around and walk back to the stateroom. Mission accomplished.

I stood there for long seconds. And then I said, "No."

He turned to face me. "What?"

"No."

He stared at me, his eyes narrowed in anger. I could see the years of rage that had been building up inside him, slowly poisoning him. "Arianna," he grated. "Go to bed."

"No." I walked over to him before he could stop me. He had time for a single angry yell before I threw my arms around him and pressed my face to his chest.

This is it, I thought. *If I'm wrong about him, this is where he smashes my head against the rail and throws my body over.*

I could feel his chest moving in big, powerful heaves as he fought with his anger. I squeezed him, willing him to pour some of the anger into me, to let me soothe him.

After long seconds, his breathing slowed. "What are you doing?" he asked.

"Trying to calm you down," I said into his chest.

He took a long, strangled breath. *"Why?!"*

I gently moved back so that I could look up into those big, beautiful, pain-filled eyes. "Because I like you," I told him. And the knowledge that it was true was like a bomb going off in my chest.

"You know what I am, now," he said. "I told you at the party that I'm a monster. Now you know what sort."

I took a deep breath. "You told me the truth for a reason," I said slowly.

He broke away from me and twisted, staring out to sea. Those massive shoulders were like a wall between us, but I kept talking. "You could have left me in Moscow and I'd never have known. You *wanted* to tell me what you were."

His shoulders set even tighter, even harder. He gripped the rail so hard his knuckles went white.

"At dinner...you said I was your *spaseniye*," I said. "What does that mean?"

I knew damn well what it meant, but I couldn't tell him that. And part of me needed to hear him say it.

He shook his head. "I was being weak."

I pressed close to him and slid my arms around his waist from behind. I could feel the tension in his body again. I molded myself to him, my breasts crushed against his back. "Tell me."

He let out a long sigh. "Salvation," he said. "It means salvation."

I didn't say anything; I just stood there holding him. When he spoke, his voice was bitter. "When I saw you in New York, so innocent..." He let out a long sigh, his big hands squeezing and releasing the rail. "I am not good with words like you."

I just waited and let him speak.

"I thought...I thought that maybe you could save me," he said. And then he snarled and kicked a folding chair someone had left on the deck. It flew thirty feet and splashed into the ocean.

"Maybe I can," I said softly.

He shook his head and it reminded me of a bull, about to charge. "*Eblan!*" he cursed savagely. "*Eblan Mudak!*" *Dumbass bastard,* he was calling himself. "*Stupid!*" he snarled in English.

"No," I said. "Brave, to say what you feel!" His anger scared me, but I stepped closer. "I *like* you, Luka."

"Even now you know?" he muttered.

I stepped right up close to him. "Even now I know."

He gradually calmed and became still. I leaned forward and we touched foreheads. He had to lean down to me to do it, hulking over me like a monster.

"You should not get involved with me," he said at last. "This is *not* wise, Arianna."

"I know," I whispered. "But I don't think I can be apart from you."

He cursed in Russian and then said, "I hurt many people."

The hairs on the back of my neck were standing up. "Would you hurt me?" I asked.

"No." And he said it with such stony certainty that I believed it. "But I might get you hurt."

Cold fear welled up inside me, ice water that merged with the ice that was already there. He wasn't a *bad boy* as in he might cheat on me or break my heart. He lived in a whole different world to me, one where people who got in the way just disappeared and loved ones were nothing more than leverage.

I felt sick. Another reason he'd always kept his relationships short-term. Being with him would be dangerous as hell, even if I *wasn't* secretly spying on him.

The smart thing to do would be to walk away.

Yet I was getting closer and closer to him and the most worrying thing wasn't that I was doing it, it was that it felt so right. Every time he touched me, every time he kissed me, it felt as if the ice inside me cracked just a little. It was a slender thread, a stupid, childish wish that I could be fixed. But it was one that I didn't want to give up on.

"I'm not scared," I said.

A tiny smile touched his lips. "You said that before. And you still are."

I still was. But I wanted him anyway. I tilted my face up and reached for him, pulling him down to me. We kissed and it was soft and slow, his size only making his gentleness more shocking. A slow-motion bomb went off in my chest. In the warm glow that followed, it felt as if each of us was drawing life from the other. I was filling in the missing parts in him, and he in me.

We'd taken a step. He was opening up to me in a way he hadn't with any of his other girlfriends. This wasn't a fling, anymore.

His hand came down to brush my cheek and suddenly he recoiled. "You're freezing!" he said. He shook his head at his own stupidity. "You're out here in a dress!"

I'd been so focused on helping him, I hadn't noticed the cold creeping in. I realized my arms and legs were growing numb. As soon as I thought about it, I gave a violent shiver.

"We need to get you inside and warmed up," he told me.

"We—" I shivered again. Now that I'd started, I couldn't stop. "We need to t—talk about this."

He shook his head. "Later." And he scooped me up in his arms, cradled me to his chest and carried me below deck.

〜

The stateroom had an attached bathroom and there was a huge corner bath. Luka started it running and then undressed me. I was shivering too much to do anything but stand there as he peeled my clothes off. It was very different to how he'd ripped and yanked at things before, in order to fuck me. This was like watching a giant undress a china doll.

When I was naked, he lifted me and slid me gently into the tub. I gasped as the water covered me, numb skin prickling painfully. But it worked—I could feel the cold receding and I stopped shivering.

We sat there looking at each other and the weirdness of the scene, of him sitting there watching me naked in the bath, made both of us smile.

I glanced down at myself—at my hair, bedraggled and damp from the sex and the sea air and now the bath; at my imperfect body; at all the broken parts he *couldn't* see, the nightmares and the fears and the insecurities. *What the hell does he see in me?* I wondered. And yet I'd glimpsed that need in him and now he'd admitted it. This wasn't just about sex, anymore. This was definitely turning into something deeper. Maybe, in time—

I suddenly caught myself. I'd completely forgotten who I was and why I was there. The moment we'd had out on the deck had let me get lost in a cozy little fantasy where I was a genuine girlfriend, and not doing all this in order to stab him in the back.

Luka frowned, concerned. "Are you okay? You look worried."

It felt as if my heart was being wrenched out. The one guy I'd connected with, the one guy who'd made me feel alive again, and I was going to have to betray him. "Fine," I said with a smile. "I'm fine."

35

I woke to the sound of a hard, heavy thumping that I couldn't identify. As I sat up groggily, I saw that I was in the bed in the stateroom. I blushed as I realized I was totally naked. Things were hazy after the bath, but I dimly remembered crawling between the sheets, exhausted.

I focused on where the sound was coming from and gasped.

Luka was stripped to the waist and hitting a punching bag that hung from the ceiling. He was barefoot, wearing only a pair of loose drawstring pants, and his muscles were gleaming with sweat.

I'd seen guys hitting bags at the gym, on the rare occasions I managed to work up the energy to go. But they hadn't looked like this. They'd danced around the bag, hitting it in different places: nifty little crosses and uppercuts.

Luka just *hit*.

The bag was old and worn and, now that I looked, it swung from a hook. That explained why it hadn't been there before—he must have had it stashed in a closet and only brought it out that morning. He was wearing hand wraps, but the material was worn, too, and they weren't even the same color, one red and one black.

I knelt up on the bed for a better look. Each blow was a powerful sweep of arm, terminating in a brutal impact that lifted the bag as if it weighed nothing. It looked as if he'd punch clear through a brick wall, given the chance. He wasn't showy or fast. He was just *strong*. And he looked as if he could keep going all day. From the sweat shining on him, he'd already been at it for hours.

I was embarrassed to feel a flicker of heat twist down to my groin. I squeezed my thighs together self-consciously, but couldn't stop looking at his muscles. There was just something about that brutal strength, that danger. I shifted and the bed creaked.

He turned suddenly and saw me. "Sorry," he said. "Did I wake you?"

I shook my head. "I didn't know you boxed."

"I don't box." He looked at the bag as if embarrassed. "I hit things." He walked towards me and began unwrapping the hand wraps. I saw his eyes flick over my body.

I realized that the sheets that I'd hurriedly wrapped around me when I knelt up had slid down. He was staring at my breasts. A hot tremor went through me.

"We will be docking soon," he said, without taking his eyes from my chest. He must have known I'd caught him looking, but he didn't try to hide it. That was the thing with Luka: he did what he damn well pleased. "We should shower."

I nodded. "Who goes first?"

He just smiled.

~

I gasped as my naked back hit the tiles. My legs were already around Luka's waist because he'd carried me all the way there. He turned the water on and the spray lashed down on us, plastering my hair to my head and racing down my body in a thousand hot rivulets.

Luka hadn't bothered to take off his drawstring pants and they were soaked through in seconds. He kicked them off. Underneath, he was naked, hard and ready. I hadn't even seen him grab a condom, but he had one in his hand and was rolling it in. Had he had that in his pocket, the whole time he was working out? Had he been planning this? The idea sent a wave of heat rolling down inside me.

I reached for him, intending to put my arms around him, but he grabbed them with one big hand and pinned my wrists above my head. His cock nudged between my slickened lips but didn't enter me yet. I groaned, my ass grinding against the wall in anticipation. I was already addicted to this man. Through the water running down my face, I stared at the tattoos on his chest, the smooth curves of his bulging shoulders and biceps. I wanted to touch them. I wanted to stroke him all over, but the feeling of being held, of just having to watch and wait and throb with need...that was even better, in some ways.

What has he turned me into?

He lowered his head and licked at my breast, running his tongue over it in hungry strokes, licking away the water only for it to be instantly replaced with more. The combination of his rough licking and then the water flowing over my nipple had me panting in seconds.

Then he enveloped my breast with his mouth, surrounding my nipple with hot suction, and started to nibble on it just a little, letting me feel his teeth but not hurting me. I tried to climb the wall, the heat churning and roiling inside me, my wrists pressing hard against the hand that held them trapped. *God, I can't escape.* The idea had me breathless. *He has me pinned and he's going to—*

He moved back enough to look into my eyes and he must have been able to see the desperate need there. I felt the head of him parting my lips and this time he slammed up into me. I panted as he slid deep....*deeper.* Filling me until I gasped and groaned and leaned forward to bite at his shoulder with my teeth.

And then he fucked me.

My legs tightened around his waist, my ankles hooking behind him as he began to stroke in and out. Clouds of steam were rising around us, caressing our bodies and leaving them glistening. Every slow, hard thrust made me hiss air between gritted teeth, delighting at the liquid friction. The feel of him right up inside me was perfect, like we'd been made to fit together, like I wasn't complete without him there. I arched my back, heaving against the hand that held my wrists, turning my face up to the spray and letting it blast me. Luka's free hand slid over my cheek and then his thumb pressed into my mouth.

I opened for him, panting around it, my lips and teeth closing on his knuckle. His thrusts got faster, my ass pressed tight against the wall. I started to lick at his thumb with my tongue. I'd never done anything even remotely like this before, but I was operating on instinct now, lost in the pleasure.

He went faster still, the muscled bulk of him forcing my thighs wider, so wide they burned, but I wanted it. I didn't mind the discomfort if it meant I could have more of him inside me. The pleasure was building and building, ribbons of it twisting together inside me, entangling my thoughts. I didn't think about what he was or what I was or the insanity of falling for him. I let those shining scarlet ribbons wrap me up entirely, right up to my brain, and then tighten into a hard little knot....

Luka's thrusts reached a peak. I'd closed my eyes against the spray but now I opened them and stared at him. His jaw was set, his eyes wild...and he was staring right back at me with a lust I'd never seen on any man. Suddenly, he pulled his hand away from my face and kissed me, hard and deep, and the feel of his tongue plunging into me sent us both over the edge. We panted into each other's mouths as we came together in long, shuddering waves. I was pressed tightly between him and the wall, his hands still pinning my wrists above me. I was utterly helpless, utterly lost, and I'd never felt so alive.

A half hour later, I was dressed and waiting nervously at the bottom of the stairwell with Luka. On the stairs ahead of us, Yuri stood looking upward, his hand raised to tell us to keep waiting.

I looked down at myself. Instead of a dress, I was wearing snow boots and tight, *tight* jeans, plus a sweater and my black coat. "Are you sure?" I muttered. "I don't feel very...dressy. Given that I'm meeting your dad."

"Trust me," said Luka. "Being warm is more important, in this place."

We both went silent. The tension ratcheted higher with every second we waited there, until I could barely breathe. Then Luka said, "Besides, I like your ass in those jeans."

I felt myself flush and gave him a half-shocked, half-turned-on look. But the truth was, I was glad of the momentary distraction. This was a whole new kind of fear.

We were waiting for the guards to tell us it was safe to disembark. They were checking the whole area for snipers. Any moment, Yuri was going to wave us forward and we'd emerge into the daylight, blinking and helpless. And pray that the guards had done their job.

"Who is it?" I whispered, shifting my weight from foot to foot. "Who is it, who might try to kill us?"

"Olaf Ralavich and his men. A rival family." He shook his head. "Not like us. They are not part of the brotherhood."

"They have less...honor?"

He looked as if he was going to spit. "They have no honor at all."

Yuri waved us forward. After long minutes of waiting, now we had to move fast. Luka went first and I almost wanted to press up against his broad back like a child, cuddling up to him until we were safely inside. But Yuri had warned us not to even hold hands, in case we had to break and run.

I took a deep breath and climbed the stairs. And found myself at the end of the world.

36

It happened while we were at sea. There's been a war, and we missed it. God, what if we're the only survivors?

That's what it looked like. Like every post-apocalyptic movie I'd ever seen.

The yacht was moored at an ugly, concrete dock. The sky overhead was almost the same shade of light gray, the clouds completely covering it. Even the sea looked a sickly gray. The gray blankness made the desolation before us stand out even more.

There had been factories, once. Now they were just shells, walls ripped down to expose their innards. There were scorch marks from fire—or possibly bombs. There was no bird song and no greenery of any kind that I could see and not even a blade of grass.

The guards marched us towards the nearest building: three men in front, three behind, guns drawn and eyes watchful. Other guards were already patrolling the cracked, crumbling road and I could see a few perched high up on walls, keeping a lookout. "What *is* this place?" I asked.

Luka shook his head. "Nowhere you ever want to come again." Even he seemed unsettled by it.

Crossing the open area felt like being a mouse crawling across a highway. My heart was a tight, pounding ball in my throat as I waited for a shot to ring out. Despite the instructions, I grabbed Luka's hand and squeezed it tight. He squeezed back.

Seconds later, we reached the building and trooped inside. I let out a long sigh of relief. Looking out through the cracked windows, I could see the yacht. It looked very small and vulnerable out there on its own. Luka had been right—it wouldn't have been safe to leave me there.

As the fear receded a little, I became aware of the cold. Luka had been right—it was *freezing*. And very, very, creepy. The sooner we got out of there, the better.

Soon, we heard a car. Luka gave me a meaningful look. I looked down at myself as if checking my appearance. I was still trying to play the new girlfriend, eager to make a good impression—and, weirdly, part of me *did* actually want that. The rest of me was scared as hell that Luka's dad would see straight through my cover. Unlike his son, he wouldn't be blinded by feelings.

A car door slammed. New guards entered, exchanging nods with our own guards. They all stood to attention and I could see the fear in their eyes. The same dread that Luka inspired in civilians, this man inspired in criminals. And then he was walking into the room, his long coat flapping like a cape.

"Luka," said Vasiliy Malakov. "It's been too long."

37

I could see immediately where Luka got his build from. Vasiliy was almost as tall as his son, almost as wide and, despite being in his fifties, he seemed to have retained most of his muscle. He was almost like a prototype for Luka—not quite as big, not quite as handsome (Luka must have inherited his gorgeous eyes and cheekbones from his mother) but still a man that made you stop and look, even at his age.

He embraced Luka and kissed him on both cheeks. Then he turned to me. "And you are?" he asked me in Russian.

I had to remember to blink and look uncomprehending.

"She doesn't speak Russian," said Luka quickly, in Russian. "She's American."

I got the sense the Vasiliy had seen enough in his lifetime that very little would surprise him, but that did the trick. He turned and stared at his son as if he'd said I was radioactive. "You brought an American *here?!* To a *meeting?!*"

"She's okay," said Luka stiffly. "She's fine."

His dad shook his head. "You couldn't keep your dick dry for one night?"

"It's not like that! She's not just—" Luka took a breath to calm himself. "I like her."

His dad sighed and laid his face in his palm. "Luka, Luka...an *American?!* She is not suitable for you." He glanced at me. "She's pretty enough, I grant you. I'd want to jump between her legs if I was a little younger."

"Father!" snapped Luka.

I willed myself not to blush. I didn't want them to know I understood Russian.

Vasiliy sighed again. "You shouldn't have brought her here. What have you told her?"

"Only that it's guns. She can keep quiet."

They'd been talking in Russian for a long time. I tried to look uncomfortable, as if I was wondering what was going on. Luka caught my look. "My father is asking all about you," he told me in English, forcing a smile onto his face. "He says you're exactly what I need."

I smiled at the lie and then smiled at his father.

"Why did you tell her that?" asked Vasiliy in Russian. "Sometimes, I worry there's too much of your mother in you. Soft like butter." He shook his head. "You'll have to dump her, when you get back to Moscow. I can't have an American sniffing around."

I felt myself tense and tried to hide it.

"She's not sniffing—" Luka began.

But his father interrupted him. He put a big, fake grin on his face and grabbed hold of me, kissing each cheek in turn. "Welcome!" he said in English. "So rude of us to talk in Russian. I apologize. Luka has been telling me all about you. You must call me Vasiliy." Then, still grinning at me, he said in Russian to Luka, "I'm serious, Luka. Get rid of her as soon as you get home."

I had to keep the stupid, dumb smile on my face even as I felt the hurt inside me swell. He hated me. Somehow, the fact he disliked me as a father, that I wasn't good enough for his son, bothered me even more than the *sniffing around* comment. *Stupid! As if this is any sort of normal relationship! As if you're really his girlfriend!*

But Vasiliy's distrust was a problem, too. I was going to have to be super-careful around him. Luka would give me the benefit of the doubt but Vasiliy *wanted* to think badly of me. The slightest hint that something was off about me and I'd be screwed.

One the guards held his finger to his ear, listening to his earpiece, then nodded to Vasiliy.

"They're here," said Vasiliy. "Let's go."

The building we were in was an old factory of some kind—big, hulking machines and stacks of old cardboard cartons. We'd been waiting in what used to be the front offices. Now we moved through a door and onto the cavernous factory floor.

A group of men approached. Wait...not a group, exactly. They kept their distance from one another, as if there was no trust between them. And they didn't seem to have anything in common. Some of them were dressed like bikers, some of them like blue-collar workers and some of them in suits. And something was off. There was something familiar about their clothes, their attitude.

"Okay," said one of the bikers. "Let's get this started."

Only he didn't say it in Russian. He said it in English, with a broad Jersey accent.

Vasiliy stepped forward and introduced himself, clasping hands and kissing cheeks. I listened to the men, memorizing their names. Every one of them was American and I heard accents from New York to California. I felt sick. The weapons I'd seen in the yacht's hold were heading straight for my home country.

"I want to thank you for making the trip," said Vasiliy in English. "Some things are better discussed in person."

I remembered what Adam had said: that Vasiliy was the figurehead now and Luka ran the business. Vasiliy would have brokered this deal and persuaded all these men to fly out here and then drive God knows how many miles to wherever the hell we were, somewhere isolated and totally private. Vasiliy was the showman and the face they'd come to trust. But, now that the pleasantries were over, it was time for Luka.

I'd grabbed Luka's hand again as we stood there listening to his dad. Now he dropped it, looking at me almost apologetically. Then he walked forward and, suddenly, he was all business, the mask coming down. I felt my heart slowly icing over again as he reminded me, word by word, what he really was.

The way things were done now, with big shipments of guns coming to America in cargo containers, was dangerous and costly, he explained. "One shipment is lost, and it's hundreds of thousands of dollars. And when the weapons *do* get into the country...what then? You still have to get them across several states to reach your customers. Every state border means another chance of getting caught." He glanced at some of the bikers. "Paying off rival motorcycle clubs, bribing the police. It's a mess." He shook his head. "No more."

"We are going to do for guns what McDonalds did for hamburgers and what Starbucks did for coffee," he said. He described a complex network of distribution, with legitimate, Russian-owned businesses trucking the guns across America to exactly where they were needed. "No more big deals," he said. "A million small ones. Too small to track, too small to trace. If one shipment gets caught..."—he shrugged theatrically—"so what?"

As I listened, my blood ran steadily colder. It wasn't just the audacity of the plan he was outlining. It was the way he sounded just like his dad. Not quite as slick or polished as Vasiliy's showmanship, but he was getting there. *In a year, maybe two, he'll be just like him.*

This was why I needed to be his salvation. But how? How could I save him when my whole purpose here was to take him down?

When Luka had finished, the Americans looked at each other. Eventually, one of them spoke up. "It sounds good," he said. "But what about Ralavich? Most of us buy our guns from him. You're taking a big slice of his business. What about repercussions?"

Vasiliy stepped forward. "I'm not scared of Olaf fucking Ralavich.

His operations in the US are a mess. I'm surprised he's lasted this long. It's time for a change."

Luka called for the guards and they trooped in, carrying the crates I'd seen on the yacht. "A sample," said Luka. "To show we mean business. Yours to keep—a crate each." He picked up a crowbar and cracked the top off one of the crates. It was filled with gleaming assault rifles.

The Americans exchanged glances, impressed. Meanwhile, I was reeling. *A sample?!* This huge pile of crates was just *a sample?!* There must have been hundreds of guns there.

I understood, now. Luka wasn't setting up a gun deal; he was setting up a business. A steady, poisonous flow of guns into my country.

Luka handed out loaded magazines and the men slotted them into the rifles. The guards placed some of the old cardboard cartons that littered the place on top of the machines to serve as targets.

A second later, the air erupted into a deafening roar as the men test-fired the guns. The huge room was lit up with flickering white fire and the windows shook from the noise.

Luka looked at me, worried. Then he put his big hands over my ears, blocking out the sound. It helped but, as I looked up into his eyes, I couldn't find the man I knew there. *You always knew he was an arms dealer, you idiot,* I told myself. But, somehow, I'd been imagining him selling a few handguns to some far-off country or maybe a tank to a Middle-Eastern regime. Not this. Not crime on a corporate scale.

I stared at him in the near silence, the thump of the guns just a vibration through his hands. My eyes pleaded with him and, just for a second, I saw the conflict start again in his face. The wish that things could be different.

I was starting to realize, with horrible certainty, that things could never be different. He was trapped in a role and so was I. He had to do what his father expected of him, just as I had to follow orders from Adam.

The guns finally ran out of ammunition and Luka gently lifted his hands from my ears. I turned to look. The men were laughing and grinning, high on adrenaline. All of them were nodding that they'd take Luka's deal.

I looked at the cartons they'd been shooting. The cardboard had been shredded by the bullets and inside—

It had been a doll factory. Naked plastic carcasses were piled in the cartons, their heads and arms and legs ripped off by bullets, holes punched clear through their bellies and chests. A thousand tiny murders, a warzone in miniature.

I turned around and threw up all over the floor.

"Who the hell is *that?*" asked one of the Americans

I could feel Vasiliy's eyes burning into me with disgust. "No one," he muttered.

38

Outside, the Americans filed into a fleet of black SUVs, still laughing and joking. Luka embraced his dad before the older man climbed into a limo with blacked-out windows. I guessed it was probably armored, too.

Vasiliy waved and gave me a big, fake smile as he got into the car. Then he pulled Luka close and I heard him say, in Russian, "She's trouble, Luka. You've fucked her—now break it off."

Luka didn't nod...but he didn't argue, either. He just closed the car door and watched as the limo pulled away. What did that mean?

It hit me that I now had the perfect excuse to end things. My mission was done, after all. I knew all about the deal and had enough information for the CIA and the Russian cops to bust Luka's business wide open. When we got back to Moscow, I could break up with him and it wouldn't seem at all suspicious. Hell, he might even break up with me before I could do it.

All simple and clean. So why did it feel as if pieces of jagged glass were being pulled from my heart?

Luka walked over to me and told the guards to give him a minute. They waited a respectful distance away, still watching out for snipers but looking a little less jumpy than before. Now that the guns and

Vasiliy—the two big targets for any rivals—had departed, things felt slightly safer.

"Are you okay?" asked Luka, taking my hand in an oddly old-fashioned gesture. His hand completely covered my much smaller one. "You"—he searched for the right word for *threw up*—"You *unwelled.*"

Despite everything, that made me smile. "I'm okay now. I just..." I shook my head. "I wasn't ready for *that.*" I could feel my face going pale again. "Jesus, Luka, you're going to flood the market."

He gave me a strange look, and I realized I'd spoken with too much authority. I didn't sound like a tourist. I tried to brazen it out. "I took some business classes," I said. "And that's what you're doing, isn't it? Flooding the market. Thousands of cheap guns. So that your competitors look expensive and you force them out, and you control everything."

He slowly nodded. "Exactly."

"But it's *guns.* So many guns. Just one of those could be used in a robbery or a murder and you're talking about *thousands.*"

"Hundreds of thousands, over the next decade." He put his hands on my shoulders. The touch would have been warm and comforting any other time, but it wasn't working now. "But I don't control what people do with them."

At that, I lost it. Hot anger bubbled up from right down in my chest. "That old excuse?"

He stared at me and I could see his own anger growing, too. "It's just business, Arianna. I'm taking the violence *out* of it. Once we control the whole market, there'll be no more fighting with rival gangs. Much better than if bastards like Olaf Ralavich control it. The deals, the smuggling—it can all be clean and bloodless."

"But it's *guns!* It's never bloodless! You're ignoring what happens when the guns get to where they're going!"

His eyes narrowed. "I didn't make your criminals want to kill each other. I didn't even make them demand guns. I'm just filling the demand."

"What about kids?" I said savagely. And, at that, I saw him hesitate and almost wince. For a second, those hard eyes softened. "What about kids of fourteen, fifteen—even younger, who get mixed up with street gangs and shot with one of the new, cheap guns? What about them?"

He glanced away, not meeting my eyes. "That is unfortunate."

"But you could do something about it! Once you control the supply, you could set conditions! Threaten to cut off their guns if they hand them out to teenagers."

He held my gaze for a split second, his eyes widening in surprise. And something else. Respect. But then he shook his head and looked away. "Arianna, you don't know this world. I couldn't do that. It shows weakness. Besides, my father would never support it."

"You have to!" I blurted. And then realized I'd said far too much already. What was rattling around my head was, *you have to, because if you're really this cold then I don't know if there's any hope for you.*

His lips pressed together in a tight line and he *loomed* at me. "I don't *have* to do anything," he said sharply. But then he stared at me for another beat, half furious and half...something else. "You're not, are you?" he muttered.

"Not what?"

"Not scared of me. No one ever stands up to me."

"I *am* scared of you," I said in a low voice. "I just...say stuff anyway."

He held my gaze a second longer and then he glanced off down the road. There was nothing in sight, but I knew what he was thinking. He was gazing at the point where his dad's car had vanished into the distance. Reminding himself that he and I could never work. He sighed. "Come," he said. "We should go."

The trip back to Moscow would be much quicker than the outward one. Now that we'd got rid of the guns and didn't have to dodge the coastguard, Luka explained, we could take a more direct route. Five hours on the yacht, a flight and we'd be home.

Luka spent most of the time on the bridge with the captain. Given that there wasn't anything to see except for the featureless gray ocean, I knew he was avoiding me. And I knew why. He was debating breaking up with me.

I lay on the bed in our stateroom and tried to figure out my feelings. *I should be happy!* The mission was nearly over and it was a complete success. I'd done everything asked of me and soon I'd go home. Some weeks or months down the line, there'd be an epic bust. I'd be hailed as a star field agent and Luka would spend the rest of his life in a Russian prison.

So why did I feel ripped apart inside?

It was as if everything good we'd had was being twisted like a knife into my guts. I'd used his feelings against him.

He was an arms dealer. He was evil. But I was worse.

Back in St. Petersburg, Yuri transferred our bags to a car and we set off for the airport. Luka and I both sat there brooding, staring out of opposite windows. It seemed like we'd sit like that for the entire flight back to Moscow, too.

Until, suddenly, Luka's cell phone bleeped. Not a call or a text— some sort of app. And his face lit up with genuine pleasure for a few seconds before he reigned himself in. He leaned forward to Yuri and muttered something I couldn't hear, and we turned off the highway.

"What's going on?" I asked.

Luka grinned at me. I could still sense the storm on the horizon— we both knew, now, that this couldn't last. But just for a second, he was happy and he wanted to share it with me. He showed me the screen of his phone—a map of the area, with an airplane symbol on St. Petersburg. "Jet is here," he said with satisfaction.

"Jet is here?" I said blankly.

"Jet is here."

"Another trophy?" I asked, eying the sleek white business jet.

He shook his head. "I bought this myself." He stroked the wing lovingly. "She was having work done on her engines—that's why we had to take a normal flight on the way here. But now she's back."

She?

On board, the pilot and co-pilot greeted us, all smiles and enthusiasm. Luka asked after their wives and kids. I saw the same fierce streak of loyalty in the pilots I saw in Yuri—for all his evil, Luka obviously treated his staff well.

He was still grinning when we sat down in the huge leather armchairs and buckled ourselves in for take-off. He took my hand and, as the engines spun up, he squeezed it.

He was...*excited*. This huge bear of a man, that nothing seemed to phase, was excited.

I blinked. I'd known there was tenderness inside him but I hadn't expected to see...*fun*. He'd always been larger than life to me, but this was the first time he'd seemed complete—a man who'd make a good friend, a good father. He hid all that away.

"You like planes," I said.

His hand loosened in mine. "What? No. Jet is to impress others. Symbol of status."

"*Status symbol*. And no it isn't. The yacht was a status symbol. You *like* this plane." I paused, studying him as we sped down the runway. "No, you love it."

He squirmed in his seat, just a little. I'd found his weakness. It was incredibly reassuring that he had one. "You've liked planes ever since you were a kid, haven't you?" I said, figuring it out. "It reminds you of those days. When you didn't have to think about all this stuff." I felt the wheels leave the ground. "It must be nice to have something pure —one thing in your life that isn't about guns and violence."

He locked eyes with me and held my gaze. I'd been talking about the plane, but it occurred to me that I'd just described myself.

"You Americans and your psycho-analyzing," he muttered. But it was a good-natured mutter. As if he didn't mind someone finding out his weakness....as long as it was me. We stared at each other and I

knew he could feel the connection as strongly as I could. That sense
that this was right, that we worked together...even though we both
knew it couldn't last. His dad had told him to break up with me and,
even if that didn't happen, I was going to betray him.

It just felt so good, though, to finally meet someone I clicked with.
I leaned over and wound my arm around his much thicker one,
spiraling them so we were entangled, and put my head on his
shoulder. He let out a long sigh—not aimed at me, but at the
situation.

"What are you doing here, Arianna?" he said. "Why not in
America with stockbroker?"

We stared at each other. We both knew the answer. "A
stockbroker isn't what I want," I said quietly.

He shook his head. "You don't want monster, either. You *think* you
do." The seatbelt sign went off. He unfastened his belt and patted
his lap.

I slowly got up. He guided me to sit astride his legs, facing him.
He folded his arms around my back and the warmth of him, after all
those hours brooding alone on the yacht, made me melt inside. "I
know what I want," I said firmly.

"Between your thighs," he rumbled. "But what about the rest of
the time? I am what I am, Arianna, just like my father."

I grabbed his hand. "*Not* just like your father. You're your own
man."

He laughed gently and shook his head. "You want me to rebel and
open a coffee shop in New York with you? That isn't how the
Brotherhood works. You don't *leave*. This is my life. This will always
be my life."

"But you could do it...I don't know...*your own way*. Like making
sure the guns don't get handed out to teenagers." It wasn't that I was
hung up on that one thing. It was that, if he could make that one
concession, I'd know there was hope for him.

He studied me. Then he leaned forward and kissed my forehead
and rested his own head against the tingling mark he'd made. "My

father ran most of Moscow for many years. Everyone respects him. Everyone fears him. I have a lot of...expectation riding on me."

I nodded, letting him feel the movement of my head against his. Both of us had our eyes closed, which I think is what made the next part possible.

"Your father's dead, isn't he?"

I nodded again, feeling the pain rise up into my throat, a jagged lump of ice.

"Your mother, too?" he whispered.

I nodded again. This time, a tear fell down between us and hit his thigh.

His arms tightened around me. "I'm sorry, Arianna." He just held me for a long time. Then he said, "My father is all I have left. I can't just go against him."

I nodded, fresh tears forming in my eyes. I wasn't supposed to know what his dad had said about me, so supposedly we were still talking about the gun deal. But I knew he was meaning breaking up with me, too. He was going to do just what his dad wanted and dump me as soon as we got back to his penthouse.

39

We landed at a tiny airfield just outside Moscow. One of Luka's many guards met us with a car and Yuri got behind the wheel.

I immediately began to translate each billboard we passed, to try to get my mind off the fact I was sitting in a car. I'd spent more time in cars in the last few days than I had in the previous few years and it hadn't gotten any easier. On the outward trip, focusing on Luka had made it bearable but now, with both of us consumed by our thoughts, there was just tense silence. Even Yuri looked uncomfortable.

I had maybe twenty minutes until we reached his penthouse. Then he'd dump me and have Yuri drive me back to my hotel. I'd call Adam and he'd get me on a flight the same day. By tomorrow, I'd be back at my desk in Langley and I'd never see Luka again. And within weeks, he'd go to jail for the rest of his life.

Everything that had happened between us was about to be wiped out.

Luka's cell phone rang. As he listened to it, I saw his body tense and coil with anger. I stared out of the window and tried to look oblivious, as if I didn't understand the flurry of curses and questions I heard. *They* had set up in Moscow. No mention was made of a name but, from the tone of Luka's voice, I suspected it was his arch rivals, the Ralavich family. The ones Luka always claimed were much, much worse than him. I heard *where* and *how many* and finally Luka told the guy he'd take care of it and hung up. He gave Yuri an address and we turned off the highway and towards a housing district.

Luka looked at me. "I must go and attend to something," he told me. "You will wait in car."

I nodded dumbly. I could see the rage in him—the way his muscles had gone hard under his suit, the fabric barely containing those thick biceps and broad chest. He looked as if he was ready to tear his way right out through the car's roof. But it didn't feel as if he was angry at *me*. What was it his rivals had done that had got him so mad?

Soon, we were driving through a residential street made up of what were once fine townhouses. The street had seen better days, but the cars parked outside were expensive. Luka leaned across me to stare at the doors as we passed, counting off numbers to Yuri. We stopped right outside number 112.

Yuri and Luka both got out. "Stay here," Luka told me, his voice making it clear he'd tolerate no arguments. I nodded dumbly.

Yuri unlocked the glove box and handed Luka a gun with what I recognized as a silencer screwed on the end, taking another for himself. I watched through the window as the two of them climbed the steps to the door. Luka knocked, hiding his gun behind his back.

The door opened a crack and I got a brief glimpse of a heavyset man with a bald head. Then Luka was shoving his gun through the crack and I could just hear the faint whisper of silenced shots.

The door opened and Luka and Yuri pushed their way inside. They closed the door behind them, but not before I glimpsed the guy who'd been guarding it lying on his back, his chest stained with blood.

I slapped my hand over my mouth, afraid I was going to throw up. I'd never seen anyone killed before. *Luka just murdered someone!* Jesus, this was a man I'd given my body to, who I'd allowed to comfort me when I was flashing back to the worst moments of my life. I knew he'd done it before, but to see it—

There was a shout from inside, abruptly cut off. Minutes passed. *God, what's he doing in there?!* I imagined him going from room to room, killing. *I have to get out of here! I have to call Adam, or call the police!* There was no way I could stay with him after this, even for just a few hours. Nothing could justify this.

Then the door opened and a woman ran out, trampling over the dead guard's body in her haste. She was naked save for a man's shirt.

Another woman followed her, this one in a red dress. She seized the first one's hand and they ran together down the street.

A third, this one in her underwear. Two more, in dresses. And a final one, her eye swollen and blackened, her wrists—

My stomach heaved. Her wrists had red marks around them, where she'd been tied.

I suddenly knew what had been going on inside the house, and why Luka was so angry. I'd thought that nothing could justify murder, but this....

Luka and Yuri burst out of the door, hauling a third man with them. He was bleeding from a split lip and his nose was broken. They wrestled him into the seat next to me and Yuri snapped handcuffs to his wrists, threading them through the grab-handle next to the door. Then Luka jumped into the passenger seat, Yuri got behind the wheel and we were screeching down the street.

I turned and stared at the man next to me. Muscled, but smaller than Luka. Blond hair, carefully styled, and a wide face with small, piggish eyes. He was glaring at Luka defiantly, but his face was pale with fear.

"You *fuck!*" Luka yelled in Russian, twisting around to glare at him. "Not women! Never women! Not like *that!*" He caught my eye for an instant and I saw something there that made me catch my breath. Fear.

Fear of it happening to me.

The man spat blood onto the spotless seatback in front of him and cursed Luka and his family. Then he turned to look at me.

"Don't look at her," snarled Luka in Russian, grabbing the man's chin. "Don't even fucking think about her!" And he punched the man in the face.

Yuri stopped the car and I saw we were in a back alley, out of view of the street. Luka came around to the rear of the car, unlocked the handcuffs and hauled the man out, handling his weight easily. He dragged him off down the alley.

"What's he going to do to him?" I asked in a small voice.

Yuri turned around and just looked at me.

My stomach lurched again. Killing the guard at the house to free the women...that was one thing. Horrifying, but maybe—I was shocked that I could even think it—maybe *necessary*. But this, what Luka was doing now...this was simple, brutal violence. Punishment.

I climbed out of the car, my legs shaking.

Yuri looked at me in amazement. "Better you stay here," he warned.

But I was already off and running down the alley after Luka. He'd dragged the guy to a lock-up garage, its door secured by a padlock and chain. Luka heaved on the chain, forearms bulging, until brute strength made one of the links give away. He swung open the door, pulled the man inside and threw him up against a wall.

"You *fuck!*" Luka yelled, swinging his fist into the man's gut. The man doubled over. Luka caught him with an uppercut under the chin, sending him tumbling backward. "You sick little bastard!" The guy was trying to get up, but Luka didn't give him a chance. His fists smashed into the man's chest and face, pummeling him, knocking him to his knees. I remembered the punching bag, aboard the yacht. *I don't box. I hit things.*

"*Luka!*" I screamed, grabbing his shoulder. "Enough!"

Luka turned to me, his eyes savage. "Wait in the car!"

"No!" I looked at the guy. Blood was pouring from his nose and lips, his face swollen with bruises. "You'll kill him!"

Luka looked at me. And nodded.

"It's enough! Let him go!"

Luka stared into my eyes. "Do you know what they were doing in there? It wasn't just a brothel. It was a rape club, for rich businessmen. Where they can do anything they like to the women, for money." He kicked the man on the ground.

I stared at the bleeding, broken man. I almost wanted to kill him myself. *What harm would it do? He deserves it. Luka's all ready to do it. Let him.*

"No," I said, my eyes burning into Luka's. "You can't. *I don't want you to.* Understand?"

He glared at me. "He deserves it!"

"I know! But I want you—I want you to be better than that! You *are* better than that, Luka!"

The man on the floor laughed and coughed up blood. He croaked something about Luka being pussy-whipped. Luka kicked him in the chest and he went quiet.

"*Please,* Luka," I begged. "I—"

Suddenly, I caught myself. *What was I doing?!* Was I really trying to change him? To reform a monster? Of course he wasn't going to change!

But I could see that momentary flicker in his eyes, the glimpse of something better inside. I wasn't trying to change him. I was just trying to help him be the man he wanted to be. He'd called me his *spaseniye.* Well, this was where I got to choose whether to be his salvation or not.

Luka shook his head at me. "I can't be weak," he told me. He picked the man up by the collar and lifted him right off the ground, his feet kicking in the air. He drew back his fist for what I knew would be the killer blow.

"If you want me," I croaked, tears in my eyes, "you have to not do this." The words were out before I knew I was going to say them.

Luka turned to me, still gripping the man. His eyes were full of that conflict I'd seen before. He was begging me not to make him choose, because he wasn't sure which life he'd pick.

I felt the heat trickle down my cheeks. I took a deep breath and stared right back at him, willing him to make the right decision.

Long seconds ticked by...and then Luka tossed the man to the floor like a sack of garbage. He grabbed my hand and towed me to the car, saying nothing. Behind us, I could hear the man groaning and cursing us.

Yuri was standing by the car, looking worried. Luka towed me straight past him and almost threw me into the back seat, getting in beside me. Yuri quickly climbed in and we sped off.

I could hear sirens in the distance. No more than five minutes had elapsed since we'd first pulled up outside the house. The adrenaline was sluicing out of my system, now, leaving me shaky and weak. I glanced across at Luka and saw the blood on his knuckles. I thought I was going to throw up again.

"We should not have left him alive," muttered Luka in English.

Yuri craned his head around, his eyes wide. "You left him *alive?!*" he asked in Russian. Then a glare from Luka reminded him of his place and he turned back to the road.

"There will be repercussions," said Luka. "He will want revenge. It would have been better if we'd finished it cleanly. Then they would have been uncertain who was responsible."

"Who is *they?*" I asked.

"The Ralavich family," Luka said. "That was Olaf Ralavich's son." He drew in a deep breath. "You have made things much more complicated for me."

I shook my head. "I'm sorry."

He stared at me, then looked down at his blood-stained hands. "Did I please you?" he said, almost under his breath.

I blinked. "I—Yes,"

"Then it is worth it."

We stared at one another as my mind exploded in slow motion. I'd made the ultimatum, but it had been a last ditch, spur-of-the-moment thing. I hadn't thought it would work. It *shouldn't* have worked, unless....

Unless I really was that important to him.

He suddenly lunged at me across the car, crushing me against the door.

40

His lips came down on mine and a little groan escaped me as I felt the need inside, the temptation to give into him. My mind was spinning. Everything was happening so fast! My mental picture of who he was, *what* he was, was constantly changing. I couldn't make up my mind whether he was a monster or not, whether he could be saved or not. And whatever he was, he was my enemy, the man I was about to betray. Whatever he felt for me and whatever I felt for him, that didn't change.

And it was about to be over anyway...wasn't it?

I broke the kiss and stared at him, panting. "When we get back to Moscow," I said, "what happens?"

His eyes gleamed. "You will come back to my apartment."

He tried to kiss me again, but I dodged out of the way. "Your dad," I blurted.

He stopped and drew back a little, frowning at me. I knew why. I wasn't supposed to know what his dad had said. But I couldn't pretend to be oblivious any more.

"He was polite to me," I said. "But I know something's wrong. He doesn't like me. Does he?"

At first, he looked as if he was going to deny it. Then he looked guilty, then sad. At last, he said. "No. He doesn't like you."

And there it was, out in the open. I waited for him to dump me.

"But I don't care," he said.

My eyes widened. "*What?!*"

He shook his head and his hand cupped my cheek. "I've never met anyone like you, Arianna. My father rules our business. It's time he stopped ruling my life."

We stared at each other for another second, his eyes burning into mine, and I knew he was serious. He was going to rebel against the only family he had left...for me.

And in that second, I didn't think about the mission being over or how I was still going to betray him. I just let out a little moan of need and, this time, I launched myself at him. I didn't care that he was a monster. I didn't care that he was the enemy. Our lips met and I wasn't Arianna Scott or Arianna Ross or a fucking CIA agent. I was just Arianna and he was just Luka and nothing else mattered.

His hands slid up the front of my dress and squeezed my breasts, making them bulge up out of the neckline. He growled in lust and released me for a second so that he could unfasten my seatbelt. I swayed in my seat, the sensation of being in a moving car making the fear bubble up inside me. Then he was touching me again and his hands melted all the fear away. His palms were sliding down my sides, down to the hem of my dress, tugging it up. At the same time, he pulled my legs towards him on the seat and I slid, flopping down onto my back.

He pulled my dress up over my panties and I felt his gaze on them, blazing through the thin fabric. I'd worn the white ones. The innocent ones. From his expression, they'd been a good choice. I was the innocent and he was the criminal and he was about to corrupt me.

I suddenly remembered there was a third person in the car. I came back to reality for a second, my head swiveling as if on a stick. Yep, there was Yuri in the driver's seat. His eyes were fixed on the road, but we were clearly visible in the rear view mirror.

Luka lowered his head and licked my inner thigh, his tongue quick and expert, drawing a blazing symbol there, and I stopped caring.

His hands separated my thighs, pushing them up and back, folding me, and I yelped in surprise, the yell growing throaty when he started to rub me right where I needed it. He pressed close, our faces inches apart, my ankles over his shoulders. He began to stroke my lips through my panties, the fabric rapidly moistening. "You are an angel," he muttered in Russian. "You don't know what's coming, but I'm going to fuck you like a cheap whore."

I had to fight very hard to look confused. I knew that I should be slapping his face, but the words only made me hotter.

His fingers stretched my panties away from my body and I gasped as I felt the air-conditioned air of the car on my moist flesh. "Careful," I muttered. "They're new."

With a sudden jerk of his hand, he snapped the waistband and tossed them away. "I'll buy you more," he said. He was on his knees on the seat, now, my ankles in his hands. He pushed them even further back and then opened them a little. His head dipped and—

I moaned as his mouth came down on my wet, ready flesh, a spasm rippling up from my groin and making me twist and thrash. His tongue covered me in quick, hard licks, dipping between my lips to taste me. I could feel the moisture flooding me there, my own helpless response to his touch.

He pushed his head closer, forcing it between my thighs, the slight grizzle on his cheeks rasping against my sensitive skin. His tongue was tracing each lip in turn, switching between them, drawing the silken flesh with it and stretching it tight. My toes curled and strained in my shoes, somewhere up near the car's ceiling. I remembered Yuri again and wondered how I looked, with my stockinged legs kicking in the air.

The tip of his tongue found my clit, teasing the hidden bud, swirling around and around it and running up and down either side but never quite lashing it directly, as I craved. He kept me on the edge while he plunged two thick fingers into me, twisting them as they speared deep. I was gasping and panting, my ass grinding against the leather seat, my hips bucking.

His fingers and tongue took me to the very edge and then, just as my climax was swollen and ready to explode, he drew his fingers from me and pushed them at my panting lips. I opened instinctively, staring up at him as he brushed them over my tongue. "I am going to do such things to you," he whispered in Russian. "If you are my salvation, then I will be your corruptor."

I tried to remember to frown at him as if confused. Inside I could feel my coming orgasm expand and stretch at his words. *Corrupted.*

I watched as he unfastened his belt and rammed down his pants. His cock sprang into view, hard and ready and intimidatingly thick.

He used his elbows to spread my legs wide as he rolled on a condom. One foot almost brushed the passenger seat. *You really do need a lot of leg room,* I thought, dazedly. Then his hands were sliding under my ass, cupping my cheeks. He lifted me—

I groaned as he sank into me in one long thrust, then groaned louder as he went deeper. I panted up at him in disbelief as he slid further—*God!* I hadn't known he could go so deep! He was hunkering over me, his body almost covering mine, our faces close together. And then the tight curls at the base of his cock were caressing my lips and he was inside me completely.

I stared up at him. He wasn't even moving, yet, but the vibrations of the car were moving me minutely around him, and that was making me tighten and spasm around his hardness. The leather seat under me was firmer than a bed and that made it feel different, too. Everything seemed more intense—maybe it was the moving car, maybe it was the fact we were properly together for the first time, more than just lovers. But I could feel every millimeter of him, every throbbing vein.

He reached up and traced my lips with a finger, following their shape. Then he started to draw back, very slowly, and the feel of him leaving me made me quiver. Every inch that he moved was a silken caress that left me panting.

I wanted it. But my hands reached for him anyway, gripping his shirt as if to slow him down.

Immediately, he grabbed my wrists, trapping them, bearing them down onto the leather above my head. I started to pant faster, staring up at him with huge eyes, pushing upwards against him. My wrists didn't budge. Neither did my hips, when I tried to lift them. He had me exactly where he wanted me, spread for him on a firm, leather seat. And now he was going to fuck me.

I could have asked him to stop.

I didn't.

He slammed back into me, his muscled body huge between my thighs, and I cried out—a high little moan that didn't sound like me at all. He began to thrust, his biceps bunched and hard, his chest wide and magnificent as he bore down into me. In the window behind him, I saw the reflection of his ass tensing and hollowing as he drove into me, filling me, and I cried out anew. I could see my own legs, too, stockinged and spread beneath him. The maiden, ravaged by the monster. The heat boiled up inside me.

His cock was like a silk-wrapped iron bar inside me, filling every millimeter of available space and then drawing out to leave a void that I immediately needed him to fill again. I began to push against his hands, trying to wriggle a wrist free. Each tiny battle resulted in him tightening his grip a little more, increasing my feeling of helplessness.

I wanted to struggle. But I didn't want to escape. *God, this is so wrong....*

He stared down into my eyes and I knew that he knew. He understood. His eyes gleamed, his thrusts coming faster and harder, forcing me down into the soft leather of the seat and leaving me breathless and shuddering. My climax was twisting as it rose, tightening into a red-hot ball of energy, and I could feel him approaching his end, too, his thrusts growing savage even as I saw his jaw tense. He leaned even closer into me, his mouth beside my ear, and he whispered in English, "You like it like this, don't you, Arianna? You like being helpless under me."

I let out a groan. The sound of that word, *helpless,* sent an earthquake through me, ripping my climax free from its bindings and letting it soar up inside me. I thrashed frantically against him and he held me even tighter and that's when it started. A choking, quaking orgasm unlike any I'd had before, one that started in my chest and rolled out to my toes, powerful and somehow cleansing. I exploded into white fire around him, my back arching and my head pushing hard back into the seat leather.

I felt him jet and pulse inside me, that sudden blast of heat that extended my own moment. And then we were slumping together, muscles slack and exhausted. I wound my arms and legs around him and we lay entangled like that until we reached his apartment building.

It was only when we got out of the car that I realized my fear had gone. The memories were still there, but simply being in a car didn't seem to be a trigger, anymore. Somewhere in that sweating, grinding chaos, I'd managed to break that link. I wasn't healed, but I was healing.

After three years frozen, it couldn't be that easy...could it?

Maybe it could be. I felt a tiny flame flicker into life, deep within the ice. In some twisted way, Luka and his brand of rough, urgent sex was good for me. And he'd let Ralavich's son live. In some way, I was good for him.

Was it possible that there was hope for us?

And then, as the afterglow faded and we ascended in the elevator, the realization hit me so hard that I stumbled and had to clutch at Luka's hand for support. I was his girlfriend, now, closer to him than Elena or Natalia had ever been. He'd made sacrifices for me, put his faith in me. He'd chosen me over his father.

And I was going to stab him in the back. I was going to send him to prison for the rest of his life.

Luka wrapped his arms around me. His warmth felt good, but even it couldn't banish the black despair that was spreading through my soul. I'd finally found a man I wanted to be with...maybe the one I was *meant* to be with. And I was going to destroy him.

But it was much worse than I could have imagined. I didn't know, then, just how dangerous being together was going to be, for both of us.

Or just how completely I'd have to betray him.

41

It was the most beautiful thing I'd ever seen: the human body as a moving work of art. The music swelled and ebbed as the ballerinas jumped and floated, weightless as ghosts.

And I couldn't concentrate on any of it because of what Luka was doing under my skirt.

"Someone will see!" I told him in a harsh whisper.

He smirked, as if that amused him. His fingers pressed a little more insistently and I groaned under my breath. And parted my thighs.

We were in a private box. A box the Malakov family actually owned, that sat empty between performances no matter how full the theater was. Apparently, Luka's dad, Vasiliy, used to take his mother here when she was alive. Now, it was used by Luka and his current girlfriend.

And now that was me. Not another willowy Russian model with laser-straight blonde hair, but a pale, awkward girl with hair you might charitably call chestnut and a body that was too heavy on the hips to be slender, but not curvy enough to catch a man's eye.

Not most men's, at least. Luka, for some reason, had claimed me for his own. And he was currently demonstrating his ownership by means of his hand between my thighs. The tips of his fingers were strumming up and down along the opening of my lips. I could feel myself moistening beneath my panties.

We'd been back in Moscow just one day. I was a gangster's girlfriend. A *moll*. If it was even appropriate to call Luka a gangster. *Kingpin* suited him better, given that he was about to take control of most of the gun trade into the US.

I knew I needed to contact Adam—urgently. But when we landed in Moscow, we'd gone straight back to his penthouse apartment for more sex and then fallen asleep, tangled in the sheets. Today, we'd lounged around the place, never apart for more than a few minutes. I didn't dare try to call Adam from the bathroom. If Luka overheard....

Then, this evening, he'd told me to dress up for the ballet. I was in one of the dresses I'd been given at the boutique, a long black number with a loose skirt and tiny beads of jet glistening blackly across the bodice. It was sexy but sophisticated and Luka had made approving noises when he saw it, and when he'd slid his hand into the high slit that run up one side of the skirt. But then he'd shaken his head. "It needs something else," he told me.

And then he gave me the necklace.

It was made up of hundreds of squares of shining silver, joined at the edges to make a shimmering snakeskin pattern that flowed like liquid as it followed the shape of my neck. It was just a few squares wide at the sides and back, but flared out to eight wide at the front. He fastened the chain around my neck and I gazed at it in the mirror. It was starkly beautiful and clearly expensive without being showy. Miles away from the bling people associated with new-found Russian wealth. But then Luka and his dad had had more time to get used to it than a lot of people.

As I'd run my fingers over it, unease had coiled and twisted in my stomach. First clothes, now jewelry. I was being seduced by him. After the violence of the gun deal and the savage beating he'd given Ralavich's son, now he was showing me the other side of his life. The one spent cruising in cars with tinted windows and in private jets. The one where we partied at the finest clubs in

Moscow, or went to the ballet or the opera. The one where everyone feared us.

I'd felt it when we'd walked into the theater. People turned and looked and then pretended to be looking at someone else. Others scurried ahead of us to open doors or quickly stepped aside to clear a path. It felt like being a princess. An evil princess. One who could order you killed with a tilt of her head. I knew Luka would do it for me in a heartbeat—he had both the physical strength and the hardness in his soul. He had killed, plenty of times, and he'd do it again.

Unless I could stop him.

It was crazy. I'd been sent to Moscow to take down a monster and, instead, I was trying to tame him. As if that was even possible. As if I could give him back his soul—and, even if I could, as if that would make a difference to Adam. He was still going to demand that the Russians put Luka in jail for the rest of his life. Luka thought I was his salvation, but I was going to be his downfall.

And he was going to be mine. I could feel myself being drawn into a world I barely understood, one where my own lust ran out of control. Women are meant to be scared of men like Luka. I *was* still scared of him, on some level. And yet, at the same time, I wanted him to—

Pin me.

Tear my clothes.

Hold me down as he—

I dug my fingernails into my palms to bring myself back. I'd never felt anything like it, before, this need to let him...*take* me. Whenever I thought about it, I flushed red and squirmed inside, ashamed of myself. And yet whenever he touched me, whenever he even looked at me in that way, I just went weak inside.

It was getting to be about more than sex, between us. I could feel the feelings deepening and branching, spreading out to every part of me and digging in deep. I knew he trusted me now, more than he ever had his previous girlfriends. He really liked me...maybe *more* than liked. And that was even more dangerous than the physical side of it.

I already felt as if I was being torn in two. What would happen when the time came to leave, to run out on him leaving some fake note apologizing for running away? What about when the police vans came for him a few hours or a few days later and he guessed it was me? It wasn't the retribution I was worried about—I'd be safely back in Virginia, by then. It was the knowledge that he'd hate me for the rest of his life.

If I was smart, I'd distance myself as much as I possibly could. I'd keep the sex vanilla and try to remain passive, staring up at the ceiling and faking my orgasms. I'd remind myself of what he was and *act,* instead of going with my true feelings.

But I couldn't do that. Being with Luka had woken things inside me, things that hadn't functioned since the day of the crash. Things I thought were broken forever. I felt as if I was a statue made of ice, and he was made of flame. The closer I got, the more my frozen heart melted. But if I got too close, if I stayed too long, I'd melt completely and be lost forever.

Luka's fingers began to move faster, stroking me through my panties. He'd used the slit at the side of my dress to gain access to me, pushing it up until the top of my stocking was showing and then sliding his arm over my thigh and between my legs. I could feel his dinner jacket and the cold silver of his cufflink against my inner thigh. As he stroked faster, I began to writhe on the padded seat, my ass tensing. "Stop!" I whispered. "Someone will see!"

I glanced around. The audience below us couldn't see us, but there were other boxes to our left and right. My lower body was hidden by the wall that ran around the edge of the box, but I was exposed from the waist up. Every expression, every soft sigh was public.

Luka glanced at me with a look that I was getting to know well. A challenging look, one that meant *say 'stop' again if you really mean it....but you don't, do you?* And I did the same thing I always did, faced with that look. I turned to warm taffy and then liquid inside and dropped my eyes.

He gave me one of his smirks and began to rub faster. I could feel my panties growing sticky and then wet. I couldn't help myself. I began to circle my hips, grinding my pelvis to meet him. I bit my lower lip and tried to focus on the ballet, determined to maintain control. I couldn't...not *here!*

His fingers slid around the edge of my panties and touched naked, slippery flesh and I knew I was lost. I tried to sit bolt upright, eyes glued to the dancers. Watching as their partners lifted them high in the air and then dropped them down—

Deep—

I gripped the arms of my seat and stared as the dancers pranced and spun across the stage—

Back and forth—

Mouth firmly closed, I panted through my nose as they—

Circled. Pirouetting around and around. Faster and faster and—

I felt my eyes widen as the orgasm thundered through me. My ass lifted off the seat and then pressed back into it, hard. My legs trembled, my heels hammering on the floor. In the box next to me, a man turned and frowned at me.

...and I went still.

"Almost silent," Luka whispered in my ear. "I'll have to try harder, next time."

～

On the way back to the apartment, I sat nestled against Luka's side, my head on his shoulder. Being in a car, especially with the freezing weather outside, still unnerved me. But it no longer triggered me as it had done before I'd come to Moscow. There were no flashbacks. *Maybe I'm cured.*

I dared to hope.

We were most of the way home when Luka's cell phone rang. He looked at the screen and then turned from me slightly, maybe unconsciously, and spoke in a low voice I could only just hear. He didn't know that I could understand Russian, so why was he going to such lengths?

Then I heard my name. He was talking about me...and I had a pretty good idea who with.

He ended the call. "My father," he said apologetically. "I said I was with you...now he wants us to come over."

"Now?" I asked. It was already late.

"Now."

Vasiliy's house had once been the home of some duke, a residence well outside from the city before Moscow had expanded and almost swallowed it up. It stood alone on a hilltop, old and grand and subtly distant from everything around it.

At the bottom of the hill there was a guard house where, even though Luka was family, the underside of our car had to be checked for bombs. The road itself snaked around the hill, its hairpin bends making it impossible to go faster than ten miles an hour. That gave Vasiliy's guards plenty of time to get ready if someone sped past the guard house.

The first floor of the house itself had no windows, just solid slabs of heavy stone. Good in the olden days for keeping peasants with pitchforks at bay and now equally useful against rival crime gangs. No one would be allowed to hurt Luka's dad.

"He barely leaves," muttered Luka to me as we approached the house. "Except for really big deals." He shook his head. "It's sad. He's almost a prisoner here."

When we got inside, even Luka got a pat-down. "In case someone strapped a bomb to me, and blackmailed me into walking into the house," he explained. He looked ridiculous, standing with his arms outstretched as the much smaller bodyguards patted his chest and back. It would have been funny if it hadn't been so completely terrifying. How much fear do you have to live in, for your own son to become a potential threat?

And then the guards turned to me. "Lift your arms," said one.

Luka shook his head. "That's not necessary."

"You know the rules," he was told. The guards looked almost apologetic...but firm.

I nodded my consent.

Two sets of hands worked quickly and efficiently over me. They were professional about it, not copping a feel. But that didn't change the fact they were both men—big, ex-military men, almost sandwiching me between them as they checked me. It was difficult to hold still, especially when it came time to check my chest and one of them ran the backs of his hands over my breasts. I could see Luka glaring at them.

They stepped back and nodded respectfully to me. I grabbed Luka's hand and, together, we walked inside.

The first floor must have been the servants' quarters originally and it seemed to serve much the same purpose today. I caught glimpses of guards sleeping in bunks and rooms that seemed to be filled with nothing but racks of guns and body armor. *God, he's got an army protecting him.* The walls and floor were bare stone.

It was only when we reached the top of the stairs and entered the second floor that the house suddenly changed. Here, it was all wood paneling and ornate windows (though I suspected the panes had been replaced with bulletproof glass). And coming down the wooden staircase from a higher floor was Vasiliy himself.

He was dressed in a suit again, but this time a little more casually than when we'd met in the old factory. His crisp white shirt was unbuttoned at the neck and he'd discarded his jacket and tie. With his ramrod posture and sheer height, he cut an imposing figure as he strolled down the stairs, whiskey glass in hand.

First, he greeted Luka, kissing each cheek. Then he turned to me. "Arianna," he said slowly, as if testing the name. Then he gripped my arms and kissed each of my cheeks, too. I caught my breath as he did it. It wasn't just the knowledge that he hated me, underneath the false welcome. It was the size of him, the strength of his fingers as he held my arms.

"I have figures I need you to look at," he told Luka, speaking in

English for my benefit. His eyes never left my face for a second. "On the screen in my study. You know the way."

Luka looked doubtfully between the two of us. He was being sent away so that his dad could talk to me, and we both knew it. I nodded to him that it was okay, even though I was terrified. I couldn't let Luka fight my battles for me.

"Come," said Vasiliy, slipping an arm around my shoulder. And he led me deeper into the house.

42

W e turned so many corners and went up and down so many short flights of stairs that I soon had no idea where we were or what floor we were on. The house was a complete maze of dark wood paneling, and the fact it was night, with the only light coming from occasional wall lights, didn't help. Vasiliy strolled through the darkened hallways, oozing calm confidence, while I could only stumble nervously alongside.

The room he took me to had no windows, just a drinks cabinet, some chairs and a table with a chessboard. Vasiliy closed the door, sealing us in. And in that moment, the mood started to change, the beginning of a subtle but important shift. I frowned, because I couldn't put my finger on it. It felt familiar and yet wrong.

"Do you play?" asked Vasiliy, waving at the chessboard as he poured me a drink. Vodka, of course. I hadn't asked for one, but I didn't feel as if I could refuse. He was a difficult man to say no to. I hadn't had the full force of his personality turned on me until now, but I could feel the power radiating off of him. Maybe it was breeding or maybe it was something he'd acquired through his rise to power, but the effect was the same: I practically wanted to curtsey.

"A little." I'd played with my dad, when I was young, because he'd enjoyed it. And then never since the crash, for the same reason. What the hell was going on? I'd been expecting him to try to push me away from Luka. Not *this*.

He handed me a glass filled with ice and vodka. "We used to be champions, before your computers beat us. It would amuse me if we played, while we talked."

Amuse him? I couldn't tell whether he was mocking himself as an old-fashioned Russian, or mocking me. I nodded.

He knocked back his drink—some sort of expensive whiskey, I noticed, not vodka. And then he looked at me as if expecting me to do the same, so I did. The vodka seemed to expand in my mouth, sending burning fumes straight up my nose and down into my lungs. But when it hit my belly, its heat melted a little of the fear.

He sat down across from me. He was black and I was white. He moved a pawn and said, "You are very beautiful."

I sort of coughed on the tail-end of the vodka fumes and looked up at him in amazement. *Did he really—*"Th—Thank you." I groped for one of my pawns and moved it.

Vasiliy moved another pawn, quick and precise. "I can see why he likes you. You are everything he's not."

I reddened and stared at the board, playing for time. I moved a knight, not even thinking about strategy. The mood was completing its shift, now, slotting into a place that was definitely familiar and definitely wrong. Very wrong.

"His other girlfriends have been..."—he shook his head dismissively—"vacuous whores. But *you*. You are intelligent. You know your own mind." He reached behind him and, as he twisted, I saw how broad his shoulders were, how his chest still had the same powerful swell as Luka's. His hair was shot through with silver, but most of it was still black.

He picked up the bottle of whiskey and poured himself another glass, as if to reassure me that he was drinking, too. And then he grabbed the vodka bottle and went to pour me some more.

I instinctively put my hand over my glass.

He grinned at me, took my hand and lifted it off and down onto the tabletop. Then he poured me another vodka. He kept smiling at me the whole time and I found myself shyly smiling, too, even though alarm bells were ringing in my head. *What the hell is going on?!*

"And you are American," he said. "Most American women do not like Russian men. They find us too..." He paused. "What is the word? Too *chill?*"

"Too cold," I said quietly. I had an awful suspicion that he'd known the right word damn well. He was just trying to appear klutzy to put me at ease.

"*Cold*. And, if the men are like Luka and me, from the Brotherhood, then we are cold *and* dark, yes?" He indicated me. "And you, you are warmth and light." He wagged his finger. "You should not be attracted to this."

His eyes. His eyes were gleaming just like Luka's.

And, suddenly, I knew what the mood had shifted to. Seduction. He was seducing me.

No! That's crazy!

I knocked back my second vodka, feeling the pleasant warmth throughout my body, now. When I was brave enough to meet Vasiliy's eyes again, there was no mistaking the look there. He wanted me. I could see it as clearly as if his thoughts were projected onto the wall behind him. He wanted to pull me up out of my chair and hurl me down on the table, chess pieces scattering across the floor. Pull up my dress, rip off my panties and—

I drew in a labored breath and stood up, staring at him. The mood shattered in an instant.

He smiled. "Interesting. For a moment there, I thought I was going to get to fuck you."

And the truth washed over me, scarcely less disturbing than what I'd been imagining. It had been a test. One I'd passed.

He looked at me and then at my chair, indicating that I should sit back down for whatever round two would bring. I stood there indecisively for a moment...and then sat down. Whatever happened, I needed to get on Vasiliy's good side. If he had a good side.

He smiled, as if glad I'd decided to play. "You suit the dress," he said, waving his hand vaguely at the bodice. "You suit beautiful things. Some of the other girls, they only like my son because he can give them nice things. But you, I think...you want something more." He moved his rook and then smiled at me again. "I think you want to get inside his head."

Shit—

He leaned forward, the muscles in his forearms bulging as he braced his hands on the table. "You are an American and you are getting close to my son. So either you are in love with him or—"

SHIT—

"You are a spy for the *C. I. A.*" He said each letter very clearly and precisely.

I stared at him in horror.

"Are you a spy?" asked Vasiliy.

"No!"

"Are you in love with my son?"

"I—"

He suddenly leaned across the table, our faces almost touching. "*What is it?!*" he snarled. "What's between the two of you?"

"I—I really like him! He likes me! He's helping me—"

"It can't have started like that! How did it start?" When I didn't answer, he slammed his fist down on the table, the chess pieces jumping and falling. "*HOW?*"

"*Sex!*" I said, my voice high and tight. "It started with sex. He—" I flushed. "He—" I couldn't meet his eyes.

"*WHAT?! What does he do?*"

"He...he's rough with me," I croaked, squeezing my eyes shut in humiliation. "He holds me down!"

"And I bet that makes you drip right down your thighs," said Vasiliy.

I opened my eyes and my hand flashed out before I knew what I was doing. It cracked across Vasiliy's cheek, leaving a red handprint. My eyes widened and I froze there, waiting for the inevitable retribution.

"Good," said Vasiliy, and sat back in his chair. He rubbed his cheek. "You hit well, for a little American thing. Make sure you do that to him, if he steps out of line."

I stared at him, utterly confused.

"I had to see if you were telling the truth," said Vasiliy. "If you really had feelings for him. I'm sorry."

I drew in a long breath. It had been another test. And in the shaky aftermath of the adrenaline, I realized it was my out-of-control feelings for Luka that had saved me. If I'd just been acting, he would have known it. "How can you live like this?" I asked in a ragged voice. "Suspecting everyone. Searching your own son for bombs. Interrogating everyone in case they're a spy?"

He sat back in his chair and stared at me. "It's no life," he said. "No life at all. And that is why you should leave my son."

I swallowed. Now, we'd come full circle. This was the conversation I'd been expecting to have when we first walked into this room. Only now, things were much more complicated. Now, I knew that he had his suspicions about me, even if they'd been allayed for the time being.

He lifted his hands and indicated the house. "Look at my beautiful, expensive prison. When I die, Luka will become the main target. And he and you will live like this, too." He nodded at my stomach. "When you give him a child, you'll have to drive him around in a car with bulletproof windows. Until he's old enough to go to boarding school—then you'll send him to England and see him every few months. Are you ready for that?"

I felt as if I wanted to be sick. I didn't know which was worse: the future he was painting or the knowledge that it was all impossible because I was going to betray the family before any of it happened.

"We have enemies, Arianna. The CIA—they're a corrupt bunch of bastards. The Russian authorities want us behind bars. The rival gangs want our business." He looked me right in the eye. "They'd kill and gut Luka, if they ever got their hands on him. But you, they'd do worse to."

I nodded slowly.

"This is not a game. This is not *exciting* or *dangerous* or *just like in the movies.* This is real. If you stay with my son, I worry that you will be killed. And that you will get him killed."

I opened my mouth to tell him that I would never hurt Luka. And then realized that that would be a lie. I was going to hurt him in the worst way possible.

"If I have learned anything, since his mother died," said Vasiliy, "it is that trying to get Luka to do something is impossible." He gave me a look that was almost friendly. "Boy has head like a bull."

"Just like his dad," I said softly.

He smiled at me. "As you say. So. You will have to be the smart one. You will have to break up with him."

The sick feeling I got in the pit of my stomach wasn't horror at what he was saying. It was the creeping knowledge that he was right. I wasn't cut out for this life. Even if I could survive it, I couldn't be sure I could change Luka and save him from the darkness that had made his father into this coldly calculating machine. And even if there could in theory be some happy ending for the two of us, the whole thing was impossible. In days—maybe as soon as tomorrow—I'd betray him.

I nodded my assent to Vasiliy. He refilled my glass for a sad farewell toast.

43

"**W**hat did he want?" asked Luka as soon as we were back in the car.

"Nothing."

Luka looked at me skeptically. "It's never *nothing*."

What would sound convincing? "He asked me about myself. Lots of questions."

"Oh." He nodded slowly to himself. "Okay. That makes sense."

I pretended to be oblivious. "Why?"

Luka sighed. "He was checking you out. Making sure you weren't a spy."

"A *spy?!*" Sounding incredulous wasn't too hard. I still felt so unlike a proper agent that it sounded ridiculous. "For one of the other gangs?"

"Or for the CIA. You *are* an American."

"I thought the CIA were all...assassinations and politics."

Luka shook his head. "Drugs and guns. They're meant to stop it, but really they control it. They're corrupt."

I blinked. His dad had said the same thing. It was weird, seeing how we were viewed from the other side, hearing the ridiculous propaganda they believed.

I nestled into his side. His dad's words were going round and round in my head. I was going to have to break up with Luka. I'd known it all along—it was the only possible outcome, ever since I'd agreed to take the mission. But back then, sitting in Adam's office at Langley, I hadn't figured on feeling this way about him.

How *did* I feel about him, exactly? Aside from the obvious lust, there was definitely something deeper. I could feel it tugging at me, whenever we were apart. I felt the sick fear when I thought he might be in danger, like when he'd run into the brothel. And, when we were together, I felt...complete. Like there'd been something missing, before. Was that love? I didn't have much to compare it to. The few relationships I'd had before the crash had been teenage fumblings and then college awkwardness. No one had ever made me feel the way Luka had. But it had only been a handful of days. Way too soon to call it *love*.

"What's the matter?" asked Luka. "Cold?"

I'd been staring determinedly out of the window. Now I looked round at him in surprise. "What?"

He glanced down at my chest. I realized I'd wrapped my arms around myself.

"You always do that in cars," he said. "Unless I'm holding you."

I stared at him. I hadn't realized I'd been doing it...but just as importantly, I hadn't realized he'd been noticing little things like that. I knew he'd been looking at my body, stripping me with his eyes. But I didn't know he'd been studying me like that, discovering all my little quirks.

"Are you going to tell me what it is?" he asked. That accent of his made the words like huge, stone slabs, ones that could shatter my fragile defenses if he wanted to. But he didn't use them in that way. He spoke gently, nudging at my layers of ice instead. It was like having a massive, powerful bear nuzzling your ear.

I might not be having flashbacks anymore, but the memories were still there, affecting me on an instinctual level. Of course I couldn't tell him about the crash. Thinking about it meant reliving it, every little detail preserved by my goddamn photographic memory.

The only way to survive was to push it way down inside and cover it with enough layers of ice that the pain was muted...and everything was frozen.

Funny how that didn't seem to be working so well, anymore.

But, even if I could tell him, and if that could somehow help me...did I deserve that? I was about to betray him in the worst way possible.

"Soon," I said. "For now...." I nestled into him and he folded his strong arms around me, wrapping me in warmth and security.

By the time we reached his apartment block, I'd unwound. Luka's arms around me started to have a different effect. I began to notice the press of his forearms against the undersides of my breasts and the feel of his muscles against my back. My whole body began to come to life, woken by his closeness.

I knew it was wrong. I knew it would soon be over between us and he'd hate me forever. But however much I told myself that, my body didn't listen. I kept looking into the rear view mirror and catching glimpses of us, his big body wrapped around my much smaller one, and the combination of his gentleness and his immense power, of how I was both protected and somehow captured by him, sent a slow, deep throb echoing through me.

In the elevator on the way up I twisted around in his arms and kissed him, soft and slow at first and then with quickly rising ferocity. By the time the doors opened, I had his shirt unfastened and my hands inside, sliding over the smooth slabs of his pecs. He gave a low growl and swept me up, one arm under my ass, and carried me inside. Then I was dumped back onto my feet on the polished wood floor and, as I stumbled in my heels—

My dress came up over my head, blocking my vision and trapping my arms for a second. Then it was gone and I was gasping and panting...and virtually naked. I'd gone for black underwear, this time, a half cup bra and a thong, both of them secured with thin ribbons.

The *va-va-voom* option, not the sweet virginal option. *Appropriate,* I thought bitterly, given that I was going to behave like a real femme fatale and stab him in the back.

But my guilt didn't do anything to slow the building heat inside me. I saw him rake his eyes down and then up my body, taking in my heels and stockings and the skimpy, glossy underwear. "Different," he rumbled after a second. "Not you. Someone else."

I nodded. I did kind of feel like someone else. Someone evil.

He stepped closer to me and put his fingers under my chin, lifting my head so that I met his eyes. "I know game we can play," he growled, his English fracturing in his eagerness. His hand cupped my breast, almost covering it completely. "Do you want to play game, Arianna?" he hissed.

This was new—he was turned on in a different, darker way than I'd seen him before. But I was panting, now, actually rubbing my thighs together to get friction. I wanted his hands all over me. I wanted his cock inside me. "Yes," I whispered.

He grabbed me and pulled me close, one hand squeezing my ass and one fondling my breast. I moaned.

Luka put his mouth close to my ear and whispered, *"I know you're CIA."*

44

It was like falling into water that was colder than any ice, a chill that soaked straight through skin and flesh to freeze your bones. I became a lifeless doll in his arms, limp and staring.

He scooped me up and started to carry me towards the bedroom.

I wasted precious seconds thinking *this is not happening, this can't be happening.* When I finally started to kick and struggle, we were almost at the door. I flung myself sideways, trying to launch myself from his grip, legs kicking and arms grabbing for the door frame.

He laughed.

I twisted around and tried to claw for his face and he trapped my wrists easily, pulling my arms behind my back until my shoulders burned. Then we were through the door and he threw me on the bed.

I didn't have time to get my arms in front of me to break my fall, so I landed with my hair in my face and the air knocked out of me. I twisted over onto my side, groaning, watching him approach. I saw his eyes track over my nearly-naked body. I was disgusted to find that there was still a dark tendril of excitement wrapped around my rising fear.

Then he was on me, using his weight to pin my legs and his hands to pin my shoulders, pushing me over onto my back. I began to fight again, thrashing and bucking under him, and that only made him grin. He reached into a drawer beside the bed and brought out something that made me freeze. A pair of shining steel handcuffs.

He wrestled my arms above my head and snapped the cuffs onto my wrists with practiced ease, hooking them around the iron bestead. A horrible, sinking feeling in the pit of my stomach as I realized *I really couldn't get free.* I heaved with my arms, using all my strength, but the handcuff chain just clinked and jingled against the iron. It was like a parody of all the times I'd pushed against his hands during sex, wanting to feel *helpless.* Except now I actually was. And my body, my traitorous fucking body, refused to acknowledge the difference. Seeing him hulking over me, still fully dressed, feeling myself bound and powerless beneath him in skimpy underwear, it responded. I could feel myself getting wet.

Enraged with myself, with him, with Adam for sending me on the mission in the first place, I lost it. I kicked him as hard as I could, but this wasn't like the woman at the club. My heel hit him in the stomach but it just glanced off the hard muscle there and he caught my ankle easily and pressed it to the bed. Then he did the same with my other leg and used his weight to pin them. Now I was held fast, stretched out on the bed with my arms above my head.

I stared up at him, my breath coming in panting heaves.

"Did you think I wouldn't guess?" he asked, his voice low and dangerous. "An American, all pretty and sweet, suddenly in my life. She acts innocent, so I'm tempted to corrupt her. But really, she's the one who's dark inside."

"I—I'm not CIA," I panted. "I swear, Luka." It didn't sound convincing even to me.

He suddenly lunged down and kissed me, forcing his tongue into my mouth. It was so unexpected I didn't have time to close my lips. His tongue brutally sought mine out and danced with it and, though I tried to twist my head away, I could feel the hot throb of pleasure go straight down to my groin. What was wrong with me?! Even now, I couldn't resist him.

He lifted his head and stared down at me. His words were like carefully sculpted weapons. "Don't lie to me, Arianna. I know you are."

My heart plummeted down through the bed. *When?* Had I not fooled his dad after all—had he tipped Luka off? Had it been on the yacht, when I'd mentioned Natalia's name? Or was it back at the party, when he saw me near his laptop? Had he known right from the start?

"I know you're CIA, sent to snake your way into my bed. Let's see you. Let's see the pretty little tits they sent to tempt me." His hand bunched in the front of my bra, there was a crack of snapping elastic and it was gone, a wadded ball of silk and ribbons in his hand, and I was topless.

He stared down at my breasts and I writhed, my head spinning. Any second, I knew, the interrogation would start. The brutal violence. Or maybe he wanted to enjoy my body one last time before he killed me.

He lowered his head and licked one breast, leaving the nipple shining, and I couldn't stop the delicate flesh puckering and hardening. He noticed and laughed. "Even now, your body's hot for me." He looked down. "Let's see how hot."

He ripped my panties away and cupped my sex, then plunged two fingers into me. I gasped and moaned, eyes wide. I could feel his fingertips sliding on my wetness. He brought them up to show me the glistening evidence of my arousal.

This was nuts. I knew he was going to kill me and I still wanted him. I wanted him no matter what.

"Now," he said. "What's your real name?"

"A—Arianna!" I gasped.

He nodded slowly, his eyes gleaming. He cupped one breast and rolled the nipple suggestively between finger and thumb, staring straight into my eyes. I started to huff air through my nostrils, panic-breathing. God, those hands were so powerful....

"What...is your real...*name?*" he asked again. And this time, he pinched my nipple. Not hard enough for it to be agony, not anywhere near as hard as he could have done. But enough for a white-hot bolt of pain to wrap around the pleasure and arc down to my groin. My back arched off the bed.

"I swear...." I panted. "My real name's Arianna!"

His eyes grew dark...and gleamed even more. "You want to do it hard way," he growled. "Well, is fine." I knew from the way his English was breaking down that he was getting more and more turned on. *God, he's enjoying this!*

He grabbed my hips and suddenly flipped me over onto my stomach. With no way to support myself, my breasts and face were mashed against the bedclothes.

"Tell me everything," he said in a hungry rasp. "Or you will know great pain."

Images flashed through my head. I knew what the Brotherhood did to traitors. There were a hundred horrible ways to die and many more ways I could be tortured before that. My fingernails could be pulled. My teeth extracted. I could be burned with cigarettes.

I knew I was going to break anyway. I wasn't some trained field agent like Nancy. I'd tell him everything I knew. Why not just do it fast and avoid some of the pain? Maybe he'd be merciful and kill me quickly.

But then I thought of Adam and how I would let him down. How I'd already let him down, by slipping up somewhere. I gathered up the shreds of strength I had left and took a deep breath. "No," I whispered.

He made a noise in his throat as if he preferred it that way. I screwed my eyes closed and waited for whatever would come next.

There was a flash of pain across my ass and a cracking sound that reverberated around the room. "*Bitch! Tell me name of your CIA handler!*"

My ass cheek throbbed and blazed. It sunk in that I'd just been spanked.

Spanked?!

Pain exploded in the other ass cheek, then faded to a dull, hot ache that seemed to soak inward towards my groin, making me writhe.

"*Whore!* I know you are spy! I find codebook in your suitcase!"

WHAT?! What codebook? I didn't have any codeboo—

And suddenly the scene reversed itself, black and white swapping over. His words from the yacht came back to me. *A sex game I used to play with Natalia. I'd be interrogating her. She used to pretend to be an American spy.*

I know game we can play, he'd said. He'd asked me if I wanted to play and, like a fool, I'd nodded.

A wave of relief crashed through me, leaving me breathless. He didn't know I was CIA at all. He was just playing the same sex game he had with Natalia. He had no idea I actually *was* a spy.

That's why it was a turn on, I told myself. That's why my body had responded the way it had. Somewhere in my subconscious, I must have known it wasn't real.

And now that I knew it wasn't real...I felt the heat soaring in my body. I pulled on the cuffs, tried to wriggle my legs from under his weight, but I was trapped. Powerless.

God...*powerless.*

Wait. I couldn't really do this. I couldn't get off on the fantasy of being caught and interrogated, when that was my greatest fear. That was too twisted. I couldn't. I really couldn't.

I couldn't. Right?

I started to pant. "I'll never talk!"

He gave a low chuckle, slid his hand underneath me and cupped a breast. Relief was still sluicing through me, leaving me weak and heady...and then he pinched my nipple, harder than before. Pain and pleasure mingled together, little white starbursts embedded in thick, dark heat. A sort of pressure was building, one I'd only felt briefly, before, when I'd pressed against his hands as he held me down. I had to let it out. But I didn't want him to stop. I wanted—

I wanted more.

"You—You Russian bastard!" I suddenly blurted. And it was like a safety valve for the pressure, while still allowing it to build.

Luka chuckled cruelly and suddenly his hand was cracking down across my ass, making the soft flesh bounce and burn. I cried out in a strangled moan.

"That's right," said Luka. "Moan like American whore." His hand came down again: *one, two three.*

I writhed and twisted under him, grinding my sex against the bed, wishing I could get more friction there. The fear I'd felt before was gone and its sudden departure had left a void. Relief had rushed in to fill it and now I was drunk on it, and that was making the pleasure and pain and lust even better.

Imagine sex on a rollercoaster, right after finding out you don't have cancer, after all.

He suddenly hauled me to my knees. My wrists were still cuffed to the bedstead, so my upper body had to stay low, my back arched and my breasts skimming the bed. My ass was thrust up into the air.

He shoved his hands between my thighs and opened me. I panted, the blood rushing in my ears. *"I—I'll never talk!"*

I heard the metal clink of his belt. The rustle of fabric as his pants fell to his knees. I tugged hard on the cuffs, the metal rubbing my wrists. "D—Do what you like to me!" I wasn't even aware of what I was saying, anymore. The heat inside me was like a furnace, melting me from the inside out. The words were just releasing the pressure, stopping me from exploding too soon. *"I'll never talk!"*

And then I felt the head of his cock splitting my folds and surging up into me and my eyes snapped wide. He drove all the way in with one long thrust and I groaned. I was already at the start of the slope that led to my release, rolling inexorably down towards it. "Never!" I shouted.

He pulled out and thrust into me again, his groin grinding against my ass, and I jerked at the feeling of being so completely filled. One of his hands slid under me and scooped up my breast, pinching the nipple between his fingers. "Beg me to fuck you," he hissed in my ear. He thrust again, making raw pleasure arc and snap from my quivering walls. Another thrust and another. *"Beg!"*

I could barely speak. This was beyond sex, now, beyond anything.

I was utterly lost, no longer even sure who I was. "Evil Russian b—bastard!" I shrieked.

His thrusts reached a peak, his hard body slapping against my upraised ass. His other hand snaked under me, his fingers finding my clit. I rocketed headlong towards my climax.

"Ah—*Please!*" I felt myself starting to spasm around him. "*I'll talk! Just please fuck me!*"

He rubbed me, playing me like an instrument as he fucked me, and all I could do was cling on as I slammed into my orgasm. I strained at the cuffs, arching my back, my fingers clutching at the bedstead. I'd never felt so completely out of control, or so alive.

The spasms lasted for what felt like minutes as he circled and rubbed at my clit. He drew the pleasure out and out for me as his hips pistoned against my upraised ass. Somewhere in my groaning and writhing, I felt him shudder and reach his own release.

Eventually, I slumped on the bed, spent. I felt him gently unfasten the cuffs and then pull me over onto my side, spooning me as my breathing gradually settled. "You'd make a lousy spy," he said with a low chuckle. "Natalia used to hold out for hours."

45

I must have fallen asleep because the next thing I remember is waking up in his arms. I lay there staring at the wall and took stock.

The pain from the spanking had long since faded—he hadn't actually hit me all that hard. My wrists were a little red from the cuffs, but that, too, would soon disappear.

What I couldn't get rid of was the guilt.

When I thought he knew, there'd been a moment when I was actually relieved. Even though I thought he was going to kill me, a little part of me was just glad not to have to lie anymore. How did other agents do this? *How does Nancy do this?!*

She doesn't fall in love with the target, I told myself bitterly.

I didn't care that it was too soon to use that word. I knew what I felt.

Stacked on top of the guilt from lying to him was the guilt at how easily I'd broken. I'd been ready to fold just at the mere threat of pain. If he ever *did* find out, I knew I'd roll over and give up my country in a heartbeat. Some spy I was. And then, when I discovered it was just a game, I'd gotten off on it. I'd come my brains out, screaming obscenities at him while he rode me harder and harder.

I was completely out of control. Not just during sex, but whenever I was around him. I needed to get out. And his father had provided the perfect excuse. I'd tell Luka I couldn't handle the gangster life, that I was scared for my safety, and his dad would back me up.

First, though, I had to talk to Adam. He hadn't heard from me since I left on the yacht. I knew he'd have people watching me from a distance, so he'd know I was okay. But he still didn't know about the scale of the arms deal.

It was time to do my job. It was time to betray Luka and finish this.

I woke him and told him that I had promised to meet a friend, someone I knew from back in the US who worked in Moscow, now. He didn't even ask her name or think that it was suspicious that I hadn't mentioned it before. That was what made it so difficult—that he trusted me so completely.

He smiled and said he'd make me breakfast. As I stumbled towards the wet room for a shower, he gave me a playful slap on the ass. "We should play that game more often," he said.

I forced myself to smile.

~

I met Adam in Red Square this time, hiding in plain sight amongst all the tourists. We stood looking up at the statue of Minin and Pozharsky, just a couple of American tourists comparing notes.

I told him about the guns I'd seen and the deal itself. He listened carefully when I described Luka's plan to take over the gun market. I handed him a tourist map on which I'd written the names of the buyers and the batch numbers of the crates of guns. He stared at it thoughtfully for a long time, then shook his head. "Unbelievable, Arianna. This is great work. Exactly what we needed."

The whole journey there, I'd been waiting for that moment. I'd been hoping that his praise would push back the awful guilt. But I didn't feel the same glow of pride I'd had in Gorky Park when I'd last met him. I just felt like a backstabbing rat.

I felt Adam's eyes on me. "Something wrong?"

I shook my head. "Just nervous. Not used to this."

He went to put his hand on my shoulder but then dropped it awkwardly. For just an instant, *he* looked guilty. "You'll be home soon," he said.

"Should I do it today?" I asked. "I mean...break up with him?"

Adam considered. "What are you meant to be doing with him, later today?"

"He's taking me out in the city, around where he grew up. He wants to show me his old apartment block and things."

Adam nodded slowly. "Stay with him for the rest of today. Make the break tonight and go back to your hotel. Make sure you keep your cell phone on, just in case I need to call you. Tomorrow morning, I'll have a car pick you up at nine a.m. and take you to the airport."

I'd known it was coming, but it was still like someone had slammed a wrench into my chest. Tomorrow, I'd go home and then I'd never see Luka again.

Two hours later, we were in Luka's car with Yuri behind the wheel. I craned my head to look out at the apartment blocks on either side: grim monoliths of concrete encircled by rusting cars, some burned out. Garbage was mixed in amongst the overgrown grass. Graffiti covered every available surface that could possibly be reached, even if it meant leaning precariously out from a balcony. The mood was somber, but it wasn't just the war-zone surroundings. There'd been a tension between us ever since I got back from meeting Adam. The knowledge of what I had to do hung over me like a storm cloud and Luka could sense it, too.

"This is where you grew up?" I asked.

"No. But I wanted you to see this first," said Luka.

We drove on, no more than five minutes. We swung into a similar neighborhood. Similar in some ways, at least. The apartment blocks were the same, but there was no graffiti at all. There were no wrecked cars and the lawns were green, the grass short. The people looked...normal. Mothers with strollers, people going to and from work. A poor neighborhood, but a good one.

"This is where I grew up. This was Brotherhood territory. Malakov territory." He looked around. "My father and I walked the streets, meeting the people, checking they were okay. Kicking out the ones who tried to deal drugs."

The guilt was churning in my stomach. I wanted to find something bad, something about him that would make me feel better about betraying him. "You make it sound like you were protecting them," I said. "But you're talking about protection *money,* aren't you? You weren't looking after them out of the goodness of your heart."

He frowned and then nodded. "Yes. The businesses paid, not the individuals. But in return, we really did look after them. No drugs where people lived. No street crime." He sighed. "I'm not saying we're good people. But we created order. You remember the neighborhood we just drove through?"

I nodded.

"Ralavich territory. They take the money and give nothing back. The alternative to order is chaos."

I tried to hate him. I tried so hard. But in this broken world where vultures like Ralavich would sweep in and tear neighborhoods to pieces, was his way really so bad?

Despite all my instincts, I was beginning to understand. The coldness I'd seen when I'd first met him was a shield, because showing weakness would be fatal in his world. The brutal violence I'd seen was horrifying...but maybe it was necessary.

I closed my eyes. Jesus, what was I becoming? Was I really justifying what he'd done? I'd seen him beat a man nearly to death— he would have killed him, if I hadn't intervened. And yes, part of me had wanted the guy dead, at that moment, because of what he'd done to those women. But that didn't make it right.

I realized he was staring at me, waiting for a reaction. I shook my head. "I can't...I understand, but I can't—"

"I never lied to you about what I was, Arianna," he said. He said it gently, but I could hear the concern in his voice. The frustration. He could sense, on some level, that I was going to end it.

I nodded miserably.

"I can show you the hospital where my mother died," he said. "I can show you where they gave me my tattoos. I'm showing you my past."

"*Why?*" I said desperately. "Why?"

"Because if I share my past, maybe you'll share yours, too." He stroked my cheek and then tucked a lock of hair back behind my ear. "I want to help you, Arianna. You are too good a person to be in so much pain." He shook his head. "Even if you won't be with me, I want you to be happy."

I don't deserve that. Even if talking about the crash would help, what right did I have to feel better, when I was about to destroy his whole life?

I closed my eyes, trying to stop the tears coming. I couldn't last until that evening. I had to do it now. "Luka," I said. "We have to talk."

And that's when the truck slammed into the side of the car.

That sickening flying feeling I'd felt once before, and countless times afterwards in flashbacks. This time, we didn't just skid and then fall. We shot sideways, Luka's body crashing against mine, our heads almost cracking together. Then there was a crunching impact right on the other side of my door and we were flipping. I lifted off my seat, weightless for an instant. The ceiling became the wall and then the floor.

We did a full turn in the air. The car slammed down onto its wheels and my spine felt as if it was trying to force its way through my head. Then silence, except for a hiss of steam from the engine.

I looked around. The air was full of choking white dust from where the airbags had fired. They were all around us, cushioning us from the sides of the car. The car itself seemed to have stayed in shape, although most of the windows were cracked. Beside me, Luka was groaning but awake. Yuri was slumped over the wheel, either unconscious or dead.

The door next to me was wrenched open and hands freed my

seatbelt and hauled me out. I was still blinking from the dust and I thought for a moment that they were police, and that we were being rescued.

Then I saw the van, with the door already open.

A bag came down over my head.

I felt myself being lifted inside, then shoved down against the van's floor. Hands wrenched my wrists behind my back.

I screamed *"Luka!"* and I thought I heard him shout my name in response.

Something hard surrounded my wrists and pulled tight. A second later, another one tightened around my ankles. Then a hard circle of metal pressed against my cheek through the bag. The barrel of a gun.

I stopped screaming.

The van's suspension sunk as Luka's muscled body landed next to mine. I heard him kicking and thrashing as they tried to secure him.

"Stop struggling," said a voice in Russian. "Or we kill your little bitch."

Luka went still.

And the van sped off.

46

I don't know how long we drove for. My heart was hammering so fast that I thought I was having a heart attack. The bag over my face meant I couldn't breathe properly and someone was still pushing a gun into my cheek.

Then I felt something against my hand. A big, strong finger rubbing against my thumb. Luka had stretched out his bound hands to meet mine. I grabbed his finger and clung to it with all my strength.

Minutes or hours later, I was hauled out and thrown to the floor. I cried out as my shoulder hit concrete. Luka landed with a grunt next to me.

I was pulled up to an awkward sitting position and the bag was pulled off my head.

Darkness. The person who'd pulled off the bag stepped back into the shadows and disappeared, leaving Luka and I alone. A lone light overhead cast a pool of light around us.

"Are you okay?" asked Luka.

I nodded breathlessly.

"No," said a voice from the darkness. He spoke English, but with a strong Russian accent. "She's not. Because she's with you."

From the echo, the room was vast. A warehouse, maybe. I searched the darkness for any sign of the man who'd spoken, but there was just blackness.

Then a single point of light exploded, glaringly bright. A match. A second later, a cigarette tip glowed orange.

He walked towards us out of the shadows. A short man in a cheap gray suit. I'd never seen him before, but his piggish eyes reminded me of his son's.

"Hello, Arianna," said Olaf Ralavich.

47

I twisted away from him, trying to get closer to Luka. He laughed and squatted down near our bound feet. I knew he was the equivalent of Vasiliy and must be about the same age. But time hadn't been so kind to the head of the Ralavich family. Where Vasiliy had maintained his muscles, Olaf was flabby. And where Vasiliy radiated a kind of cold, calculated charm, Olaf was all swagger and brutish violence. A thug, not a criminal.

And he was staring right at me with those dark little deep-set eyes.

"So you're the one who saved my son," he said to me. His English surprised me—it was at least the equal of Vasiliy's or Luka's. But he spoke with a sneer I couldn't imagine either of them using. Vasiliy might have hated me—maybe still did—but he'd never sounded like this. Olaf spoke as if I was a lower species, as if all women were.

He turned to Luka. "I heard you were letting some *blyadischa* order you around," he said, glancing at me as he casually called me a whore. "But I didn't believe it until now. What is it she's got between her legs, Luka, that gives her such power? Shall we see?"

Luka kicked out viciously, but Olaf dodged it easily, laughing. My blood ran cold. We were all alone here, tied up and powerless. Easy targets for whatever Olaf and his men wanted to do to us.

Olaf walked around to our heads and squatted down again. "My son is still in the hospital. They may not be able to fix his face. Only the whores will want to fuck him, now."

"He was chaining up women," said Luka in a low growl. Even bound on the floor, he managed to exude menace. If he was scared, he didn't show it. "Letting men pay to rape them. I should have killed him."

"If you had," said Olaf mildly, "I would have killed you already. But since you just made him suffer, I'll just make you suffer. I'm going to teach you a lesson, Luka. About how you and your father can't just steal our business."

Shit! This wasn't just about Luka beating Olaf's son. This was about the gun deal. But how did they even know about that? I stared at Luka, terrified. Now they'd beat him, right in front of me.

Two men stepped out of the shadows and grabbed Luka's shoulders, then hauled him up to his knees. He struggled, but they knelt behind him, their knees grinding painfully into the backs of his legs, pinning him there. Then they wound their fingers into his hair so that his head was held still.

Olaf pulled out a knife and my blood turned to ice water. But then he crouched down and cut the zip-tie that bound my ankles. I looked up at him in confusion and hope.

Olaf grinned. "She's going to have to open her legs," he explained.

I remember screaming—a single, long wail of horror that left my throat raw. Then I started shuffling away from him across the filthy concrete floor.

Someone behind me put their boot against my shoulder, stopping me from moving any further.

"Don't you *touch her!*" screamed Luka. For the first time, there was fear in his eyes. He hadn't cared what they did to him. But this...I knew this would tear him apart.

I tried to struggle to my feet, but my hands were still bound behind my back. Olaf grabbed the front of my dress and pulled it away from my body, as if he was going to lift me up by it. Then he slashed with the knife again, cutting it all the way down the front. My bra strap was sliced through and then I felt the cold of the knife against my groin and my panties were cut.

I writhed in disgust, trying to hide my nakedness from him, trying to turn over. He put his shoe on my bare shoulder and slammed me back down onto my back, then hunkered down over me. He stared into my eyes, but spoke to Luka.

"First," he said, "I'm going to fuck her. Then my men will fuck her. Then we're going to take her to one of our places—you know the sort, Luka. The ones that made you so angry. We'll chain her up and let the suits play with her. They'll like a nice American girl. We'll get her some new dresses, so they can rip them off. *Again and again.*"

Luka thrashed and pulled at the men holding him, almost tearing his hair out by his roots. But they held him fast.

I stared up at Olaf. This wasn't anything like the games I'd played with Luka. All I felt was sick, cold fear.

Olaf unfastened his belt. "Hold her down."

The room suddenly burst into light and noise. It was as if dawn had broken in fast-forward, a slice of light sweeping across the floor until it filled the whole room. It was so bright, after the darkness, that I couldn't see a thing. There was a rumbling like the end of the world and the roar of car engines. I twisted and tried to cover myself, screwing my eyes closed and pulling myself into a tight little ball on my side. For long seconds, all I could hear was gunfire. I prayed for death. That would be better than what they'd been going to do to me.

Running footsteps and shouting in Russian. Then a voice I recognized.

Yuri.

Something soft dropped over me. I opened my eyes.

The first thing I saw was a man I didn't recognize—one of Olaf's men, I presumed—lying on the floor just a few feet away. He'd been shot through the head.

I turned away from him, trying not to throw up.

Yuri was standing behind Luka, cutting him free. The last time I'd seen the head bodyguard had been in the car, after the crash. "I thought you were dead," I croaked.

Yuri grimaced. "Death would have been less painful," he said. He was bleeding from a cut on his head and I saw that he was using only one arm, the other hanging at an odd angle. Somehow, though, he'd managed to pull off his suit jacket to lay over me.

Free at last, Luka got to his feet and ran to me, sweeping me up into his arms. I looked around, blinking in the sudden light.

We were in a warehouse, as I'd suspected. But now the huge door at one end was open, letting in daylight. Two black SUVs were parked just inside. The whole place was swarming with men in black combat fatigues. Vasiliy had sent an army.

I looked back to Yuri. "How did you...?"

Yuri snorted. "Idiots think I'm dead in car and don't put bullet in my head. I wake up and you and Luka are gone." He nodded at Luka. "I track his cell phone and call Vasiliy for backup."

I looked up at him in wonder. I'd always thought of Yuri as just a big, dumb lunk. I was just realizing he was a superb bodyguard, something he hid behind his dour manner. Probably deliberately.

Yuri caught my look. "Is not—how you say it?—is not my first rodeo."

Luka looked down at me and tenderly stroked my cheek. He didn't ask if I was okay—I think he could see that I wasn't. He just stared into my eyes, his own full of guilt and pain.

One of Vasiliy's men staggered up to us. "Olaf got out the back."

Yuri swore and kicked one of the dead bodies. Then he nodded us towards the SUVs. "We go. Before police arrive."

Luka carried me towards one of the SUVs. I looked around at the devastation as we went. Six dead, two of them Vasiliy's men. I started to shake in Luka's arms.

"It's okay," he whispered. "It'll be okay."

I knew it wouldn't be. I saw now just how brutal his world could be. Tomorrow, I'd escape it forever...and lose Luka forever. And with Olaf gunning for him like this, I knew it was only a matter of time until this world killed him.

48

"*Those fucking fucking fucks!*" yelled Vasiliy in Russian. "*Who the fuck do they think they are?!*"

The SUVs had taken us directly to his house—Vasiliy had insisted. There was an antique suit of armor at the top of the stairs and I watched as Vasiliy kicked it apart, sending metal clattering down the stairs. "*Fucking fat little jumped up son of a whore thinks he can threaten us?!*"

He spun to face me, his chest heaving with rage. "You sure you're okay?" he asked in English.

I nodded. I was wearing a spare set of combat fatigues which Yuri had found for me. They were enormous and looked ridiculous, but at least they covered me and that made me feel better.

"*No one*," spat Vasiliy, "messes with my family." He said it in English and he met my eyes as he said it. There was regret there, beneath the anger. An apology for not trusting me, before. I was one of them, now, and the thought send an unexpected flood of warmth through me.

I'd never really been conscious of how much I missed having a family until that moment. And then I remembered how I was about to betray them, and I wanted to be sick.

"He won't stop," said Luka. "Not unless we abandon the gun deal." His voice didn't leave any shred of a possibility that that was going to happen. He was as stubborn and as proud as his dad.

Vasiliy started to curse again, talking about payback. Then he remembered me and sighed, shaking his head. "My apologies, Arianna. You do not need to hear this. The maids have prepared a room for you and Luka. Please."

Being able to take a hot bath to wash Olaf's touch off me sounded like the best thing in the world. But first, I gave Luka a long hug. "You'll stay right here?" I asked. "You won't go off on some stupid revenge attack?"

He touched his forehead to mine and let out a long sigh. "There will have to be retribution. But not tonight, *myshka*. I'll be here." He hugged me close and then took my face between his hands. "I never meant to let my life hurt you, Arianna. I'm sorry."

I felt hot tears welling up in my eyes. *He* was sorry, and I was about to destroy him. I nodded quickly and turned away, trudging up the stairs to the next floor.

I knew that the next morning, just as I ran out on him, he'd be ready to go and attack Olaf and his gang, turning this into a full-on war between the families. Maybe, *maybe* he'd survive the next few days...just long enough for the authorities to arrest him. I actually started to wish that I could betray him sooner. At least in prison, he'd be safe.

Or would he? I knew that the gangs controlled the prisons. Did the Malakovs have the right influence in the right places? Was it better that Luka was shot in a gang war or stabbed to death in a prison yard?

I sighed and shut myself in the bedroom. Like the rest of the house, it was luxuriously appointed. There was a bathroom with a huge corner tub and I immediately ran a deep, hot bath. I stripped off my clothes and climbed in, letting the heat soak into me. It made me feel cleaner on the outside...but it didn't do anything to lift the deep, dark stain that was spreading through my insides.

I was lying almost completely submerged when a noise from the bedroom startled me. My cell phone ringing. It was in my purse, which had been with me in the car when Olaf had attacked us. Now the purse was on the bed—Yuri must have salvaged it from the wreckage.

I jumped out of the tub, naked and dripping. For Adam to be calling, something must be wrong. Maybe he couldn't extract me tomorrow. I grabbed the phone and was holding it in my hand, about to answer, when a thought echoed in my head. Something that had been swimming around and around ever since the warehouse. *How did Olaf know where to ambush us?*

My phone had been with me in the car. And Adam had told me to make sure I kept it switched on.

He'd tracked me and guided Olaf right to us.

I fell to my knees in defeat as I answered the call.

"Hello, Arianna," said Adam.

"You're working with Olaf Ralavich," I whispered.

49

I sat there naked, the water drying on my body, as the pieces dropped into place. Vasiliy and his dad had both talked about the "corrupt CIA" who controlled the guns and drugs. It had never occurred to me that it might actually be true.

Adam knew Russia. He'd worked in Moscow for years. When he moved up to head of the Special Activities Division at Langley, he was in the perfect position to help his Russian friends get their guns into the US. Hell, he might have even sought the position for that exact reason. He'd probably been squirreling millions away in Swiss accounts, a cut of every gun deal the Ralavichs had done.

Until he'd heard that the Malakovs were trying to muscle in, of course. Then he'd panicked. He'd needed someone to get information on the deal. Someone utterly disposable, someone too naive and eager to please to question why Malakov was such a high priority.

I'd been a pawn, right from the start. Roberta, Nancy...they'd tried to warn me something was wrong and I'd ignored them.

"You don't want Luka arrested," I said. "You never did. You want him dead."

Adam made a scoffing noise. "I don't give a shit about Luka.

Vasiliy still controls the deals. Without his face and name, the buyers will come running back to Olaf." He sighed. "Fucking Olaf. I told him trying to scare Vasiliy off wouldn't work. So we'll just have to move to plan B."

"You're going to kill him," I whispered in disbelief. "You're going to kill Vasiliy."

"No," said Adam. "You are."

50

"After this call," said Adam, "you'll take the back off the cell phone and remove the battery. There's a capsule filled with liquid. You're going to dump that into Vasiliy's drink."

"Poison."

"A drug. He'll have a heart attack a few hours later."

"Never. Jesus, you must know that. You know I won't do it."

"Oh, but you haven't heard the best part," said Adam. I could hear the victorious smile in his voice. "You haven't heard what I'll give you in return."

"I don't want it!" I almost shouted it. "Whatever it is, I don't want it!"

He paused for effect. "You get Luka."

There was silence for a moment.

"I only want Vasiliy," said Adam. "Luka walks. And with the gun deal in pieces, I'm sure someone as...*persuasive* as you can tempt him away from crime. You can have a life together."

I sat there stunned. It was everything I wanted. Luka and I could jet off into the sunset. He'd never need to know I was CIA. I could be with him.

If I killed his father.

I shook my head, ashamed that I'd considered it even for a split second. "Go fuck yourself," I hissed.

Adam sighed. "Then you leave me no choice. I'll have both Vasiliy *and* Luka taken out."

"You—-You said you didn't care about Luka!"

"I wanted to do it clean and quiet, with no questions from the authorities. A heart attack does that. But if you're going to force me to openly kill Vasiliy, I might as well take his son, too. Wouldn't want him coming after me for revenge. And you know I have the resources to do it. I just wanted to exhaust every other avenue first."

"*Please!*" I begged.

"Don't be pathetic, Arianna. Make a choice. We both know which one you're going to choose."

I slumped against the wall, my brain racing, searching for a way out and finding none. The thought of killing Vasiliy made me sick. But the idea of losing Luka as well....

My silence was all the answer he needed.

"Good girl," said Adam. "I'm proud of you, Arianna. I always knew you had potential."

I wanted to hurl the phone across the room, but I couldn't because I couldn't risk damaging the capsule. I wanted to howl in anger but I couldn't risk Luka hearing. So, as Adam ended the call, all I could do was thump my fists uselessly on the bed. And then slump to the floor, the shame of my own stupidity coming out as hot, painful tears.

51

By the time I'd cleaned myself up, it was nearly time to do it. I couldn't risk Vasiliy going to bed. If he was still alive in the morning and Adam got wind of it, he'd think I'd double crossed him and kill Vasiliy and Luka as well.

A brand new dress and underwear had been discreetly hung on the doorknob of the bedroom while I'd been bathing—Luka must have sent one of the maids out to buy them. With them on and the necklace Luka bought me around my neck, I felt a little more human.

For a second. Until I remembered what I was about to do.

Yuri was at the foot of the stairs, cleaning one of his many guns. His arm was in a sling. He looked up at me. "Okay?" he asked gruffly.

I nodded.

"I'm sorry," he said. "I should have sent more men to the back of the warehouse. Olaf should not have got away." He pushed the magazine into the gun with a vicious snap.

"It's okay," I said comfortingly.

He jumped to his feet. He wasn't quite as big as Luka, but his size was still intimidating, especially when he was angry. "Is *not* okay." He stared at me. "Bastard takes Luka, takes *you*...he needs to die. He's pure poison. Always has been."

There was something in his eyes—a more intense version of that sadness that always seemed to be there. I suddenly knew who'd given him the scar across his face.

I put a hand on his arm. "You did great, Yuri," I said softly. "You rescued us. Without you...."

I didn't want to think about what would have happened without him. I could still feel Olaf's hands, cutting my dress away. Before I was even aware I was going to do it, I pulled the big man into a hug, wrapping my arms around him and patting him on the back. He responded awkwardly, as if no one had hugged him in a very long time.

When I unwound myself, he said, "Luka likes you."

I nodded.

"I think that maybe you are what he needs," said Yuri.

I nodded again.

"But I'm there to protect him," said Yuri, the loyalty fierce in his eyes. "From everyone."

"I understand," I said levelly.

He nodded solemnly, as if to say that we'd never mention this conversation again, and went back to cleaning his gun.

I found Luka and Vasiliy in the drawing room, looking at something on a laptop. Blueprints of a house, presumably Olaf's. Luka reached for the lid to close it as I walked in....and then relaxed and left it open.

He trusted me. He finally trusted me enough to have no secrets from me. Just as I was about to destroy his life.

He came over to me and put his arms around me. "What's the matter?" he asked. "You look worried."

I stared into his eyes and drew in a long breath. "I—" *Tell him.* "I —" *Tell him!*

Vasiliy was looking at me, too. He walked around from behind his son. "Arianna," he said, his accent rolling around my name like rocks grinding it smooth, "I owe you an apology. When you came here before, when you indulged me by playing chess...I did not trust you."

He suddenly grabbed my hands, squeezing them in his. I felt as if I was contaminating him with my sins. My own hands felt like cold, dead flesh. "Luka was right about you," he said. "And I am honored—*honored*—to welcome you into our family."

My mouth moved soundlessly. I could feel the tears rushing towards my eyes. *God, no! Don't do this to me! Not now!*

"Leave her alone," Luka muttered. "She's been through enough without being pressured."

Vasiliy smiled kindly at me and released my hands. They throbbed from his warmth. "I'm sorry. Don't mind me, Arianna. I'm not looking for you to marry him."

"Father!" Luka's cheeks were flushing.

"Not yet, at least."

"*Father!*"

Vasiliy's eyes were twinkling. Any other time, it would have been funny and wonderful. Now, it just made me want to vomit up all the darkness inside me. No, I wanted to run to the stairs and hurl myself over the edge, down to the bare stone floor below. Maybe I'd crack my skull open and maybe then I wouldn't be a threat to them anymore.

But even that wasn't an option. Ever since Adam's phone call, we'd all been locked into our fate. The only question was how many of them I was going to kill.

And really, there's only one answer to that. I'm a geek at heart. I know how to do math. One death is better than two.

"Maybe we could have a drink," I said, surprised at how level my voice was. "To celebrate."

Luka looked at me, surprised, but then smiled. Vasiliy led us down the corridor to the tiny room where he'd questioned me, and poured whiskey for himself and vodka for us.

I had the tiny capsule in the palm of one hand. The two of them were so happy, it was easy to pick up Vasiliy's glass for a second and crush the plastic against the rim so that the clear fluid dribbled into the whiskey.

"To family," Vasiliy said, picking up his glass.

"To family," Luka repeated.

"Family," I said in a hollow voice.

We all raised our glasses to drink.

Time seemed to stop. I was in the car again, the wheels sliding over the snow. Falling and falling, the ground coming up to meet us.

I couldn't do it.

I slapped Vasiliy's glass away from his mouth, cracking it against his teeth and spilling the drink down his shirt. He cursed in Russian and frowned at me.

The glass hit the floor and shattered.

With anyone else, in any other country, Luka's next words would have been *What are you doing?!* But he was Luka Malakov and this was Russia, and both he and Vasiliy had been living this life for far too long.

I turned to Luka to see his face going pale. I could feel the tears forming in my eyes, too powerful to stop. "I'm sorry," I managed to get out.

"What did you do?" said Luka.

I shook my head.

"What did you do?!" Luka thundered.

"They're going to kill you," I whispered. "They're going to kill you both." I looked at Vasiliy. "Killing you was the only way to stop it." I looked back to Luka, trying to drink in a last glimpse of him through the blur of tears. "I'm sorry. I'm CIA."

He stared at me for three quick breaths. Then he stepped behind the table, pulled open a drawer and grabbed a handgun. He pointed the barrel right at my head.

I closed my eyes and waited for the bullet.

"Get out," I heard at last. Luka's voice, but choked up with so much emotion that it barely sounded like him.

I opened my eyes and stared at him, tears coursing down my cheeks. "They're going to kill you!" I sobbed.

"GET OUT!" he screamed. I saw his finger tense on the trigger.

I turned and ran, blundering down the stairs. I staggered on my heels, half-blinded by tears. I finally made it to the front door and out, past the bewildered guards.

I ran. I didn't know where I was going or even where I was. I had nothing but the dress I was wearing.

I was still running when the cell phone Adam gave me rang. I stared at it in disgust for three rings before I answered.

"I had someone watching the house," he said. "They saw you run out. I'm disappointed, Arianna."

"Fuck you," I told him with bravery I didn't feel.

"No," he said coldly. "You see, you no longer work for the CIA. You've been officially recorded as switching sides to the enemy. You're on your own. Arianna Ross no longer exists. If you try to use her passport or credit cards, the authorities will pick you up for fraud. And, as far as we know, Arianna *Scott* is an unemployed languages graduate who's still in the US."

I shook my head. "You can't do this—"

"So really, Arianna, it's fuck *you*." And he hung up.

Seconds later, the cell phone went dead, its number disconnected.

I staggered to a stop by a payphone and tried calling the CIA main switchboard. None of my access codes worked. I'd been completely erased.

The CIA had disavowed me as a traitor. And that meant that I could never convince them of what Adam had done.

Vasiliy was still going to die and now, Luka as well. I'd condemned him with my own weakness. And Adam was going to get away with it. He'd keep on making millions from the gun trade and that bastard Olaf Ralavich would take control of the whole of the North American gun trade—only his smuggling would have all of the violence Luka had been working to end.

I was only wearing a dress. It was starting to snow, the flakes turned into little daggers of ice by a bitter north wind, stabbing the cold into my exposed arms and face. But I was past caring. The cold soaking into my body from the outside was nothing compared to the way I was freezing up inside. All the parts of me Luka had brought back to life were shutting down again, this time forever. I'd lost him, the one man who could have saved me.

I slumped down beside the payphone, hugged my knees and sobbed.

The wind scoured my skin and pushed the warmth inside me deeper and deeper, like an animal withdrawing into its burrow. I could feel myself losing feeling in my hands and toes, but the loss of caring was worse. I no longer saw the people passing by on the street —my eyes just stared fixedly ahead. I no longer felt the sidewalk under me as I sat, or smelled the exhaust fumes from the traffic as it rushed past. I felt as if I was floating.

The warmth receded and receded inside me. My head grew swimmy and my thoughts slowed and became big, lumbering barges creaking through ice. I don't know how long I sat there—an hour? More? I shivered at first, but then I stopped and just felt sleepy.

I was sitting in the snow on a windswept street with the temperature well below zero. My thin dress was soaked through and just made the cold sink in faster.

Somewhere, on a very distant level, I knew I was going to die.

But I'd been there before, trapped in a car, screaming, and this creeping cold was easier and quicker. I could just let my eyelids close and go to sleep.

52

There was a particle in the darkness of my mind. Orange-red and glowing, defiantly alight despite the freezing wind that whipped around it. I couldn't go to sleep until it flickered out and it was taking its sweet time.

That little spark of warmth hadn't been there, back in the crashed car. It was something new. And the more the coldness pressed in around it, the brighter it burned, until it glowed bright enough that I could see its shape.

Luka.

Insane. A man who hated me. Who never even knew the real me. Who I'd used and betrayed. Who I'd thought of as a monster and tried to change, when the real monster was me. To cling onto his memory was pathetic. *If he was here right now, if he found me like this, he'd probably put a bullet in my brain.*

I waited for the spark to go out...but it wouldn't. Not even the thought that he hated me stopped me loving him.

I didn't want to see him die. It wasn't much of a wish, even as deathbed wishes go, but it was all I had. I knew I'd lost him; I knew I was as good as dead myself, from the cold or Luka's people or

Ralavich's people, if any of them saw me. But I didn't want to take Luka with me.

The cold was welcoming me with open arms, drawing me down into it. But I couldn't give myself up to it completely. My love for him wouldn't let me.

I opened my eyes.

At some point, I'd slumped onto my side. I was half-covered in snow, huddled up against a low concrete wall. The sun had set.

I tried to move and found I couldn't. Nothing worked. My muscles wouldn't respond. I lay there like a puppet with her strings cut.

A woman walked past and didn't even look at me. I was just another passed-out whore sleeping off the drugs, or dead.

I tried to twitch a leg and felt the sick, lurching fear of being paralyzed. My body had completely shut down. My heart had probably slowed so much it had almost stopped, my breathing, too. Anyone finding me would think I was dead. In another few minutes, they'd be right.

I thought of Luka and the ballet and the stateroom on his yacht. Of the restaurant and the ice rink and the party and the way he'd held me that time in the car.

I heaved with every ounce of will I had and my left leg shifted a few millimeters. It felt like lead. And then the pain started, exploding up through my calves and thighs. Every nerve felt as if it was being shredded. But pain was good. Pain meant I was still alive.

It took long minutes, but I managed to roll onto my front and then get to my knees. My legs were too shaky to carry me. The wind was whipping the snow into a full-on blizzard, my clothes plastered white.

I crawled to the edge of the sidewalk and knelt there, my arms held straight up above my head, and prayed a cab would stop. I was about to give up hope when headlights bathed me and an aging Mercedes pulled up. The driver looked at my dress, filthy from lying in the street, and at my snow-soaked hair. He must have wondered whether I was a well-dressed hooker or a debutante who'd been mugged. "You have money?" he asked in Russian.

I had nothing. I'd run out of Vasiliy's house without my purse. But I was wearing the necklace Luka had given me and I managed to lift it away from my neck to show him.

He grumbled and then got out and lifted me into the back seat of his car. We drove through the streets with the heater on full blast and, gradually, I thawed out. More pain, as the feeling came back, and then the shivering started. I took off the necklace and gave it to him. "Thank you," I said in English.

He stared at me in surprise. "You American?" he asked in English. He looked again at my bedraggled appearance. "You want go embassy?"

I shook my head. My brain was finally starting to work again. "I want you to take me somewhere there's a payphone," I said in Russian. "And I need you to loan me a little money."

Given that the necklace probably cost more than his car, the cab driver didn't grumble too much about handing over the equivalent of fifty dollars. He even took me to the taxi company and let me use the phone there and bought me a cup of coffee. It was scalding hot and strong and the best thing I'd ever tasted.

I knew it was no good going through the CIA switchboard—I didn't exist anymore, to them. But I'd called her at home before and I only need to see a phone number once to memorize it.

"Hello?" said Roberta.

It was the middle of the day, there, and she was at home. That was good for me and almost certainly bad for her.

"I fucked up," I croaked. I hadn't been ready for how hard it would hit me. Hearing a familiar voice was a reminder of everything I'd lost. If I closed my eyes, I could almost pretend I was back in the safe little languages department again.

"*Where are you?!*" Roberta said. Then, just as fast, "No! Wait!"

Seconds ticked by as she thought.

"Stay by the phone," Roberta said. And hung up.

Thirty seconds later, the phone rang. "OK," said Roberta. "This is one of my emergency cell phones. Bought it for cash so I'm pretty sure it's not tapped. Now what the fuck is going on?"

She kept "burner" cell phones around, just for emergencies?! I'd always thought of Roberta as a mother hen, as comfortable in her safe little world of languages as I was. This was a reminder that she'd been a field agent, once.

"What do you know?" I asked. "What's happening there?"

Roberta took a deep breath. "Adam says you switched sides and ran off with Luka. Everyone's been told not to speak to you. *I* shouldn't be speaking to you. Hell, I've been suspended while they investigate!"

"Roberta, that's not what happened! Adam's working with Luka's rivals—I think he has been for years. He tried to get me to kill Luka's dad. He's going to have both of them killed."

Roberta went very quiet. "Do you have any proof?" she asked at last.

I bit my lip. "No. None."

Silence.

"Do you believe me?!" I begged.

Roberta sighed. "Yes. I knew you were in over your head, but I didn't think you'd betray us." Her voice hardened. "Jesus...*Adam.* I always hated that prick."

The tears started. I think it was hearing that she believed me. That *someone* out there was still on my side. "You were right all along," I whispered. "You tried to tell me. You tried to persuade me not to come. I'm sorry, mom."

I sniffed and then realized I'd called my boss *mom.* It hung in the air between us, but she was nice enough not to mention it.

"Roberta," I said, "he's going to have Luka killed. His dad, too. I have to save them."

"No. The smartest thing you can do is get far, far away. Get outside Moscow and wait it out. I'll wire you money—"

"I'm in love with him."

When Roberta spoke again, her voice was soft. "Arianna—"

I cut her off. "I know it's wrong, okay?! I know I haven't known him long enough! *I don't care!* I know how I feel and I have to save him! Now, are you going to help me or not?"

There was shocked silence for a moment.

"I may have underestimated you, Arianna," she said, a hint of a smile in her voice. "Okay. What do you need from me?"

Roberta had been suspended, but she had enough loyal friends at the CIA that she could get me what I needed: satellite imagery of Vasiliy's house, earlier that evening. I needed to know if Luka was still there. When she told me that he and Vasiliy had left an hour ago, my stomach contracted into a tight little knot. Vasiliy spent most of his time cooped up in that fortress of a house. Why would he leave it now?

And then it hit me. I'd told Luka that his life was in danger and he had responded with exactly the sort of arrogant swagger that made everyone fear him. He and Vasiliy weren't going to hole up at home. They were going to go right out in public, where everyone could see them. And with most enemies maybe that bravery would have worked. The gangs kept most of their violence off the radar. Even Ralavich had taken us off to a warehouse to kill us.

But they didn't realize how determined Adam was, or what levels he'd stoop to.

"Find out where they went," I pleaded.

Minutes later, Roberta had followed the car to its destination. She said the name of the restaurant and started to give me the address, but I was already running to the cab driver and pleading with him to take me on one more trip. I knew the restaurant. It was where we'd had lunch, our first real date.

I was going to finish this at the same place we'd started it. And I knew there was a very good chance I wouldn't come out alive.

53

I'd managed to clean my face up a little. But my dress was still soaking wet, my hair was a tangled mess and my face was almost as white as the snow outside. I saw the doormen hesitate as I walked up the steps to the restaurant.

"I'm with Luka Malakov," I told them. One of them doubtfully showed me in. I'd told the cab driver to leave me there—however this worked out, it was going to be dangerous and he'd done enough for me.

Luka and Vasiliy were at the same table I'd sat at with Luka—his usual table, I guessed, although something looked different. There was food already on the table and wine, too. The tables around theirs had fallen into a sort of awed hush as people realized who they were sitting close to.

Yuri was standing just a few feet behind them, keeping watch. He spotted me first and said something in Luka's ear.

Luka had been looking down at his food. Now his head snapped up and he looked right at me. My breath caught in my throat. Even with everything that had gone wrong between us, my heart gave the same lurch and then mad rush that it always did when I saw him. But

God, the ice in his eyes, the raw, hot anger that shot across the space between us—it tore me apart.

I put my hand up in front of me. "I'm sorry—"

Luka stood, pushing his chair back so hard it clattered to the floor. He half-turned, reached his hand under Yuri's jacket and returned holding a gun. A gun he pointed straight at me.

People around me started screaming. For all they knew who Luka was, for all they'd heard about the Brotherhood and their crimes, they didn't expect to actually see things happening right in front of them. No one would be crazy enough to shoot someone in a crowded restaurant.

But if there was one person powerful enough to do it and get away with it, it was Luka.

"I'm not here to argue with you," I managed to say. "You need my help."

"I don't need you at all." His accent and anger combined to twist the words. It was almost a snarl.

"*Listen* to me! My old boss was working with Ralavich. He's going to have both of you killed."

"He can try," said Vasiliy quietly. "You should go, Arianna. I'm running thin on reasons not to kill you myself."

"*Please!* You don't know him!" I stared at Luka. "I don't want to see you get hurt!"

"You tried to kill my father! You lied to me!"

"*I'm sorry!*" It was useless. I'd thought that maybe I'd be able to reason with him and persuade him to lie low for a while, but he was far too angry to listen.

And then, as I glanced around the room in frustration, I saw what was different. Like many places around the city, they'd brought in portable heaters to keep the place warm despite the blizzard outside. But last time I'd been here....I shut my eyes to make sure, going back to that day we'd had lunch. Yes...there'd been two heaters, one in each corner of the room, pumping out hot air.

Now there were three.

Luka still had the gun on me but I forced myself to turn away and shout to a waiter. "When did the extra heater arrive?" I asked in English.

He looked blank.

Well, I guess it didn't matter anymore. "*When did that extra heater show up?*" I demanded in Russian.

The waiter stared at me as if I was crazy and then shrugged. "A few minutes ago. Some guys in overalls."

When I looked back at Luka, his face was thunderous. *Yes, I could understand all your Russian. Sorry.* Just another lie I'd told him.

I took a step towards the heater. Luka raised the gun a little.

I took a shuddering breath. "I think it might be a bomb," I said, saying it in English so I didn't panic a hundred jumpy Russians. "If you're going to shoot me, then shoot me."

And I walked over to the heater. Luka tracked me with the gun the whole time.

There was no hot air coming out of the heater and the surface was stone cold. I didn't dare try to open it, but I looked through the vents.

There were wires and bricks of gray stuff even I recognized as plastic explosive.

I stood up. "Tell them all to get out!" I yelled.

Luka stood there, the gun still pointing at my head. And now I could see the hurt in his eyes, the anger that came from a deeper place.

"You can kill me later," I told him. "Just get everyone out."

He held my gaze a second longer and then lowered the gun. Then he shouted, full volume, for everyone to get out, shooting into the ceiling a few times for good measure. The diners and waiters stampeded for the door. Luka, Vasiliy, Yuri and I were left standing there until the end. Then Vasiliy and Yuri grabbed Luka and pulled him and he pulled me, and we all stumbled down the steps and onto the street.

When we came to a stop, I found myself right up against Luka, as close to him as I had been that time at the party, back in New York. He was breathing deep and hard and he suddenly grabbed me by the upper arms. I tensed, staring up into his furious face.

One of the diners tried to run past us, back inside. Yuri grabbed her arm.

"*My son!*" she screamed. "I think he's in the bathroom!"

I took a step towards the restaurant, but Luka shoved me back against Yuri and ran up the steps. Yuri tried to follow his master, loyal to the end, but Vasiliy pulled him back.

We watched as Luka disappeared into the restaurant. Seconds passed. Vasiliy put his hand on my shoulder and it was comforting, even with the knowledge that he probably wanted to kill me.

The restaurant exploded. I had to close my eyes as a hot wind blew fragments of glass and china and wood right at us. I felt one slash my cheek. But I was focused on the image behind my eyelids, the snapshot my perfect fucking memory had burned into my brain forever: the windows of the restaurant caved outward by orange fire.

I'd killed him. My heart collapsed down like a black hole, sucking everything else that I was down with it. I didn't dare open my eyes because, when I did, he would truly be gone.

I heard the mother's hopeful sob. My eyes flew open. As the smoke cleared, I saw Luka lying flat on the ground just in front of the restaurant doorway, where he must have hurled himself as the bomb went off. His body was hunched protectively over something and the back of his suit was smoldering.

I ran over to him and slapped out the flames. He lifted himself from the young boy he'd shielded and the boy staggered off towards his mother.

"I thought you were dead!" I croaked.

Luka got slowly to his feet, wincing a little.

"We Malakovs are not so easy to kill," said Vasiliy. "Come. Get in car."

Yuri grabbed my shoulder and started walking me towards a car, where more of Vasiliy's men were waiting.

"You want me to go with you?" I looked at Luka, but his face was unreadable. "For what? *Luka?!*" He didn't answer.

I looked at Vasiliy. "What's he going to do with me?" I asked.

Strong hands pushed me into the car.

"Whatever he wants," Vasiliy said grimly.

54

By the time we arrived back at Vasiliy's house, the blizzard had slowed traffic to a crawl and the guards outside were wrapped up in thick coats. There were more of them, standing at the gates and watching from balconies. They knew the threat to their masters was real, now. And they all knew it was somehow connected with me, that I'd betrayed Luka. I could feel their anger blasting down at me in hot waves as we walked the short distance from the car to the front door. Out of all of them, only Yuri didn't seem to hate me.

Inside, Luka grabbed my forearm and pulled me upstairs to the room he was using. As soon as the heavy oak door was closed behind us, he shoved me away from him, making me stagger, as if he couldn't bear to touch me anymore.

I looked at him. Swallowed. Opened my mouth to defend myself but couldn't come up with the words.

"I should kill you," said Luka, his voice shaking with anger. "*Sooka.*"

Which can mean *traitor* or *bitch* or *whore*. All of which were sort of accurate. Handy of the Russian language to combine all three in one word.

"You betrayed me," he snapped. "You slept with me. You made me think—" He broke off and glared at me.

"What?" I asked, my voice weak. "What did I make you think?"

He shook his head and muttered *Wed'ma* under his breath. It meant *witch*. Crazy, because I'm the last person who'd ever be able to cast a spell on anyone.

"I'm sorry," I said. I knew it wasn't enough, but it was all I had. "I was wrong. I thought I could..." I closed my eyes. "...*be* with you and not feel it and—I couldn't." I shook my head.

He let out a disbelieving snort. "I think you good person," he said, his rage making his English slip. "You seem like an innocent."

"I *am!* I am an innocent. I've never done anything like this before! This is my first mission!" I opened my eyes and shook my head, blinking back tears. "I'm not even a real agent! I'm just a languages geek!"

He took a step towards me. "Then why would you agree to do this?"

I let out a long groan of self-hatred. "I thought I was working for the good guys."

He shook his head, but gently, as if he understood. "There are no good guys, Arianna. Only different bad men."

I nodded. I got that, now.

He stepped right up against me. That big, strong hand came up and settled on my throat. I knew he could throttle me without even breaking a sweat. "So tell me. Why did you spill his drink? Why did you change your mind?"

"Because I'm in love with you," I whispered.

He stared into my eyes. I've never felt so connected with anyone my entire life. There were no secrets, no doubts. Everything I was, was exposed to him.

And he knew I was telling the truth.

Has hand stayed on my throat but his mouth came down on mine, tasting my lips, then devouring me completely, taking control of me.

I melted into him, clinging to his back. The heat was raging inside him, throbbing through his skin, that dangerous energy that had scared me so much, at first. Now, I gave myself up to it. I let it soak into me, right to my very soul, and thaw the parts of me that had been encased in ice for so long.

We kissed for a long time, exploring each other, turning slowly, our hearts thumping gradually faster and faster, in rhythm with one another. We twisted so that he was the one with his back to the wall, and it was almost as if we were a couple of normal, regular lovers. His hands traced down my back to my ass, pulling me in close, and I let out a long, slow breath at the touch of those big palms there.

Then he suddenly twisted us again and slammed me up against the wall. The mood shifted to a more primitive need.

We stared at each other, neither of us daring to move. His eyes, burning into me. Telling me what he wanted to do to me. Every filthy way he wanted to corrupt my innocence.

And me, for the first time, daring to meet his gaze full-on and telling him that I wanted it.

He grabbed my waist and lifted me straight up, my feet kicking in the air. He pinned me against the wall like that, my ass pushing against the cool plaster, my chest heaving with fear and heady arousal. Then he mashed his body against mine, pressing his legs between mine, holding me there with the pressure of his flat, taut stomach against my groin. I felt myself go squishy inside, my sensitive flesh rubbing over those firm ridges of muscle as I struggled.

Why am I struggling?

I flushed. *Because it's more fun.*

His hands bunched in the neck of my dress. It was funny because I almost had a vision of him ripping the thing in two, but it was quite strong fabric and—

His muscles bunched and the material screamed and gave, seams popping and stitching wrenching loose. It ripped straight down the front, baring my bra-clad breasts. He got it all the way down to my navel and then, with three savage tugs, he ripped it right down to the hem and it fell apart. Air made furnace-hot by his presence wafted against my exposed stomach and thighs. I could feel myself throbbing—God, *moistening* under my panties.

He kissed me again, gripping my hips to lift me a little more, his mouth hungry and fierce at my lips. His tongue plunged deep, meeting mine. I was being plundered, ravished. Fantasies I hadn't even known I had, fulfilled.

I could feel him panting through the kiss. His hands ran up and down my body in long strokes, lifting and fondling my breasts through my bra, then sliding down to the softness of my inner thighs, then back up in a rhythm that had me writhing.

He broke the kiss. "You understood all the things I said in Russian?" he asked in Russian.

I nodded. *"Da." Yes.*

The tiniest hint of a blush as he remembered some of the things he'd said. But a deeper gleam of lust in his eyes as he realized that I'd understood them...and I'd come back for more. *"All* of them?" he asked.

"Even when you said you were going to make me beg you to stop," I whispered. "And then make me beg you for more."

He growled low in his throat. And then picked me up by the waist and threw me onto the bed.

The shreds of my dress flopped around me, half-hiding my body, but he was on me in a second, rolling me onto my face and stripping it off me. A second later, I was back on my back, drawing in shuddering gulps of air.

He looked down at my chest. Then he folded his thick fingers around the front of my bra and pulled, hard. It stretched away from my body for a second, the straps pulling painfully tight, and then they snapped and my breasts were naked beneath his eyes. He stared down at them for a second, feasting his eyes, and the feel of him looking at me sent a hot wave soaking through me. Then he lowered his head and began to lick in long strokes, covering all of my breast but each lick crossing my nipple. I moaned and kicked and writhed beneath him and reached for his head, intending to pull him down against me harder.

He grabbed my wrists in one big hand and pinned them to the bed above my head. A moment later, his other hand bunched in the thin fabric of my panties and ripped them away. I groaned and tossed my head, feeling the heat rising up inside me, filling me. It was too much. My legs opened and wound around him but, at the same time, I shook my head and said, "I don't understand this."

He froze and stared down at me. "What is there to understand?"

I flushed. "Us two, together. *This*. This...thing, this game—"

"Is not game,"

"That's worse! Or better, I don't know. Like, is it BDSM and should we have a safeword and is it wrong that I like it? I mean, I'm not sure *why* I like it and *MMFF!*"

The last was because he'd put his hand over my mouth.

"Shut the fuck up, Arianna," he told me.

I went stiff and quiet.

"You Americans analyze every fucking thing," he said mildly. "You like it—yes?"

I nodded.

"You know I would never, ever hurt you?"

I did, but hearing it lit a warm glow of reassurance inside me. I nodded again.

"Then that is all that matters. Now shut up and kiss me while I fuck you like dirty slut."

My mind exploded as his lips replaced his hand and his tongue slid into my mouth. I wasn't Arianna Scott or Arianna Ross anymore; I was just his. I wasn't going to be judged for wanting him to be rough, for wanting to play at resisting him. I could just enjoy it.

I pressed up against his hand with my wrists but it felt like his hand had turned to rock. I was held there, helpless, until he damn well chose to let me free, and the thought made my groin roll and grind against him.

His free hand tangled in my hair as he kissed me, then stroked down my cheek. He lifted his lips from mine and stared at me with those icy-blue eyes. "Beautiful," he said in English, and my heart soared. He kissed me softly on my neck. "*Sooka,*" he whispered and the heat tightened and twisted inside me. He kissed me again, this time on my collarbone. "Innocent," he said. Another kiss, on the top of my breast. "*Shalava,*" he whispered.

He kept going, alternating between telling me how beautiful I was and what a dirty, filthy slut I was, with kisses for punctuation. By the time his mouth reached my groin, I was a hot, panting mess.

He put his mouth very close to me, until every hard-accented syllable was like a caress on my ready, throbbing sex. "You will tell me," he said.

"What?" I was so turned on, I slurred it.

"You will tell me exactly what you want," he said, his voice like cold steel.

My eyes widened. Every time we'd had sex, I'd basically let him do all the talking. *His* voice I got off on, but I couldn't say that sort of stuff. "I can't," I said hopelessly.

He lifted his eyes to meet mine. "You will. Or I will stop."

He licked me and my back arched like a bow, hot pleasure rippling up through my body to explode in my mind. *What?!* He wanted me to—My cheeks reddened. I couldn't—

He stopped.

I instinctively humped my groin towards him, but I couldn't quite reach that hot, expert tongue. "I *can't!*" I insisted.

"Say it in Russian," he told me.

Russian. Maybe that would make it easier.

And so I told him in awkward, halting phrases, how I wanted him to lick me. And as he did, the words came a little easier, the heat inside me melting away the barriers. My Russian came in little flurries of words and then in desperate, rushed sentences and then in a gasping litany that rose to the ceiling as I begged him not to stop, begged him to go deeper and faster and OH GOD harder. I wouldn't have had a hope of knowing some of the words... if I hadn't listened to his phone sex over and over again.

Wrestling against his hands was my safety valve, enabling the pleasure to go on and on without me exploding too soon. His shoulders held my thighs wide apart as his lips sucked on my aching clit and his tongue plunged deep. I could feel it building, building, the blood rushing in my ears, my breath coming in desperate pants. I was rolling my hips, bringing my body up to meet him. Just as I thought it couldn't get any better, he slid two fingers into me. I felt myself shudder and go over the edge and then I was bucking and twisting, straining with my wrists against his hand. The pleasure rolled up my body in waves, stretching every muscle taut and then letting it dissolve into warm goo. I flopped onto the bed, spent.

When I looked up, he was unbuttoning his shirt. I started to sit up.

"Stay!" he commanded. A hot rush went through me. I stayed where I was.

He pulled off his pants and shorts and stood naked in front of me. My eyes locked on his cock, long and thick.

"Turn over," he said. His voice was thick with lust and the thought that it was me doing that to him, that I was making this ice-cold man lose control, was electrifying.

I slowly turned over onto my hands and knees. But when he climbed onto the bed behind me, he gently took my wrists and drew them behind me. Wait, what was he—

I felt the touch of cold metal. Handcuffs.

He locked them on and something about the feel of it made my insides flip over and then melt, that familiar combination of fear and lust. My groin tightened and throbbed in a way it never had before. The fact we were together, now, with no secrets, took it to a new level —I felt connected to him as never before. I felt myself begin to pant. My shoulders sank to the bed and the position made it even better, my breasts helplessly pressed against the covers, my face turned to the side. I was helpless. *He can do anything he wants to me.*

The bed creaked as he shifted position and then rolled on a condom. My ass was high in the air, utterly exposed. He ran his palms over my cheeks and I shuddered. Then his thumb moved inward, *between* them—

Oh God! Is he thinking of—I panted, unsure whether to stop him or—

He chuckled. "Another time."

And then I felt the satin-smooth hotness of him pressing into me, dividing my lips and pushing deep. Presented to him like that, I was utterly his for the taking and he sank into me all the way in one long thrust. He slowed at the end, coming to rest against me with his groin tight against my ass, the size of him making me gasp.

He moved his hands to my hips and began to fuck me.

I knew I wasn't going to last long. I was still coming down from before and, in this bound position, I couldn't do anything to control the pace or hold him back. Every silken stroke of him into me ratcheted the heat inside me higher and higher. Every hard thrust made my breasts rub against the covers until my nipples were achingly hard. I pulled and pulled at the cuffs, jerking my wrists as if I wanted to get free, but all I wanted was for it to continue. My climax was twisting and swelling inside me, ready to burst, leaving no room for conscious thought. I found myself pushing back and meeting each thrust, grinding and swirling my hips as I danced my ass against him. He drove himself into me faster and faster and the sound of our bodies slapping together filled the room. I could feel everything slipping away, teetering on the brink like a rollercoaster at the top of a hill.

Suddenly, his hands were scooping under my breasts, squeezing them, his thumbs rubbing my nipples. "Let it go," he hissed in my ear. "Let it all go."

And then he pinched my nipples between his powerful fingers and the exquisite mix of pain and pleasure sent me soaring past the point of no return. My eyes screwed shut, my head went back and I cried out his name, only to have it muffled as his lips found mine. I shuddered and quaked and panted out my orgasm as he filled me again and again, and then he, too, was grunting and gasping as he exploded inside me.

I felt his fingers undoing the cuffs and then, as soon as my hands were free, he rolled us gently onto our sides, my back against his chest. His arms wrapped around me protectively...and warningly.

"Arianna," he said. "You are mine, now. No one else's."

And I knew he wasn't talking about other men. He meant other loyalties.

I didn't even have to think about it. I'd made up my mind hours ago, lying in the snow. "I'm yours," I told him. "Always."

He leaned down and kissed me. "Then let's stop these sons-of-bitches."

At that moment, there was a knock at the bedroom door. Luka went to open it, unashamedly naked. When he opened the door, I couldn't see past his wide shoulders to see who was there.

"A message from your father," said Yuri. "'Which do you need: a sheet to wrap the body, or a wedding ring?'"

I gasped.

Yuri heard and took it completely in his stride. "I owe your father a bottle of whiskey," he deadpanned. "He is downstairs when you're ready."

Given that my dress was in shreds, we had to borrow clothes from one of the maids. I struggled into a slightly tight sweater and jeans. "You can't just keep ripping clothes off me," I muttered.

"Yes I can," he said immediately, and a wave of heat rolled through me.

Vasiliy watched the two of us walk down the stairs, his face carefully neutral. When we reached the bottom, I went over to him. I was squeezing Luka's hand for strength. "I owe you an apology," I said in Russian. "I tried to kill you."

"But you saved me. You didn't let me drink. Then you saved me again at the restaurant." He sighed and shook his head. "I know who the real evil is, Arianna.' He exchanged a look with Luka. "I hope you do, too."

I nodded. "My boss's name is Adam Kinlen." I was breaking every oath I'd taken when I joined the CIA. But he'd betrayed me *and* the agency. "He's right here in Moscow. I think he's been helping Ralavich for years."

I saw Luka's massive body tense. "Bastard." There was murder in his eyes. "We always thought Ralavich had US help."

"What will they do, with you still alive?" I asked.

There was a shout from outside and then a gunshot.

"They'll try again," said Vasiliy grimly. "Get away from the windows! Get upstairs!"

More shouting from outside and more gunshots. Running footsteps as Vasiliy's guards raced outside to defend the house.

"*Here?!*" Luka's voice was disbelieving. "They'd attack us *here?!* This place is built like a fortress. The police will come."

"Not if they've been ordered to stay out of it by the government," said Vasiliy. He looked at me. "I bet they received a special request from a Mr. Kinlen at the CIA."

I died inside. This was all my fault. By telling Adam all about Luka's gun deal, I'd motivated him to destroy the family once and for all.

Yuri ran to join us, gun drawn. We backed up the stairs...but before we were halfway up, there was a massive crash as the front door was kicked down. Gunfire filled the air, horrifyingly loud. Ralavich's men swarmed into the house, guns pointed right at us.

And behind them, swaggering into view, was Olaf, a flashy, chrome-covered handgun dangling from his meaty paw.

"Nice house," he yelled in the silence that followed. "I'll take it."

55

There were far too many of them. Luka signaled to Yuri to drop his gun. He did so reluctantly.

Olaf walked slowly up the stairs, the wood creaking under his weight. "I see you didn't kill her, Luka," he said in Russian, "even though she betrayed you. All friends again?"

Luka stared at him, his eyes full of fury. I could see that he was seconds away from launching himself at the man...and that would mean death for all of us. Olaf had a gun and three of his men were walking up the stairs with him, their own guns drawn. I wrapped my arm around Luka's waist, partially to hold him back and partially for comfort.

"Have you welcomed Arianna into your family?" Olaf asked Vasiliy, reached down and cupping my chin. My skin crawled. "Quite pretty, even if she is an American. I bet you were tempted to fuck her, too."

Vasiliy gave a snarl and charged forward.

Olaf raised his gun quite nonchalantly and fired. Vasiliy staggered back and fell, a red stain spreading across his shirt.

I screamed and Luka yelled in rage. Olaf ignored both of us. "Take them through there," he said, motioning with his gun towards the nearest bedroom. One of the armed thugs dragged a groaning Vasiliy while the other two herded us towards the bedroom door.

It was the same bedroom Luka and I had used earlier. They dumped Vasiliy against the foot of the bed. His face was already deathly pale, the blood spreading steadily across his snow-white shirt. Luka's fists were bunching and unbunching—he was going to go for Olaf and, when he did, I knew he'd be killed. I was beginning to see that this was Olaf's way, to taunt his victims into a rage and then finish them.

Olaf's eyes lit up as he noticed the rumpled bed...and then something else. "Oh! I see what sort of games you've been playing, Luka!"

I looked behind us and my chest went cold. We'd left the handcuffs on the bed.

Olaf stepped close to me and stroked my cheek. "You must have enjoyed being tied up in the warehouse. Were you sorry when you were rescued?"

I glared at him. I wanted to scream at him, tell him how he couldn't be more wrong. How Luka was the polar opposite of him and his men.

"Don't worry," said Olaf. "When we're done with these two, I know just where I'm going to take you. You've been there before, when your boyfriend beat up my son. You'll be a very popular attraction."

I spat right in his face. He stepped back, staring at me in disbelief. Then there was a flash of chrome and my head snapped back. It felt as if I'd been hit by a truck. I staggered sideways into one of the gunmen, tasting blood. I groggily realized I'd just been smacked across the face with a gun. But it had been worth it, just to break the arrogant bastard's cool.

And it had an unexpected bonus. With everyone looking at me, Luka had a second to launch himself at Olaf, knocking him to the floor. Yuri knocked the heads of two of the thugs together and they crumpled to the floor. That only left the one I'd stumbled into, and he was still off balance. Vasiliy kicked out his legs and sent him crashing down.

We were free—but in a few seconds, they'd all get to their feet and we'd be dead. And we were still trapped—God knows how many armed men were downstairs.

"My room," snapped Vasiliy as Yuri hauled him to his feet. "Quick!"

Luka punched Olaf once in the face. He looked as if he'd gladly carry on all through the night, but he obeyed his dad and grabbed my hand, picking up one of the gunmen's handguns at the same time. The four of us staggered out of the room and across the landing, then through another bedroom door. As soon as we were inside, Vasiliy threw himself against the door, slamming it shut and sliding thick bolts across. A half-second later, the first of the gunmen slammed his fist against the other side.

My eyes scanned the room. There was one door, half-open, leading to a bathroom and no other way out. Why had Vasiliy brought us in here? To buy time? The men outside pounded and kicked at the door. They'd be through in seconds.

Vasiliy clutched at his chest, the red stain on his shirt spreading rapidly. He nodded Luka towards the ornate, cast-iron fireplace. Luka crouched, gripped both edges of it...and hauled the entire thing away from the wall.

It hadn't been fixed there, just rested there under its enormous weight. Behind it was an opening to the chimney...and the rungs of a ladder.

I looked at Vasiliy.

"Is not first time people try to kill me at home," he said in English, the pain making him pant it out. He waved Yuri to the ladder and the bodyguard started to descend. Then Vasiliy himself. He touched his bloody chest by way of explanation. "If I fall, I won't take you with me."

I went next, followed by Luka. The rungs were iron, bolted into the wall and coated with a thick layer of dust. Far below, I could hear water.

We climbed quickly but as quietly as we could. We knew there were still gunmen waiting downstairs and, if they heard some noise from behind the walls, they'd know where we were. But there were also the men trying to break into Vasiliy's room, above us. All they had to do was reach the fireplace and fire down into the hole—we'd be fish in a barrel.

At last, I reached the bottom and splashed down into freezing, knee-deep water. We were in a tunnel with a curving roof, scarcely big enough for me to stand up in. The men had to crouch-walk. "Is old sewer," said Luka in my ear. "Don't worry—not used anymore."

We could hear voices above us—were they into Vasiliy's room? We stumbled down the sewer towards blinding whiteness....

...and emerged into crisp daylight. The snow had stopped and we were crunching our way out of a small opening set into a muddy bank by the side of the road. The dash across the landing and the climb had taken its toll on Vasiliy. He was stumbling now, his face deathly pale.

Across the street was a car—an ancient Soviet-era thing. Yuri reached underneath and found a hidden key, then helped Vasiliy into the passenger seat.

Vasiliy read my amazed expression. "Is so that no one steals it," he told me, nodding at the rust and peeling paintwork. "Is BMW underneath." Then he reached out and clutched Luka's hand. "We have to split up. Take her out of Moscow," he said. "Out of Russia, if you can."

Luka gripped his dad's hand hard. "I'm not leaving you to die."

Vasiliy looked offended by the idea. "I'm not going to," he said. "Yuri will get me fixed up. But I'm out of the fight." He clapped his son on the shoulder and glanced at me. "*You* are the Malakovs, now."

And they sped off, the car's engine roaring like a showroom model.

Luka pulled me in the opposite direction, towards a tram station. There was a tram just pulling in. "Don't turn around," he told me.

In seconds, we were mixing with the crowd. I could hear shouts behind us as the gunmen emerged from the tunnel and started to hunt for us. The tram was crowded and, for a few horrible seconds, I thought we were going to be left behind on the platform, easily visible.

But then Luka reached in and just scooped out a couple of paying passengers, quieting their protests with a glare, and the doors closed and we moved off. I had a glimpse of one of Ralavich's men kicking the tram sign in rage and then we were speeding into the heart of Moscow.

We transferred to the metro and got on one of the main lines racing along deep beneath the city streets. Our plan was to go straight through Moscow and out the other side, then keep going. On board the quiet, gently rocking train, everything just...stopped.

I flopped down onto a seat, resting against Luka's side. The headlong rush from the house had been sheer adrenaline. Now it was seeping away and I just felt utterly drained. The stark reality of our situation started to sink in. Vasiliy was dying, possibly dead. Olaf Ralavich, backed up by Adam's CIA influence, was seizing control, starting with Vasiliy's house and finishing with the Malakov's gun business.

I looked across at Luka. In the space of a few hours, he'd been transformed from the crown prince of a criminal empire to a man on the run. And, thanks to me, he was facing enemies he'd never had before—not just a rival gang but the entire might of the state. With Adam nudging them, the government would pull out all the stops to catch the two of us. Luka was a major criminal, after all. He'd just been ignored by them for all these years because he'd paid off the right people. Now, it was open season.

I pressed harder into Luka's solid, reassuring body, winding my arms around him. The exhaustion and the fear, the hopelessness of our situation—it all weighed me down like heavy chunks of ice, pushing me beneath the dark water.

Luka's hand stroked comfortingly through my hair...and I slept.

I had happy, brightly-colored dreams of Luka and me together somewhere—New York, maybe. We did all the things couples are supposed to do: running through parks, rolling over and over each other in the grass. Birthday parties. Roller coasters. But the dreams kept being invaded by men with guns.

I woke, but I didn't open my eyes immediately. I didn't want to face up to the reality of what was happening. The dreams only made it worse—they were a world I'd left behind when I'd joined this new society based on violence and fear, honor and respect. People like Luka—people like *us*—didn't get to have lives like that.

Luka nudged me in the ribs. "Trouble," he whispered in my ear.

I opened my eyes and sat up and he shook out the stiffness in his arm—he'd been holding me cuddled into his side, my head on his shoulder, for an hour or more. He was staring through the window as we pulled into a station. Police officers were waiting for the train, watching who got off.

"This is the edge of the city," Luka whispered. "Adam must have them looking for us. We can't get out of Moscow. We're trapped."

56

We took the metro back into the city and went up into the streets. With the stations and presumably the roads out of the city under surveillance, we'd have to hole up in the center while we figured out what we were going to do. But, as soon as we got above ground, Luka swore under his breath and nodded ahead of us. One of Ralavich's men, marching determinedly towards us. We turned and there was another one behind and more getting out of a car across the street. Between them and the police, they had the whole city locked down.

Luka pulled me towards the street. I didn't know what he had in mind until he pulled open the door of a man's car and pointed his gun at him. The man scuttled out, hands over his head, and Luka pushed me into the driver's seat.

I stared at the steering wheel in horror. I hadn't driven since the crash. Luka flung himself into the passenger seat. "I can't," I told him. It was night. Snow was falling. I was going to have a full-on flashback. Just being in a car might not be enough to trigger it, anymore, but this combination of stress and fear sure as hell would. And if I had a flashback at the wheel, we could both be killed.

Luka grabbed my head between his hands. "You have to," he said, waving the gun. "I have to shoot."

My eyes bugged out. *Shoot?! Shit! Shit shit shit shit—*

My whole body was stiff with tension. I clumsily put the car into gear, then tentatively pressed the gas. We shot forward and smashed into the car in front. Luka swore.

"I told you!" I snapped. Ralavich's men were running towards us, now.

An irate driver climbed out of the car ahead of us. Luka pointed the gun at him and he climbed back in.

There was a bang and a crash of shattering glass. Bits of the rear window were in my hair.

"Arianna!" Luka's voice was commanding and calm despite the chaos. "We have to go! *Now!*"

I hauled on the wheel and pulled out into traffic, drawing honks and shouts. I prayed and floored the gas. We screamed forward, pinballing off parked cars but pulling away from the car behind us. For a moment, I thought it was going to be okay. Maybe I really was healed.

Then a corner came up, way too fast, and we slipped and skidded on the hard-packed snow. The past rushed up to meet me, the horrible feeling of the wheels leaving the ground.

I could feel the memories rushing up to engulf me, bright and sharp as the day of the crash. The feel of the seat under me. The creak and crunch of tortured metal. I squeezed my eyes closed but it was too late. I was with my parents, the car skidding towards the cliff—

"Arianna!" It was Luka. "Stay with me!"

I focused on his voice, on the exquisite, perfect *solidness* of him, my anchor in the here and now. I opened my eyes and I was out of the flashback and back in Moscow.

I hauled on the wheel and managed to get us round the corner, though we clipped a parked truck. Luka gripped my arm hard, keeping me in the present. He was firing out of the window with the other hand.

I sped through the twisting streets. There were several loud gunshots, but all I could do was stare at the road ahead, go as fast as I could and pray a bullet didn't hit me in the back of the head. After a few more corners, the sound of the car chasing us seemed to fade.

"There!" yelled Luka, pointing. "Go *there!*"

I looked. A big, open doorway led to an indoor market. I aimed for it and then hit the brakes as soon as we were inside.

We came to a stop with the car half-covered in rugs and carpets and a guy yelling at us in Russian that we'd ruined his stall—but at least no one was hurt. Luka pulled me out and carried me through the crowd, then planted me down on my feet and grabbed my hand. By the time the other car caught up with us, we'd disappeared into the crowd.

"We have to change our appearance," I told Luka. We'd left the market through a rear entrance and were moving through a maze of alleys.

He blinked at me. "You really are a spy."

"I can talk in Russian, remember?" I said in Russian. "Less conspicuous." Although my Russian accent wasn't great. I'd only had to understand Russian, back in Langley, not speak it and convince people I was a local.

I was shutting out the panic and fear, now, and going step-by-step through what I'd learned in my basic training. All the stuff Nancy used every day, the stuff I'd never thought I'd need. Thank God for my memory.

Luka's phone rang. He grabbed it and put it to his ear, pulling me into an alcove. I could feel the tension in his body....and then he relaxed. "My father is okay," he said.

I let out a long breath. Given how pale Vasiliy had been, last time I saw him, I'd feared the worst. "Yuri got him to a doctor?"

"Yuri *is* the doctor."

I stared at him.

"It's fine. Yuri was a medic in the army."

"At least tell me they went to a hospital?!"

He shook his head. "A safehouse." He looked at my expression. "It's fine. Yuri will have knocked him out with vodka and then dug the bullet out and stitched him up. It's his third—no, fourth time."

"Please say this hasn't happened to you!"

"No. Well, only once. Bullet hit my leg. Hardly counts."

I shook my head in disbelief. It was a miracle any of the Malakovs were still alive.

We found a department store that was open late and I led him through it, buying up clothes and make-up. Then we found the grottiest, seediest hotel we could, a place where they'd take cash and not ask questions.

57

A half hour later, I stepped out of our room's tiny bathroom. Luka was sitting on the battered bed, his face lit up by the weak bulb in the bedside lamp. He came to attention when he saw me. "*Wow,*" he said.

What I'd done wasn't subtle.

I'd based the look on the people I'd seen at the *Underside of Heaven* club. Rich and yet cheap and tacky. With everyone looking for us, trying to be inconspicuous wouldn't work. We had to be so obvious and loud they'd look right past us.

I was in white knee boots with a towering heel and a ridiculous number of laces up the front. Fishnet stockings, then a tight dress in metallic blue made of some gleaming, sparkling fabric that had to stretch to allow me to walk. Over the top I had an ankle-length padded jacket in shiny black, like a latex fetishist's sleeping bag. I'd gone heavy on the make-up, my lips a vivid red and my eyes dark and smoky. The crowning glory, though, was the wig.

It was gleaming, silky and blonde. Blonde like only one of Luka's old girlfriends could do. Arrow-straight, the hair reached right down to my mid-back.

"Wow," said Luka again.

I'd dressed him in expensive black pants and designer boots, with a flashy belt and an eggshell-blue sweater that matched his eyes. He'd drawn the line at a chunky chain around his neck but the effect still worked. We looked like a pair of rich kids out for a good time. Or, possibly, a hooker and her pimp. Fashion-wise, there wasn't all that much difference.

He held out his arms to me and I climbed onto the bed. The springs squeaked—given the sort of hotel this was, they probably saw a lot of action. As if to back up my suspicions, a rhythmic banging started in the room next to us.

Despite everything, I laughed. "Who do you think they are? Two lovers, on their honeymoon?"

Luka snorted. "More likely boss and his secretary. Wife thinks he's working late." He looked at me. "Or hooker, with client."

He kept looking at me and that familiar heat washed through me. I was kneeling up on the bed and I was very aware of how tight the dress was on my thighs. "Are you implying I look like a hooker?" I asked in my best *I'm-really-offended* tone.

"No," he said. "You're too beautiful to be a hooker."

The heat throbbed down to my groin. Sex had been the last thing I'd been expecting. I wouldn't have thought getting turned on was possible, when you were running for your life. I hadn't realized that danger is an aphrodisiac, that having adrenaline pumping through your system for hours leaves you itching to do something with all that nervous energy. Suddenly, I was like a cat in heat. "Well, you're too good looking to be a client," I said.

"I know," he deadpanned. He sat up fully, so we were just inches apart, and traced my cheekbone with one finger. "What would you call yourself, if you were a Russian hooker?"

"Natalia," I said, shaking out my long blonde hair.

He blinked. "I had a girlfriend called Natalia, once."

"I know. I remember the phone sex."

He stared at me. "You listened to—"

"Many times."

He just looked at me for a moment, anger flaring in his eyes and then turning slowly to lust. "So, *Natalia*. How much would it cost to sleep with you?"

"A lot," I said. "Millions of dollars."

"I have millions of dollars," he said, leaning even closer. His lips were almost brushing mine. "So I could hire you and fuck you."

I was quaking now, the heat rolling through me. This was all getting very kinky, very fast. It was like sex always was with him: dark and dangerous and edgy...and wonderful. It felt different now that we were together. The sex we'd had at Vasiliy's house had been the tipping point, when we'd actually dared to talk about our sex games. I felt free, free to share my fantasies—if I dared. The potential was huge but the timing was awful—sex should have been the last thing on our minds.

But maybe, I realized, it was exactly what we both needed.

"Yes," I said huskily. "You could. And I'd have to do anything you said."

"Oh, would you?"

"Yes. Anything." My head was spinning from the raw lust in his voice. *God, how does he always do this to me?*

He moved back on the bed, sitting up against the scratched wooden headboard. And then he glanced down, just once, to the bulge in his pants. "*Susi hui,*" he instructed me. *Suck me.*

My cheeks flared. He was being crude. Deliberately crude. And for some reason, that only made me hotter. I glanced around the room, seeing the torn wallpaper, the glowing neon sign outside the window. I really could be some Moscow hooker, kneeling over her client, preparing to suck him to pay my rent.

I took a deep, shuddering breath and unfastened his belt, pulling down his pants and then his shorts. His cock sprang out, thick and already erect, and I gazed down at those strong, muscled thighs. I slid my hands over them, pushing his pants lower. Then I slowly took him into my mouth.

It wasn't the first time I'd done it. But doing it for him was completely different. With my boyfriends in the past, it had just been a part of sex—mechanical, almost. This felt...*dirty.* But in a good way.

Like I was demonstrating how filthy I could be by doing it, and he loved me for it.

I rolled him around in my mouth, using my tongue, and he groaned and called me a good little *shalava*. I added my hand, his shaft hot and slick with my spit, and he began to stroke my long, blonde hair. Every time I looked up at him with my big, painted eyes, I could feel him grow harder in my mouth. We stared at each other as I bobbed my head, the tension building and building. God, I felt so dirty...and yet it felt utterly safe. Because, however much he played at being the callous, unfeeling customer, I'd seen the real him.

He suddenly pulled my panting mouth off him and then lifted me onto the floor so that I was standing, facing the bed. He put a hand on my back and pushed me down so that I bent at the waist, my hands braced on the bed and my ass high in the air.

I caught a glimpse of us in the mirror and scarcely recognized myself. Some blonde hooker, bending over for her client. I recognized him, though. Luka Malakov, big-time criminal, wanted arms dealer. As I watched, he stripped off his sweater and shirt, kicking off his pants so that he was naked. His tattoos gleamed in the dim light and, as he moved in behind me, the sight of his muscled body made me catch my breath. A mafioso, using one of his girls. Using *me*. It was exactly how I'd imagined him back before I'd really known him, before I'd seen past his defenses. Pure darkness. I'd seen the good in him, now, but that didn't mean he couldn't be—my groin tightened —*evil*.

He kicked my legs apart and I cried out in shock as I dropped lower. Then he was jerking my dress up over my thighs, baring my ass. I felt my panties shoved aside. God, I was already wet for him. There was the rubber sound of a condom and then—

I gasped as he drove up into me, filling me in three hard thrusts. His hands hooked around my hips, drawing me back onto him, his thumbs rubbing along my lower back. I writhed and groaned at the feeling of him inside me, that combination of size and hardness, just the right side of *too big*.

He was hard and brutal—just the way I needed it. His breathing turned from gasps to sharp, almost angry grunts as he pounded me. He stroked my ass, his hands soft and tender, a stark contrast to his plunging cock. I could feel the pleasure flooding outward in warm waves, soaking into every part of me from my toes to my fingertips. I dared to open my eyes and the sight of us in the mirror, my blonde hair tossing, his muscled body tight up against my ass, rocketed me forward towards my orgasm.

His strokes sped up until the wonderful smooth friction seemed to blur and loop in on itself, becoming endless. My hips were grinding back against him and he was calling me filthy names in Russian and English. The words soaked into my brain and exploded in my groin.

And then, just as he reached his peak, I felt his hands spreading my ass and gently rubbing me *there* with his slickened thumb and I lost it completely. I yelled and screamed and I think I called him names, thrashing and grinding against him until I flopped on the bed, exhausted.

From the other side of the wall there came an angry knocking and a voice telling us to *keep it down!* We both laughed.

Afterwards, I said, "It's never been like *that* before."

"Maybe you just needed to let go."

I thought of the way he usually took control, pinning my hands or throwing me on the bed. That let me let go. Pretending to be his whore had, too. Maybe he had a point. I imagined a future with him, with glorious long nights in some penthouse somewhere, learning more about letting go. Hell, forget the penthouse: my old apartment in Virginia would do just fine.

What I wanted was him. But, unless we could figure a way out of this, we had no future at all. It was only a matter of time until either Ralavich's men or the police caught up with us.

We lay there in silence for a few moments. Then he said, "Arianna?"

"Yes?"

"What's your real name?"

I turned and looked at him, gaping. *He still didn't know.* Ever since the restaurant, he'd trusted me, even though I was CIA, without even knowing my real name. That made my heart swell until I thought it was going to burst.

"It's Arianna," I said breathlessly.

"Your *real* name," he said patiently.

"No, it really is Arianna." I laughed bitterly. "That's how lousy an agent I am. They didn't trust me to keep up a real alias. They just changed my surname. I'm Arianna Scott."

He stared at me for a long time and then sort of grunted. "Good."

"Good?"

He rolled over onto his side. His hand traced down the length of my body. "Because I like you as Arianna. I was worried I might have to get used to a new name."

I stared into his eyes. "I'm sorry. I'm sorry I lied to you."

"Lying was your job."

"I don't think I want a job where I have to lie, anymore."

He rubbed my cheek with his thumb. "I think you can do anything you want to, Arianna."

I shook my head. "They've disavowed me. My passport's been invalidated. Even if I could get home, there's nothing for me there, now. If they want to, they could try me as a traitor."

"Where is home?" he asked.

"Virginia. But I'm from Wisconsin, originally."

"What's Wisconsin like?" It was almost like we were on our first date.

I had to think about it. It had been a long time since I'd been back there. I'd told myself, ever since I'd started working for the CIA, that Virginia was now my home. It was only now that I realized I'd been lying to myself. "Wisconsin's beautiful," I said. "Lakes. Cows. Do you like the country?"

He blinked. "I don't know," he said, quite serious. "I've never really been there."

My heart went out to him. All he'd ever known was the city, his world of crime feeding off the population.

His fingers knitted with mine. "If we get out of this," he said, "I'll take you there. I swear to you, Arianna. Even if we have to smuggle you back into America. No one should have to be separated from their home."

I knew it wasn't going to happen. I knew he was just trying to make me feel better, offering me a slender straw to clutch at. But I loved him for trying. "We could go swimming, in the lakes."

"We could go thin-dipping."

"*What?!*"

"Without clothes."

"*Skinny*-dipping." I laughed, but there were tears in my eyes. It sounded so good. And so impossible.

He brushed the tears from my eyes with the back of his hand. "Will you tell me, now?" he asked. "Tell me what happened to you? Do you trust me enough?"

I stared at him. "Is that what you thought? That I didn't—God, Luka, of course I trust you. I just can't—" I caught myself and shook my head. "I *couldn't*. But now, I think, I can."

And, gripping his hand for strength, I told him.

When I reached the part about being trapped in the car, he pulled me onto his lap and wrapped his arms around me, surrounding me with his warmth. And even though the memories were so sharp and clear they felt like they could cut me, I didn't feel in the same danger from them. I had a shield between them and me, now, and he was strong enough to protect me from anything.

Afterwards, as we sat there in the near-darkness, I felt...not healed, but more cemented in the present. As if the past had loosened its grip on me just a little. And it felt as if, the longer I stayed with Luka, the easier it would get.

I could feel the tension in him, the anger at how I'd been hurt and the frustration at not being able to change the past. "What can I do?" he said at last.

"Will you just hold me?" I whispered.

He tightened his grip and nestled my head into his shoulder, and it felt so good that I was asleep in minutes.

58

The next morning, the cracked ceiling made me frown for a second until I remembered where we were. Then it all came back to me like cold lead dropping from above, pounding me down into the depths.

We'd bought some toiletries from the department store so we could scrape a wash. Breakfast came from a battered vending machine, normally only used by the hotel's prostitutes between clients. I noticed all the gum was gone.

Luka passed me a scalding cup of instant coffee and offered me the choice of the last two chocolate bars. "That one has raisins," he said, deciphering the unfamiliar brands for me. "That one is sickly, but I used to like it when I was a child."

I took the raisin one and we sat on the end of the bed. It was an odd sight, watching a huge, tattooed arms dealer eating a candy bar. I wondered what Olaf was doing, at that moment.

"Do you think Olaf's still at your dad's house?"

Luka nodded bitterly. I imagined Olaf sitting at the huge dining table, tucking into an extravagant breakfast like a conquering king.

"It's the staff I worry about," muttered Luka. "I don't care about the place, but the people...."

"The staff?" I asked.

He looked at me, pain in his eyes. His hands were tightening into fists. "The maids."

I remembered what Olaf and his gang liked to do to women and my stomach turned over.

"Do you think he'll move in?" I asked.

He nodded. "My father's house is nicer than his place. That's how it works. You take over and you take what you want. Trophies."

"Like you with the German's yacht."

He nodded and then kicked a chair. "He'll take the jet. Everything. Then he'll build a fucking empire in the US based on *our* gun deal. First guns, then drugs. Then, when he owns the local police, his fucking rape clubs. We paved the road for him!"

Guilt knotted in my chest. This was all my fault: I'd sleepwalked into the middle of a war and helped the wrong side to win. I'd been so hot for Luka, I'd not seen the way I was being manipulated. I fell onto the bed on my back and stared at the ceiling. "There's nothing we can do, is there?"

He shook his head sadly. "What I want to do is kill that bastard."

For the first time, the idea of killing didn't disgust me. Maybe that meant I'd finally been corrupted. Olaf Ralavich deserved to die.

"But he's too well guarded," said Luka. "And there's only two of us. We'd have to get him alone."

"So we just sit here and do nothing?" I asked bitterly.

He turned slightly and looked at me, then down at my legs. Flopping down on my back had made the short hem of my dress ride up. "We don't have to do *nothing,*" he growled.

I had to love him for that, for still being his brutish, horny self even when everything was lost. And God knows I'd happily tear his clothes off and make enough noise to piss off the couple next door again, but—

Something was scratching at the back of my mind. Two things he'd said that, in combination....

He leaned down to kiss me, but I put a hand on his chest to stop him. His eyes clouded with lust. "Are we still playing that game?" he asked. "Want me to interrogate you?"

Just those five words, combined with his accent, were enough to turn my insides to liquid heat. But I shook my head and sat up. "Wait," I said. I was sifting through my mind like a gold panner, trying to find the few tiny gold flakes and crush them together. "He'll take the jet?" I asked slowly.

Luka nodded. "It's my prize possession. Everybody knows that."

I thought of the jet and its luxurious leather seats. The smiling pilot—

That was it. That was the other thing that had sparked something when I'd heard it—when Luka had said he worried about Vasiliy's staff. He cared about the people under him. I remembered how the jet's crew had responded to him. "They're loyal to you, aren't they? The pilot and co-pilot?"

He looked puzzled. "Yes. But once Olaf arrives and tells them he's taken over, they'll have no choice."

"But if you contacted them...maybe they could help us?" I grabbed Luka's arm. "Maybe they could help us get Olaf alone?"

He blinked at me twice. Then he suddenly kissed me, wrapping me up in his arms and pulling me against his chest. "I love you, Arianna Scott," he said.

And then we just stared at each other. It was the first time he'd said it. My eyes searched his and the flame within those clear blue pools of ice was burning bright, now. I knew he meant it.

I kissed him, slow and deep. We explored each other as if it was our first time. If we'd met without all the baggage, in some other universe, *this* is the point we would have reached—all sins forgiven, all defenses down. His warmth was soaking into me through every place we touched, from my lips to my groin, and I felt the ice inside me shudder and finally explode. Underneath, the parts of me I'd thought were lost forever started to glow and swell, alive again. It felt like we'd found our way onto the path we were always meant to be on. And it was the best feeling in the world.

When we finally broke the kiss, he held my head between his

hands and just looked at me, letting me know that this was *it,* that we'd be together forever, now. If we survived.

He pulled out his cell phone and started the app that located the jet. "Good. They haven't disabled my account, yet. I can still check— Yes." He smiled. "There's a trip scheduled. From my usual airfield to New York." He showed me the screen. Six passengers were listed. Four of the names I didn't recognize—bodyguards, presumably. But two of them I did. Olaf and Adam.

"If we could get Adam," I said, "And some evidence, maybe his laptop...I might be able to prove to my people that he was a traitor."

"Everything we need will be on that plane," said Luka. "They're leaving in two hours. Let's go."

59

The airfield was just outside Moscow. That meant going through a roadblock staffed by a mixture of police and Ralavich's men. I grabbed Luka's hand as our taxi drew close. I was pretty sure I wasn't recognizable in the wig and make-up, but Luka still looked pretty much like himself.

"It'll be fine," said Luka, not very convincingly. He fingered the handgun under his jacket. I counted four armed men at the roadblock. If it came to a shootout, I knew we'd last a few seconds, at most.

As we neared the roadblock, I suddenly threw myself on top of Luka, straddling him. His knees pushed the hem of my dress up a little.

"What—" he started

"Shut up and kiss me," I said. And kissed him hard and deep, trying to keep my head between his face and the window.

His hands came up to grab my ass, then slid up to my waist. His tongue danced with mine, my own desperate, scared pants mixing with his.

The cab driver muttered something about us paying extra.

We stopped again. I kept my eyes tight closed, but I knew we must be at the roadblock. Right outside the window, they'd be watching us, comparing us to the descriptions they'd been given. I kissed Luka frantically, grinding on his lap, praying it would be enough to distract them.

There was a knock on the window. *Shit!* I could feel the eyes of the men outside.

I broke the kiss for a second. "Pull my dress down," I panted frantically into his ear, keeping my eyes closed.

Luka hesitated. He could feel them staring at us, too.

"Do it right now," I panted, "Or we're both dead."

He yanked the shoulder straps of my dress down, taking my bra with it. My breasts spilled out, throbbing in the freezing air. I bucked and ground against him, feeling the men's eyes on my naked chest—

Someone knocked twice on the roof of the cab and the driver pulled away. I waited a few seconds to be sure, then climbed off Luka and slumped breathlessly beside him. I could feel the driver watching me in his rearview mirror and quickly pulled my dress up. We drove on down the road, the roadblock receding behind us.

"Tease," panted Luka, his eyes gleaming.

By the time we reached the airfield, it was snowing again, thick flakes reducing visibility down to just a few car lengths. Perfect for what we needed to do.

We got the cab driver to drop us near the perimeter fence and watched as the cab's tail lights disappeared into the blizzard. We were miles from anywhere—if this went wrong, we had no way back to the city. But if this went wrong, we were going to be dead anyway.

Security was a lot laxer than at a big commercial airport. We found a place where the fence was rusted and Luka tore the metal strands apart. Luka's private jet was sitting on the runway, just visible through the snow. Most likely, the tower wouldn't give them clearance to take off until the blizzard died down. Two black SUVs were parked nearby. I could see Ralavich's bodyguards, too—four of them. They were probably meant to be patrolling, or spaced out around the jet keeping watch until it could depart. But they didn't have Yuri's loyalty or resolve. Two of them were huddled against the SUV, trying to stay out of the wind, while the other two had given up completely and were sitting inside it, smoking. There was no sign of Olaf or Adam, which meant they had to already be on board.

Luka took out his phone and dialed a number, then spoke quietly in Russian. He spoke slowly and earnestly. Asking for help, but not demanding that the pilot risk his life. At last, he nodded and solemnly gave his thanks. Then he nodded to me. It was on.

We crept through the snow. I was grimly aware of how completely unprepared I was. I was in a dress and heels, for God's sake, the padded coat already plastered with snow. I didn't have a gun. I barely remembered my unarmed combat training.

But there was no way on earth I was letting my man go in there alone.

When we were thirty feet from the jet, the pilot lowered the rear cargo door. We crept inside the tiny hold and Luka called the pilot again. Seconds later, the door closed, plunging us into darkness.

"Stay behind me," whispered Luka. "And whatever happens...I love you."

I clung to him for a second. And then the plane began to move.

From the passenger cabin, we could hear shouts of anger and alarm. Answering shouts from the bodyguards outside. Running footsteps. They couldn't understand why the plane was taxiing for take-off without them aboard.

Luka took a deep breath and pushed open the door to the cabin.

Olaf and Adam were the only people inside and both of them were staring at the runway as it flashed past outside the open passenger door. The steps were scraping along the ground, sparks flying. "*Hey!*" Olaf was shouting towards the cockpit, "*What the fuck are you doing?!*"

Just a few feet from me, Adam had his laptop out and—my heart leapt—he was checking his bank accounts on the screen. Routing numbers. Amounts. Everything he'd been paid by Ralavich for helping him over the years. It was exactly the evidence I needed; all I had to do was get that laptop back to the CIA.

He looked round and saw us. His strangled cry alerted Olaf, who turned...to find Luka pointing a gun at him.

"My father's going to live," Luka told him. "And we're going to take back everything you stole from us." I saw his finger tighten on the trigger.

Adam suddenly yelled and jumped forward. Luka turned but didn't shoot—he knew that Adam had to go back to America alive if I was to clear my name.

Adam hurled his laptop. Luka awkwardly deflected it, but it opened him up for Olaf to charge at him, knocking him to the floor. The laptop landed on one of the plush leather chairs by the door.

Olaf straddled Luka, punching him in the face and trying to pry the gun out of his fingers. I winced—and then Adam grabbed hold of me around my waist. I thrashed and struggled but he was a lot stronger than I was, dragging me towards the open door. We were almost at take-off speed, now, the runway whipping past outside and the jet engines deafening. "Stop!" he yelled. "Or I throw her out the door!"

Luka froze and then went limp. Olaf pried the gun from his fingers and stood up, pointing it at him.

No!

Adam's arms were like a steel band around my waist. All I had were my arms, and I didn't have anything I could use as a weapon.

Then I saw the laptop, still sitting on the leather chair next to the door. The evidence I so badly needed.

As Olaf leveled the gun at Luka, I stretched forward and grabbed the laptop. Adam leaned instinctively back out of the way, so that I couldn't hit him. And Olaf was staring at me. If I threw it at him, he'd see it coming.

But there was one thing I *could* do with it. One thing that might save us...or kill us all.

I twisted as hard as I could, managing to turn Adam around as well. I was now right in the open doorway, the freezing wind scouring my face, the roar of the engines pounding my ears. The runway was just a blur.

I threw the laptop into the jet engine and watched as it was sucked inside. The whole plane trembled for a split-second and then the engine exploded into a million jagged pieces.

The blast hurled Adam and I back inside and across the cabin. The whole plane slewed to one side. As I'd hoped, none of us could keep our feet. Olaf went staggering into Luka, who grabbed the gun and pushed him away.

Olaf stumbled backward and made a grab for me, perhaps intending to throw me out of the door. Before he could, four wet, red flowers erupted on his white shirt. He looked down in disbelief...and fell backwards out of the door, his body bouncing as it hit the runway.

Adam was still reeling from the explosion. Luka grabbed the front of his shirt, then punched him just once with the other hand. He dropped to the floor like a puppet whose strings have been cut.

The plane started to slow. Through the open door, I could see the SUVs finally catching up with us. The bodyguards inside were wide-eyed in panic. They'd just seen their boss's body hurled out of a plane and, unlike Yuri, they weren't thinking about honor and vengeance; they were thinking that they'd backed the wrong side. Luka approached the door, gun raised. As soon as they saw he was still alive, the drivers stamped on the brakes, turned and drove away as fast as they could.

The jet finally stopped. The pilot unlocked the door from the cockpit and tentatively looked out. He looked at me, then at the groaning Adam on the floor, then finally at Luka. "Are things back to normal, sir?" he asked.

Luka drew in a long breath. "Yes, captain. Thank you for your help."

Adam spat a tooth across the cockpit. "You can't prove shit," he panted. "It was all on that laptop."

I slumped down into one of the leather chairs. "You know, I always thought it was Roberta who underestimated me," I told him. "But the whole time, it was you. Don't you remember *anything* about me?"

EPILOGUE

One Week Later

"Arms up," said Yuri.

Roberta raised her arms without complaint. The pat-down was standard practice but I knew that wasn't the only reason it was being done. This was the first time Luka and Vasiliy had ever—knowingly—met someone from the CIA. They wanted to remind her who was in control.

Yuri stepped away and nodded her over to our table. He was still solemn—he was *Yuri,* and that would never change—but he did seem just a little lighter, since Olaf had died, as if a door to his past had finally closed forever. I'd even caught him smiling, once.

We were in a coffee shop that, until a few moments ago, had been full of customers. They'd all cleared out as soon as we'd arrived. Word had spread of the fall of Olaf Ralavich. If they'd been scared of us before, now they were terrified.

That didn't bother me as much as it used to. There are worse things in life than being feared. People are going to be scared of *someone.* Better that that's a family with some notion of honor and justice.

Luka sat on one side of me, hulking over the table like a bear. His untouched coffee looked comically small in front of him. He looked as if he might smash the table in two at any moment, his hatred for the CIA barely contained. But I wasn't scared of that anger, anymore. I'd seen the man inside, the one who'd always been there. He'd just needed the right person to bring him out.

On my other side sat Vasiliy. He'd insisted on forgoing his painkillers that morning so that he could be sharp, although he'd then proceeded to kill the pain with vodka instead. He stared at Roberta with as much venom as his son...and with a hint of something else, too, something I couldn't quite read.

"Mr Malakov...and Mr. Malakov," said Roberta as she reached us. Then, to me, "Arianna."

Silence. I kicked Luka under the table.

He inclined his head. 'You may call me Luka," he growled.

Roberta turned to Vasiliy. "And may I call you Vasiliy?"

Vasiliy gave her a strange smile. "No. You may call me *Mr. Malakov,"* he said. His voice was velvety smooth.

Roberta blinked at him and sat down. It was strange, seeing her outside Langley. It reminded me of when we'd first met, when she'd recruited me. Once again, she was in a sharp suit—actually, an even sharper one. Of course, she could afford the upgraded wardrobe, now.

"They promoted you, I hear," I said.

She nodded. "Things are a little...chaotic, back at Langley. That's why they wanted me to come over here and make our position clear."

"You mean, explain why a senior CIA man was working with arms dealers," said Vasiliy sweetly. "I think our government is wondering the same thing."

From what I'd heard, there had been a lot of very embarrassed diplomats rushing back and forth between the US and Russia over the last few days. There were rumors of desperate bargaining behind the scenes and the whole thing had narrowly avoided making it into the press.

"Adam pled guilty last night," said Roberta. "He didn't have a lot of choice, given the evidence." She looked at me. "Well done."

The thing about a photographic memory is, it's always on, whether you want it to be or not. I'd seen Adam's laptop screen and all the account numbers and amounts were burned indelibly into my mind. That was more than enough for Roberta to go to her superiors and demand they subpoena the banks, and that had started a domino effect. Adam's whole career of deceit had come spilling out.

Roberta put her hands flat on the table. "We wanted to acknowledge the part you played, as well," she told Luka and Vasiliy. I could tell this wasn't easy for her. "And to let you know—off the record—that the CIA won't be pursuing investigations into your trading at the present time."

"Meaning you'd rather have us around than scum like Ralavich," muttered Luka.

"Meaning keep it clean," said Roberta, a warning tone in her voice. She stared at Luka, but kept glancing meaningfully at me. "Play nice. Be respectful. And we won't have to get involved. Am I clear?"

I could feel the motherly concern and disapproval coming off her in waves. Even Luka was a little subdued by it. He nodded and I couldn't help but smile.

"And you," said Roberta, turning back to me, "are free to come back anytime." She tossed me my Arianna Scott passport. "There's a job waiting for you, if you want it."

I looked at Luka. "I don't."

She looked at the two of us and a sort of world-weary smile touched her lips. "Well, I'm there if you need me," she said.

"And I'm here if you need *me*," I said. I meant it, too. I owed her one. And I figured that an American in Moscow, under the protection of one of the most powerful families in Russia, was probably quite a useful thing to be.

She nodded gratefully and was about to say something else when Vasiliy interrupted her. "And what about you, Roberta?" he asked. His voice still had that smooth tone. "I can call you Roberta, can't I? Can I tempt you away from the CIA? I'm sure I could find something for a woman like you."

He locked eyes with her.

She flushed.

Oh.

That was what was going on. I stood up quickly and made *let's go* motions at Luka. Luka being Luka, he took his sweet time to get up, nod a goodbye to Roberta and allow me to lead him away from the table. We left Roberta looking panicked, as if she couldn't decide whether being left alone with Vasiliy was the worst thing in the world or the best.

"Your dad better not sleep with my boss," I told Luka.

"Ex-boss," he rumbled. "It's out of my hands. You think this is first time he's done this?" He grinned, just a little cruelly. *Goddamnit, he's enjoying this!* He seemed so much less troubled now, and it was more than just the Ralavichs no longer being a problem. It was finally having someone to open up to and trust, after all those years alone. I understood that, because I was feeling it, too.

Being together, though, hadn't cooled off the sex one bit. I'd taken the precaution of adding a safeword to our games, because that seemed sensible. But Luka's big hands were still shredding plenty of pairs of panties, and sometimes whole dresses, and that was just the way I liked it.

I glanced back at the table. Vasiliy was leaning forward a little; Roberta was leaning forward a lot. *Oh, good grief.*

"She'll be fine unless he shows her his gunshot wound," said Luka knowledgeably. "Then, all is lost."

I glanced back again. Roberta was nodding. Vasiliy started to unbutton his shirt.

Oh shit.

"We Malakov men know how to handle American women," said Luka proudly.

He'd find out, soon. Nancy had promised to visit in a few weeks. And once Vasiliy had fully healed up and could spare him, I was planning to take Luka on a trip to the US and show him Wisconsin—cows, rain and all. And there'd need to be business trips, too—to New York, first, and then all over the US, to finalize the gun deals. With Ralavich gone, we could take over his US gun business cleanly and without violence. Soon, we'd be the main pipeline into the country.

The idea didn't scare me as much as it once had. Russian guns were coming into America one way or another—better we controlled it than someone like Ralavich. We could at least do it with the minimum of bloodshed. Once we controlled the whole supply, there'd be less need for in-fighting. And I'd persuaded Vasiliy to introduce my *no guns to gangs who employ kids* rule—it was a small victory, but at least it let me know we were heading in the right direction.

"Oh, you know how to handle us, do you?" I asked.

In answer, he pushed me up against a wall. Dammit, we were still just about within sight of Roberta...although, she *was* looking quite distracted. I looked back at Luka, feeling myself rapidly getting lost in those fiery, ice blue eyes. I could feel my breasts pillowing against his muscled chest, the hard bulge of his cock pressing against my thigh....

"Oh, the hell with it," I muttered. And kissed him.

The End

The Malakov family return as guest stars in *Kissing My Killer*.

Find all my books at helenanewbury.com

Made in the USA
Las Vegas, NV
14 February 2023

67542211R00194